PRAISE FOR
Born of This Fire

"A beautifully-crafted love story coupled with authentic background history of the Anthony Family siblings, *Born of This Fire* is palpable, nestling into our bones and marrow and nourishing our minds, while energizing our collective human spirit." Almeta Whitis, African-American storyteller

"Librarians will recommend this book to patrons seeking books about strained marriages, women's courage in the face of loss, and the moral challenges of a divided nation. It lends itself well to book club discussions and reading circles seeking astute women's historical fiction. . .With its sterling reflection of powerful personalities whose choices influenced the era, *Born of This Fire* is hopeful, invigorating, and hard to put down." Diane Donovan, *Midwest Book Review*

"Gehret has done meticulous research onsite in Leavenworth and in Susan B. Anthony's hometown of Rochester, NY. A successful mixture of American history, historical fiction, romance and Annie's *bildungsroman*—her development and growth as a woman. It will appeal to a broad audience, especially in women's fiction." Andrew Coyle, librarian and Managing Editor, *Rundelania.com*

"Jeanne Gehret brings history & historical settings to life in *Born of this Fire*. I feel as if I'm in Leavenworth, Kansas living with the Anthonys, seeing and feeling everything that's happening in and around their lives. Only a great historian could find so much information about the lives of Daniel, Annie and Susan B. Anthony, the history of Leavenworth, and how the border war with Missouri and the Civil War impacted Kansas. Gehret's intertwining history and fiction make for a great read that's hard to put down, and I hope there's many more books to enjoy." Anna Smith, Kansas Alliance of Professional Historical Performers

BORN OF THIS FIRE

Jeanne Gehret

VERBAL IMAGES PRESS

ISBN (ebook): 978-1-884281-21-1
ISBN (trade paper): 978-1-884281 20-4

In this book, terms such as *Negro, slave, colored*, and *Indian* mean no disrespect but reflect expressions of the era. May we continue developing language that honors all people.

Cataloging information: Gehret, Jeanne. | Born of This Fire.
Title: Born of This Fire / Jeanne Gehret
Description: Trade paper and ebook. | New York: Verbal Images Press, 2025
Subjects: Daniel and Anna Osborn Anthony | Bleeding Kansas | Marriage | Civil War | Susan B. Anthony
BISAC: FICTION/ Historical. | FICTION/ Marriage. | FICTION/Civil War

Dauntless Series Reading Order

Book titles listed in italics
Prequel: "Songbird in the Marsh"
Book One: *Secrets to the Wind*
"Trust in These Vows"
Book Two: *Born of This Fire*
"Christmas in My Heart"

Book Three scheduled for fall 2026!

Series Companion: *Susan B. Anthony and Justice for All*

Stories available to newsletter subscribers at JeanneGehretAuthor.com

Dedication

To Mary Ann Sachse Brown, whose friendship and intrepid research have inspired me to write this trilogy

CHAPTER ONE

Annie

Leavenworth, Kansas: February 16, 1864

Nineteen-year-old Annie Osborn Anthony stepped down from the stagecoach in Platte County, Missouri, gripping her husband's strong gloved hand like a lifeline. She drew a slow breath, her teeth pressed tight against the cold. Though she had traveled fifteen hundred miles from an island in the Atlantic Ocean, it was this final stretch—the last fifteen hundred feet—that nearly undid her. From here, she could see Kansas, the state Daniel had sacrificed so much to keep free. But between her and its shores lay a vast obstacle, the frozen Missouri River

.

However, the impending river crossing wasn't her only source of concern.

Here in Western Missouri, slavery gripped many homes, fields, and back rooms like a vice. Daniel had taught her to read the telltale signs—the weary movements of Black men forced to haul trunks, the wary glances exchanged along depot benches, the silence that clung to those who had "no right" to speak.

"I'll be right back, my dear," Daniel said, striding away before she could even acknowledge his words.

She anxiously watched his retreating broad-shouldered back, the wind biting through her cloak. He cut a fine figure, towering over the man bundled in thick layers standing next to a sleigh and pair of horses.

She shivered, brushing aside stray strands of honey-colored hair that had escaped their pins, and stepped toward the river's edge. Her heart pounded. This was no familiar shoreline. The ice looked solid, but she knew how it could deceive. Coming from the coast of Martha's Vineyard, Annie knew water—knew ice, too. She had seen it swallow a man and his cart without a trace.

Daniel approached, brushing frost from his beard. "Sleigh's ready."

She followed him down the slope, boots crunching through crusted snow. The sleigh waited at the riverbank, runners sunk deep, horse shifting nervously in the traces. She couldn't help feeling much the same at the prospect of trusting the treacherous ice for their crossing.

"No bridge?" she asked, trying to keep the rising panic from her voice.

"Not here. Ice is thick enough. We'll ride across."

She bit her lower lip. "Are you sure it's safe?"

"Would I risk losing you if I wasn't sure?"

Smiling to cover her nerves, she gave him her hand so he could support her up into the sleigh. Then he climbed in beside her and tucked the blanket across their knees.

The driver flicked the reins, and the sleigh jerked forward. Wind swept across the open river, cold and sharp. Annie braced against the seat, watching for cracks, listening for change.

At the midpoint, the river almost blinded her. She twisted away from the glaring sunlight bouncing off the surface and gazed in wonder at the miles of ice stretching in either direction. Her bonnet ties flew out behind her, streaming straight in the biting wind. She looked back; Missouri glinted under the winter sun—a land still ruled by chains.

Ahead lay Kansas, a free state. Her husband was a Union patriot. Her new life had begun.

The sleigh runners rasped across the ice, smooth but uneasy. Daniel leaned close, his breath warm and moist next to her cheek. "There's the Planters Hotel. It'll be toasty."

"If it's not, I'll expect you to warm me, as only you can."

He returned her dry wit with a chuckle and reached beneath the blanket to envelope her thinly mittened hand in his large one, infusing it with heat. She cast him a grateful smile. She'd chosen her husband well. He would always take care of her.

Annie stepped onto the snowy bank below the Planters Hotel, Daniel's hand steadying her. The wind eased its bite, slowed by the trees and structures of Leavenworth's shore, and she nearly wept with relief. The hotel porter swung the door wide, and at last—blessedly—they crossed the threshold.

Heat enveloped her. Firelight flickered across gleaming floors. The scent of roasting meat and beeswax polish rose to meet her, mingling with the faintest trace of pipe smoke. For a moment, she just stood there, blinking at the golden grandeur: velvet drapes, brass sconces, a crystal chandelier that glittered like ice without the danger.

Daniel removed his hat and announced, "Planters House, Mrs. Anthony. I told you it would impress."

She was too weary to answer with a quip. Instead, she gave a subtle nod and tried to absorb the moment. It had been days since she had stood in a place meant for comfort rather than endurance.

A tall man in a velvet-trimmed coat strode toward them with a broad smile and a jovial clap on Daniel's back. "Welcome back, Mr. Mayor," he said. Then, turning to her, he swept a courtly bow. "And you must be Mrs. Anthony. I'm Jep Rice. We've been expecting you. Your rooms will be ready within the hour. In the meantime, we've added clam chowder to the menu—just for you."

Tired as she was, Annie knew the importance of making a good first impression. Summoning her best smile, she said, "That sounds divine. Thank you."

She sank into a brocade dining chair. As Daniel pushed it in for her, the tension in her shoulders eased for the first time in days.

"Thank you, my love."

"Of course, my dear." He took his own seat and picked up the menu the waiter had left.

Annie retrieved her own menu, but could barely focus. She wasn't on the road anymore. And yet, even as her limbs rested, her mind drifted eastward—back to the mercurial Atlantic Ocean, the salt air of Martha's Vineyard, the well-tended lanes and whitewashed fences. Everything she had once called home now seemed impossibly distant.

Across the table, Daniel studied his menu intently. When the waiter arrived, he ordered pork and sauerkraut for both of them, then reached across the table and enclosed her hand in both of his.

She smiled. "A penny for your thoughts, husband."

His gray eyes softened as they met hers. "You. Here. You're the answer to a dream I've carried for years, Annie Anthony." His voice dropped to a hush, as if afraid the moment might vanish if spoken too loudly. "I've waited so long to bring you to Kansas."

She pursed her lips in amusement. "We only met in August."

"I know"—the corner of his mouth turned up slightly—"but I was looking for you long before that. And now you're here—more than I hoped for. Better than I dreamed."

His words curled around her like a shawl, warming her deeper than the fire in the grate.

"Flattery will get you everywhere, Mr. Mayor," she teased. "But for now, I can't wait to see the places you've told me about, and meet the people who matter to you."

Later, after sharing a slice of chocolate pie and lingering over coffee, Annie followed him out to a waiting carriage for a tour of the city. Warmed and revived by lunch at the Planters, she now found the wind brisk rather than biting, its sharpness waking her instead of wearing her down.

After handing her into her seat, Daniel climbed up next to her and took the reins himself.

"Ah. That's better," he said, wrapping the reins around his leather gloves. "Now, let's get you oriented."

He tapped the reins to set the horse in motion, and Annie turned her attention to absorbing her surroundings.

When Daniel had proposed marriage, he'd painted a vision of taming the wild edge of civilization—a mission that made her heart beat faster.

But it wasn't just his dreams of Leavenworth that stirred her. It was his bravery. His stories of storming Confederate farms and rescuing enslaved people from bondage had ignited something deep within her. His fire and righteous fury drew her like a river pulled to the sea.

Her first glimpse of the levee district sobered her idealism.

Warehouses sprawled along the river like sentries—stark, utilitarian, and colorless. The rutted roads, bare of trees, carved lines through the landscape. She watched the scattered buildings go by—some hastily erected and unpainted, their mismatched facades jarring to her Vineyard-bred eyes, accustomed to established neighborhoods and charm.

"What are those ugly buildings over there?" She pointed.

Daniel followed her finger with his gaze. "Warehouses. People stock their wagon trains here before setting off on the Santa Fe trail."

"I see. Don't those shopkeepers know that paint preserves buildings?"

"The city's growing so fast, they don't have time to paint. They barely have time to hang up their shingles before the customers flock in."

Annie nodded, pondering the potential reasons for such quick growth. She was about to ask Daniel when he began speaking again.

"The river runs east of the city." He indicated the frozen track through the valley with his chin. "All the north-south streets are numbered—the further from the water, the higher the numbers."

He gestured as they rode, but to Annie, each direction felt the same. The carriage jolted over a rut, and she straightened the lap robe across her knees.

"They named the east-west roads for Indian tribes," he continued. "Main Street stands in for First."

Annie listened, but the landmarks blurred together. Back home, she needed no compass—just the sea on either side to tell her where she was. Here, everything was flat. Directionless.

Still, she lifted her chin. In time, she would learn to love this place. Perhaps, in time, its people would love her too.

They drove past a stone building with commanding columns. "That's Clark Gruber Bank," Daniel said. "Milton Clark's the president—we're having dinner with him and Lydia tomorrow night. And over there is the telegraph office. That's the opera house on the corner . . ."

Opera? Her brows rose. "I'd love to go to the theater. Especially if they're doing Verdi."

"We'll go," he promised, before continuing the parade of names and places. Hotels. Bakers. Dry goods sellers. "That one burned down last year . . . The man who ran this shop died on a trip back East, and his widow took over . . . The *Commercial* newspaper office—an old friend from Rochester owns it. And here's the post office."

He pointed toward a corner window. "That's my office."

She smiled at him. "So this is where you mailed me all those love letters."

"And where I paced back and forth waiting for yours," he replied, flicking the reins.

"You care as much about this town as you do your family in Rochester," she teased, nudging his shoulder with a smile.

Only three days had passed since they left his mother's house, but the visit clung to her thoughts—especially the hours spent with Daniel's sister Susan. When Annie met the well-known advocate for equal rights and women's suffrage, she'd braced herself for a firebrand. Instead, Susan B. Anthony—as she was known by both allies and adversaries—was a woman of conviction and careful words. Her fire burned low and steady, guided by a calm diplomacy that could defuse a room without raising her voice. By contrast, Daniel blazed bright and hot—sharp-edged, intense, and often unfiltered. They were siblings, yes, but different kinds of flames.

"Shhh—Susan might hear you," he said, glancing theatrically over his shoulder. Then he grew serious. "You're my family now, Annie. I want you to be happy here."

"I'm sure I will be." His devotion warmed everything except her fingertips, which once more ached from cold. "I need to warm up again. Can we go back to the hotel?"

"Just one more stop, my dear. I promise, it will be worth a few extra minutes of discomfort."

She nodded, wondering what could be a higher priority than thawing her numb hands.

In Leavenworth, the Civil War had made its presence known. Horse-drawn carts groaned under the weight of army supplies. Union troops threaded through throngs of refugees, while newsboys shouted battle headlines on the corners.

At City Hall, Daniel turned up Fifth Street, then rounded onto Pottawatomie. The street ended at the river. He stopped the horse.

"There," he said. "That's the land I bought. This is where we'll build our home."

Annie swept her gaze across it. Scrubland, scraggly brush, no trees. No garden path or hedgerow. She tried to picture a house rising here—one with porches and rose trellises—but the image wouldn't come. Still, he sounded proud, and she didn't want to dampen his spirits.

"It has a good view of the river," she said.

He nodded, satisfied. "Better than that, it's right across from Leavenworth's first park." A row of saplings lined a narrow green strip. "One day," he said, "I hope this'll be a peaceful border with Little Dixie."

"Little Dixie?" she asked.

"The slave counties along the border."

She shivered. "So close."

He gave a grim nod. "Too close."

Daniel gave the reins a subtle shift and clucked once. "All right, boy—let's go."

The horse responded without hesitation, easing into the harness with a steady pull. Annie watched from the seat beside him, struck by the quiet authority in Daniel's voice. No need to shout or jerk the reins—just a murmur and a motion, and the great animal obeyed.

There was something reassuring in it, this quiet command of his. Not the bluster of politics or the fire of an argument, but a steadiness she hadn't noticed before. Looking downstream, she saw the Planters Hotel—its very presence promising hot water and a place to change her clothes.

After freshening up and unpacking some of her things, Annie entered the Giacomini Restaurant on Daniel's arm. Faces turned. She lifted her chin, every inch the mayor's wife. By some miracle, she had managed to subdue her curly strawberry-blond hair without the aid of a proper hairdresser.

A dapper man rose from a corner table. "Someone's finally caught Leavenworth's most eligible bachelor," he said, his eyes warm behind his round glasses. "Welcome, Mrs. Anthony. I'm Milton Clark, and this is my wife, Lydia."

Lydia's dark hair gleamed, pulled back into curls that framed her cheeks. She looked to be a few years older than Annie's nineteen years and had a warm sparkle in her eyes.

"I once tried to match D.R. with a friend from Nebraska," Lydia said with a laugh. "But he insisted on marrying someone from back East. And here you are! What has he shown you of Leavenworth so far?"

Annie described the carriage ride.

"Pish," said Lydia. "Typical man. Telegraph offices and City Hall! I bet he didn't tell you where to get Godey's Ladies Book, or the best confections or linens, did he?"

Annie shook her head, laughing.

"Then you must join me on a ladies' tour tomorrow morning. It will be the perfect preparation for the "at-home" reception we've planned for you in the afternoon." Lydia arched her pretty brows and cocked her head. "Say yes?"

"How can I resist?" said Annie, charmed and relieved. When Daniel had first told her about the event he and Lydia had planned, she had felt nervous. But spending time with this new acquaintance beforehand would ease her fear of meeting so many strangers at once.

"Thanks, Lydia." Daniel gave a slight nod of his head before turning to Annie. "Until you're better acquainted with the city, I'd rather you not go out alone."

Annie nodded, lulled by the firelight and the clink of silverware.

Over dinner, they discussed the women she would meet tomorrow, the customs of Leavenworth society, and the larger party Daniel planned to throw once she'd settled in.

"I hope many of tomorrow's guests become your true friends," Lydia said. Reaching into her reticule, she brought forth a box of calling cards with Annie's name on them. "You can give these to whomever you wish tomorrow. The reception begins at two."

"How thoughtful," Annie murmured. She handed one to Lydia with a smile. "I hope you'll call on me often."

As Annie drifted off that night, nestled in a hotel featherbed at last, she thought of her stepmother back home, and her best friend Cora. She missed them. But perhaps—perhaps—new friendships would take root here.

She pulled the quilt up to her chin.

She had chosen this life. Chosen this man. The real question was not whether she loved him—she did—it was whether love would be enough in a land as raw as this.

As snow began to drift across the windowpanes, Annie closed her eyes and whispered the only prayer she dared.

"Let me be strong enough to stay."

Tuesday afternoon's reception took place in the Planters' small parlor downstairs, a comfortable room furnished with many small refreshment tables and groupings of velvet chairs for conversation.

By four o'clock, Annie had already encountered several women who assisted their husbands with various tasks, such as selling tickets for the railroad and taking photographs. She discovered that Daniel's black stallion, Bully Boy, was quite the admired creature in town. Rumor had it that Daniel, in his role as postmaster, had significantly enhanced the speed of letter delivery. She received two invitations to dinner and a caution about a particular establishment near Fort Leavenworth, which posed as a restaurant yet was, in reality, a house of ill repute.

"They also have cockfights there," Lydia said, shuddering. "Can you imagine anything so barbaric?"

As the last parting pleasantries faded, a quiet hope stirred in her chest. Maybe she could find her footing here, build a circle of friends, a place to belong. Though she missed the familiar faces of Martha's Vineyard, her time with Lydia reminded her of the giggles, whispers, and plans she had shared with her childhood companion Cora. She would do her best to plant seeds of friendship in this new soil.

After dusk that evening, Daniel returned from work bearing a letter. "It's from Martha's Vineyard . . ." he teased, holding it just out of her grasp. "Uh-uh—I need a kiss first. Otherwise, I'll never again bring your mail early. Like everyone else, you'll have to wait a full day for the carrier to sort the sack."

With a smile, she flattened herself against his chest and stretched her arm along the length of his. His other arm folded around her, the envelope pressed against her back, while he kissed her firmly.

As soon as she got her hands on the letter, she exclaimed, "It's from Cora!" Overjoyed, she bounced on her toes.

He smiled. "I bet you'll get one from Eliza soon, too." Annie had already sent two letters to her beloved stepmother during their wedding journey. "How was your reception?"

"Lovely, although I thought it best to decline an invitation to Mary Stillings' sewing circle—since I don't sew." She paused, recalling new names and faces. "Sally Harvey said she works in the lobby downstairs and can usually accompany me when I want to go out."

"Good," he said. "She works at the ticket booth in the north corner."

She wondered which way was north. "I did accept an offer to attend a book club. And do you like to play euchre? We were invited to a card party."

"Great game." He eyed her with mock resignation. "I guess now that you have a new letter, you'll be too preoccupied to take a short outing after dinner."

"That's an odd time to make a social call, isn't it?"

"Yes, but I thought you would like to meet this fellow as soon as possible so you can resume one of your old habits." He arched his brows, waiting for her reaction.

"What old habits of mine do you know about, Colonel Anthony?" she mused, cuffing him playfully. "We've only been married three weeks. Not even that. Do you mean having lemon with my tea for breakfast, or brushing my hair a hundred times, or . . ."

"I was actually thinking of your love for horseback riding."

"Oh!"

"On that abominable saddle, swathed in that riding costume that you ladies call . . ." He made a prompting motion with his hand to elicit the desired word from her.

"A habit!" The double meaning clicked into place, and laughter bubbled up within her. She loved his wordplay. "So who is this fellow you wish me to meet?"

It was dark by the time they walked down to the livery where, the day before, Daniel had introduced Annie to Bully Boy, the large black stallion that had maneuvered him through the war. As they entered the barn, the sweet smell of hay transported her back to the livery where she stabled her mare on Martha's Vineyard.

A man in dusty brown pants looked up from the account books he was working on. "Colonel, Mrs. Anthony." He nodded.

"Evenin', Sweeney. We'd like to look at the new black gelding that came in today. Where is he?"

Sweeney pointed.

Making their way down the aisle, Daniel explained that a horse sired by Bully Boy's father had come up for sale and he had claimed first rights, pending his wife's approval.

Daniel moved inside the stall they had reached and called out, "Annie, I'd like you to meet Bill. Bill, this is your new mistress, if she'll have you."

As he led the animal out of the stall and tied the bridle ropes to opposite posts, she marveled at the horse's height. Stroking Bill's nose, she said, "He's beautiful. But I've never ridden a horse this size."

"This is the West, Annie," he teased, "and everything is bigger—the land, the horses, the spirit of the people. He's been well trained, but if you think you can't handle him . . ."

Remembering some heart-thumping rides she and her mare had taken along the Atlantic shore, Annie thought being a horsewoman was a part of the West she could adopt with enthusiasm. Bill was built for speed. "I'm up for the challenge. Thank you!" She kissed his cheek.

He paid for it on the way out, and they headed home with her arm nestled into the warmth of his side.

Chapter Two

Annie

February 17, 1864

"I'll see you at the bank at one o'clock," Daniel said at half-past five the next morning as he buttoned his shirt. "It's just one block south and one block west of here. Can you find it on your own?"

Raising herself on one elbow in bed, Annie watched him with a heavy heart as he prepared to leave her alone for another whole day. "Yes, Lydia and I passed it the other morning."

"Good. Oh, by the way, I've arranged for some friends to meet us at the farm on Saturday afternoon. It would be best to wear an old skirt."

Annie caught her breath. If separating from him at dawn was almost more than she could bear, going to a farm on Saturday was beyond endurance. "Why? What are we going to do there?"

He bent to look in the dresser mirror, combing back his wavy hair and smoothing his mustache. "I just like to get away from the city now and then. It's a nice break from politics." He put his wallet in his pants pocket.

"But it's the middle of winter! What can you possibly be growing now?"

"Not the middle of winter, the end. In a month, the wagon trains will be back in town, outfitting themselves for the Santa Fe Trail going west. To answer your question, I'm growing apples. They have to be pruned before active growth begins, and now's a good time to start."

"I was hoping we could do something fun," she said, taking hold of his pillow and hugging it. "Like taking a ride. Or going to the opera."

"I have horses to ride at the farm, don't worry. And there's nothing playing this week at the opera." With his hand on the door to the main hall, he said over his shoulder, "Anyway, you'll like Chas and Ella." Annie nodded, recalling the kind officer who had escorted her and Lydia back to the Planters.

After Daniel left, Annie got up, unbraided her hair, and began to brush it as her sadness and irritation grew. She missed the intimate moments of their honeymoon when he had eyes for no one but her. Now she had to share him with the whole town.

Staring at the ceiling as she reviewed their last conversation, she frowned. She had not brought any old clothes to Leavenworth. How could she possibly lay her hands on a suitable skirt in only three days? Though Lydia might have loaned one, she was much shorter than Annie. And what would she need it for, anyway? Thinking of manure, she wrinkled her nose.

Daniel hadn't asked; he'd told her, matter-of-fact, as though her time were his to arrange. The sting of it sat hot in her chest. She wasn't a child to be managed. She was his wife.

She rose a little too quickly and caught her reflection in the mirror. There it was—that pout. Hardly a becoming expression, but an honest one. She didn't even have plans of her own for Saturday, and that only made it worse. Still, today wasn't over.

At three o'clock, Lydia would take her to the Sanitary Commission meeting in town. Leavenworth's version of the soldier-aid circle she'd known on the Vineyard—familiar territory. Maybe it would lead to real introductions—women with names and voices, neighbors who might become friends.

If someone invited her to call, she would go. Daniel wasn't the only one who could make plans.

In the meantime, she would find a skirt suitable for the farm. She went to the lobby to ask Sally Harvey to join her on this errand and they planned an outing for one o'clock. By the time she had lunched alone with a book, it was time to meet Daniel at the Clark Gruber Bank to open her very own bank account. During their brief visit to the Anthony homestead on the journey to Leavenworth, Susan had advised her to do this in case something happened to Daniel.

After finishing up at the bank, Annie went right to Sally's booth in the Planters' bustling lobby. Situated on the river, the hotel was the locus for travelers by steamer, rail, express wagon, stagecoach, and the ferry that ran in better weather.

The diminutive Sally met her with a swift apology. "I'm sorry, but my husband has stepped out for a few minutes, so I'm the only one here right now. I can't go with you, but I can recommend some shops to try."

Annie backed away so Sally could wait on an approaching traveler. "I'm sure I can find something on my own, Sally. Thanks anyway."

On Shawnee Street, Annie entered Fisk's, the first dressmaker shop she found, and browsed while the middle-aged clerk chatted quietly with a customer who, by the look of her, was having gowns altered for her advancing pregnancy. "Yes, I expect she will be looking for a modiste to make her dresses and hats. But I want nothing to do with that homewrecker or his wife. Imagine him torching the whole town of Pleasant Hill! And now he wants to settle down. Men of that age often marry for money, you know." She gave a knowing look.

Annie felt sorry for whomever the dressmaker was maligning. She would have to be careful not to give this woman anything to gossip about her.

Sumptuous silks, soft velvets, and crisp sheer fabrics invited her touch as she moved about the shop. She especially liked a blue riding habit. The tailored jacket would hug her curves while the wool skirt would drape beautifully over her legs and the horse's hind quarters.

She and Daniel had not discussed a clothing allowance yet, but he would surely be generous, judging from his praise for some of the clothing she already had. And, of course, she had her inheritance, but she preferred not to touch that except for an emergency. As mayor, he would understand her need for gowns for evening entertainments and official events. She looked forward to wrapping herself in styles fashioned by this woman's skillful hands. Today, however, she needed a plain farm skirt that did not show dir t.

Would the dressmaker be too busy to make her something for the weekend? If she knew Annie was the mayor's wife, maybe Mrs. Fisk would put Annie ahead of her other customers.

The customer who was expecting excused herself to look at ribbon, so now it was Annie's turn to make the dressmaker's acquaintance. When the dressmaker's eyes turned appraising eyes Annie, she was glad that she had unpacked her favorite suit for this excursion.

With a practiced smile, the woman said, "That blue velvet would suit your eyes beautifully."

"I love your work." Getting right to the point, Annie extended her gloved hand and said, "I just moved here. I'm Mrs. Colonel Anthony."

The smile vanished from the modiste's face as if she had erased a chalkboard. Annie felt a warning chill.

"Ah, yes. I heard the mayor had taken a young wife. I'm sorry, I can't assist you today."

"But all I need is a farm skirt."

In a clipped tone, the modiste answered, "We don't do that sort of sewing here; we are more devoted to modern fashion." She turned and began to move away.

Annie wanted to disappear. Immediately. Unfortunately, she didn't know where else to turn for the clothing she needed now. "Is there another shop that could help me?"

The woman sniffed. "Amelia Bennett on Shawnee between Second and Third might assist you. Her clientele tends to be more practical-minded."

Outside, the cold rejection stung more than the cold wind that blew down her neck. Why hadn't Daniel's name elicited the respect she had anticipated?

Turning up her collar for protection and trying to get her bearings, she almost tripped a one-legged man with a crutch.

"I'm so sorry," she gasped, wondering whether he had sustained his injury in the war.

The shop owner had described her destination on Shawnee Street as one block north, two blocks east. But how was Annie supposed to know which way was north when the noonday sun was at its apex? She began by heading the way the woman had pointed, keeping the tallest structure in town—the Planters Hotel—in view.

She always knew where to shop on the Vineyard, and the streets were in better condition because many were paved with shells, which allowed water to drain quickly once the snows receded. But here she risked turning her ankles on late-winter ruts of mud crisscrossing the roads. She had meant to accomplish a small task in obtaining her farm costume. Instead, she had wandered into a maze of uncertainty.

Chiding herself for not memorizing the Indian tribe streets in sequence, Annie crossed an alley. In an open doorway there, a woman in a worn dress and green shawl was stuffing something into her cloth bag. She darted a glance at Annie before hunching over her prize and hurrying away. The poor woman must be starving to pilfer food from the rubbish.

As the wind settled down and she turned a corner out of the shadows, she marveled at the February temperature. She hardly needed gloves. But as she crossed the road, the mud threatened to suck the boots right off her feet. Just before she reached the sidewalk, she recoiled as a passing coach splattered her skirt with muck. She brushed off what she could, her spirits sinking once again.

A hundred yards later, she stopped short. Where was she? Looking around she spied the welcoming sight of the Planters rooftop behind her. Though she couldn't see the name on the top of the building, she still recognized it from this angle. She soldiered on.

Her heart began to thump harder, and her palms became moist inside her gloves. Nothing at street level, however, looked familiar. She replayed the directions in her mind—counting streets, noting turns—but Shawnee Street wasn't where it should have been. Had she gone too far? Or not far enough? Leavenworth was so much bigger than Edgartown!

Then, at last, she saw it—the small sign of the Amelia Bennett shop. Relief crashed over her so suddenly that her knees nearly buckled. She pushed open the door, the chime of the bell above sounding a gentle welcome in the midst of her inner chaos. The warm scent of polished wood and lavender sachets wrapped around her, and the tension drained from her shoulders.

She was safe. She was here. She'd found it.

Mrs. Bennett's was indeed a shop for the practical-minded, with serviceable fabrics and few embellishments for sale. After examining the workmanship on the mannequin's plain outfit, Annie approached the counter.

When she inquired about the skirt and blouse on display, the shop owner smiled and nodded. "As luck would have it, I am just finishing a spring outfit to replace that one."

While she was folding Annie's purchase, a man came in lugging a shipping crate of goods. When she asked him to suggest her return route to the hotel, he stood by while she wrote it all down. Calmed and fortified by the couple's kindness, she set out with renewed confidence.

On this return trip, Annie took the time to study the buildings lining the street. Unlike the neat brick and clapboard buildings of Edgartown, many of the buildings on the main streets of this frontier city looked as if someone had thrown them together in a hurry. Leavenworth's business district was noisy and distracting, but she did like the large variety of things they had for sale.

She coveted that riding crop with a jeweled top and the hat with streamers on the back. Such beautiful leather boots. More intriguing than anything else, however, was George Kohn Furniture across the street, with its window showcasing a carved table and chairs fit for King Arthur.

She longed to settle into her very own home with Daniel. He had promised that construction would start after he began his second term as mayor. That wasn't too far away, was it? Surely it wouldn't hurt to simply peek at some of the furniture brands available at this crossroads of civilization. Visiting such a treasure trove would be worth the chore of removing more mud from her skirt later.

By the time she left Kohn's with a mental list of furniture she liked, she had only twenty minutes left before meeting Lydia for the Sanitary Relief Commission. A tall storefront blocked her view of the Planters, but she was as certain of its location as she was of the sun in the sky. She pressed on until an especially muddy intersection prompted her to take a detour.

Five minutes later, in a somewhat unsavory section of town, Annie admitted to herself that she was lost. There were no inviting shops here, just grimy businesses. Raising her eyes in desperation, she searched for the rooftop of the Planters, but couldn't see it. Her heart pounded and breath quickened.

Then, glistening in the sun and sparkling clean, a carriage emerged from the nearby livery. She beckoned to the driver, who stopped and lifted his cap.

"I wonder if you could direct me," she began, a tremor in her voice. "I seem to have lost my way to the Planters Hotel."

"I'm headed over that way to pick up someone now. Would you like a ride?" said the driver—a dark-haired man who held the reins with beautiful leather gloves. Noting the name "Bauer Brothers Livery" in gold letters on the carriage door, Annie blushed. She had never hired a ride for herself.

He eyed the mud on her skirt and boots. "On second thought, I don't have time to clean out the carriage after you," he apologized. "Would you mind sitting up here with me? It's just a few blocks. No charge. I'm Martin Bauer, by the way."

Cheered by his professional appearance and demeanor, Annie hesitated no longer. "That would be so kind! Thank you."

Mr. Bauer jumped down and helped Annie up next to him in the driver's seat. Her panic gave way to calm when she recognized the familiar landmark of the Clark Gruber Bank. She gathered her package and purse when hoofbeats pounded up beside her, then slowed to match the pace of the carriage.

Her heart quickened with joy at spotting the rider.

"Daniel!" she called over the din. "What brings you out of the office at this time of day?"

Ignoring her, Daniel leaned across his horse to shout at her driver. "Bauer. Stop the carriage." Annie had never seen her husband wear such a menacing face.

Bauer said, "Leave me alone. I'm headed to the Planters to pick up a fare." He did, however, pull back slightly on the reins.

"Stop right there, Bauer." Drawing his pistol, Daniel aimed at Annie's companion.

She stared, horrified.

"You got no call to harass me," snarled Bauer, bringing the carriage to a jarring halt.

In front of the hotel, a bald man stood in the middle of the street, aiming a revolver toward the vehicle. Despite the winter chill, Annie began to perspire. What was all the commotion about? Was Mr. Bauer a dangerous criminal?

From the other direction, another bystander drew a gun on Daniel, demanding, "What's the problem?"

Annie shifted fearful eyes from one pistol to the other.

In seconds, a knot of townsmen stood with arms folded, staring at Daniel. Another man pulled out a pistol and trained his sight on Martin Bauer. Annie sat wide-eyed, her pulse galloping along in alarm. Daniel was the mayor, in charge of the whole town. Who would dare challenge him?

When the bald gunman ran up, panting, she noticed a marshal's badge glistening on his chest. He was not aiming at Daniel. Good. Two colored officers fell in behind the lawman, their revolvers all pointing at Bauer. Now the stakes were even.

Through gritted teeth, Daniel fixed his eyes on the driver. "Bauer, if this carriage moves one inch, I'll shoot your hand off. Understand?"

"Confound it, Anthony, I'm not even armed." The driver raised one hand, keeping hold of the reins with the other.

Now Daniel shifted his gaze to Annie. "Step out of the carriage, Annie, and get behind the officer."

The man with the badge gently helped her down. From the corner of her eye, she spotted Lydia approaching in her blue cape and waving at the front of the hotel.

Seated on Bully Boy, Daniel occupied the highest position in the throng. The glare he conferred on Bauer was enough to make any man squirm. "Now, suppose you tell me *where* were you planning to take my *wife?*"

"Your wife?" Bauer echoed. "I had no idea you married such a young girl." When his eyes flicked to Annie cowering behind the man with the badge, she wanted to dissolve into the mud.

"Where were you taking her?" repeated Daniel.

"To the Planters. She stopped me to ask directions. I offered her a ride."

Daniel swiveled in his saddle to look at Annie. "Is this true?" he demanded, his eyes drilling into hers.

"Yes," she replied, hating the squeak in her voice. "I was late to meet Lydia. This man was very kind." She waited for whatever would happen next, barely daring to breathe.

The bystanders began to disperse, but not before one of them said, "Suppose, Mayor, that you apologize to this innocent citizen and allow him to pick up his next customer?"

Daniel nodded awkwardly to Bauer. "As you were." Then he instructed the bald man with the badge. "Follow her to the Planters." He returned his revolver to his pocket.

Annie avoided Daniel's gaze when he told her, "Wait for me there." As the officer turned her by the arm toward the hotel, Bauer pulled to the side of the road and rehashed his grievances with his friends.

Her cheeks flaming, Annie lowered her eyes as she and Lydia, arm in arm, followed the marshal toward the hotel. Behind her, Bauer sneered, "Anthony does nothing but cause trouble. If he hadn't ruined my homestead, I wouldn't have to drive for a living."

Striding along ahead of her, the lawman turned briefly to Annie and introduced himself as City Marshal Charles Goodman. Even taller and brawnier than Daniel, he looked equal to any task. Before taking his leave at the hotel, he mentioned that he and his wife would accompany the Anthonys to the farm on Saturday.

As soon as he left them in the Planters lobby and the women reached the Anthony suite, Lydia rounded on Annie. "We're too late to join the Sanitary Relief Commission now. Where have you been? I waited in the lobby for you and even asked Sally Harvey if she'd seen you. She said you'd gone out by yourself. Finally, we sent a courier from Milton's office to see if the colonel knew anything of your whereabouts."

Annie's lips formed a flat line of dismay at the furor she had caused. Before she could reply, Daniel burst into the room.

"Annie, what in tarnation were you doing over on West Seventh? Do I have to watch you every minute?"

Blushing, Lydia mentioned somewhere she had to go and quickly excused herself. Annie was left alone to face her husband, who paced like a lion about to roar.

Chapter Three

Daniel

Later that day

As soon as Lydia left, D.R. spun around to face Annie. Hang it all, why couldn't she understand the dangers here? His heart had nearly stopped when he'd spotted her in Bauer's carriage.

Throwing up his hands, he said, "Why were you out alone? I thought you were coming back here from the bank to wait for Lydia." He spoke gruffly, wanting his words, his fear, to get through to her. If she kept venturing into trouble, he'd never sleep again.

"Is Leavenworth so very dangerous, then? You scared the dickens out of me, pointing your gun like that." There was no mistaking the fury in her eyes—blue fire, hot and sudden, aimed straight at him.

D.R. blinked, fighting the urge to gape at her. His sister Susan was the only woman who'd ever spoken to him that way in the past. But now, Annie.

Her rosy cheeks flushed crimson as she continued, "Have you lied to me and brought me to a town where I can't go outside by myself? We were surrounded by men with guns! Where did they come from?" She swept her hand around the room.

If only she knew how complicated that question was. But he'd keep it simple for now. "Some were my friends, some were Bauer's."

"In Edgartown, men can disagree without pointing revolvers." Her nostrils flared as she jabbed her finger toward the ground, condemning his beloved town. "What's so different here?"

He had to make her understand. Had to find the right words.

"If your enemies carry guns, you need one, too." There. Simple enough. He shrugged, waiting for reason to dawn on her. "You can't just go walking into a hornet's nest without some protection."

"So Leavenworth is a hornet's nest?" Her voice rose higher. "Do you plan to keep me imprisoned in this hotel? Going out only with an escort? Is *that* your plan? Because my plan isn't to be some hothouse flower!"

Indeed, to him, that was just what she was: a rose, tender and fair, reared in that white mansion by the sea, sheltered from every harsh wind. Her honey-colored hair had slipped from its pins, falling about her face like a gentle halo. The thought of harm coming to her struck him like the desecration of something cherished—something he'd vowed to keep safe.

But there was no denying her unholy fury. When she paused for breath, he saw his chance to defuse it. He took a seat and evenly stated, "Of course not! I wouldn't bring you somewhere dangerous and lock you up. It's just that . . . this isn't Martha's Vineyard. As you just said."

The calmer he grew, the more her temper spiraled. "Another thing that's different from Martha's Vineyard is there *I* decided where I went, when, and with whom. No one dictated a schedule to me. Or told me when to get out of a carriage. I'm not one of your soldiers you can order around." Her eyes flashed defiantly. "What other plans have you made without telling me? Do you know how difficult it is to come up with a . . . a . . . *farming costume* in only three days if you don't have a dressmaker?"

Farming costume? D.R. stared blankly. "What is a farming costume?"

"You know. An old skirt, like you said. If a woman doesn't bring an old skirt to Kansas and she doesn't know anyone her size, how is she to acquire one?"

The absurdity of it almost made him laugh. "So you went out to acquire this item—er, costume?"

"Well, yes. But Mrs. High and Mighty on Shawnee Street wouldn't help me. She was so unfriendly."

"You mean Matilda Fisk? Yes, she would be." He studied Annie from the horsehair sofa, noticing her anger fade.

Curiosity flickered in her eyes. "And why is that?"

"Did you introduce yourself?"

"Yes, I believe so." She drifted closer to him now.

He blanked his mind from an image of the widow Fisk at the cemetery. "Her son died while serving under my command, and she blamed me. Then her husband got cholera. Now she's alone and, if I hear correctly, struggling to make ends meet."

"How sad." Annie's expression softened before she resumed her tale. "So, finally, I found my way to Amelia Bennett's on Osage, where I got a serviceable skirt and blouse.

"Everything was fine up to that point. But then I had to detour around the mud." Her voice softened, turning a little rueful. "Leavenworth's bigger than Martha's Vineyard. I never get lost there. But here . . ." She trailed off, and something in the way she said it tugged at him.

"You were lost? In Leavenworth?" The words slipped out before he could stop them. "But the streets are *numbered!*"

The instant he said it, he saw the way her head dipped—but not before he caught the slight tremble of her lip. His chest tightened. That's why she'd ended up in that part of town. Of course. But still—the streets were numbered.

He couldn't imagine it. Not knowing where you were, how to get back. He read his own surroundings without thinking—to take in landmarks, directions, the subtle shifts of a place. That instinct ran so deep, the idea of losing his bearings felt . . . impossible.

But she had lost hers. And the vulnerability in that, in *her,* struck something in him.

Without thinking, he reached out his hand, and finding her waist, eased her onto his lap. She didn't resist. Didn't pull away. When he stroked her back, slow and steady, he felt softening of her body, the quiet way she melted into him. And when her arm slipped around his shoulder, it was all the answer he was waiting for. He held her a little closer. Just in case she needed it.

Her warmth against him calmed his own tension. "If you don't want to be pampered in a hothouse, then I guess I'd better equip you to be a sunflower."

"What do sunflowers have to do with it?" Though she grumbled, much of the fight had gone out of her.

"It's the Kansas state flower. Grows on the prairie like a weed."

She flicked her fingernail gently against his ear. "So I've degenerated from a flower to a weed?"

Her touch sent a pleasant shiver through him. "Sturdy as a weed, but still as beautiful as a flower." He leaned closer to her ear. "Good for many seasons of pleasure."

As his lips brushed her neck, warmth radiated from her skin. When he pulled back to look at her, the blush that had spread across her cheeks pleased him immensely.

Shifting her off his lap, he rose and rummaged through a drawer until he found what he needed—a detailed city map. "I doubt you spent much time at the docks on the Vineyard, right?"

"True," she admitted.

"It's the same here. Most places are fine for you to walk, but ladies avoid this neighborhood." He circled the dangerous section where she'd strayed. "Go around this way instead. Perhaps I should pencil in some landmarks?"

She liked that idea. "Landmarks are much easier than all that north-south-east-west business."

After marking a few more notes for her, he paused to pull out his pocket watch. "Hang it!" he declared.

"What's wrong?"

"I'm late for a meeting." He pressed a swift, earnest kiss to her mouth, her softness a comfort he hated to leave. Even as duty tugged at him, he savored that fleeting taste of home, his lips memorizing her warmth in that moment of borrowed time.

Then, he hurried down the hall and took the steps two at a time down to the street.

When they went for a stroll after dinner, arms intertwined, D.R. took time to explain his reaction to seeing her with Bauer.

"He hates me because I was in the cavalry." The memory still burned. "In Missouri, he used to have a tobacco plantation, farmed by slaves. And fine horses—far more than he needed for that kind of farm. Not plow horses, but built for speed, like Bully Boy."

They walked two blocks west to Third Street and turned left, their shoulders occasionally brushing in the cool evening air.

"My commander ordered us to destroy any support that bushwhackers—militant secesh—received from Missouri townsfolk. We reckoned the Bauers corralled horses and stored excess crops as reinforcements for the Confederates. So, we disposed of everything according to army policy. We wiped out most of Bauer's family fortune. And most of the other farms in that town."

"What's a secesh?" she asked.

"Sorry—short for secessionists, or Confederates."

She was quiet for a moment, taking in what he'd said. "How did he end up in Leavenworth?"

"He has a brother who lives out by Salt Creek, a Union man. Not too far from my apple farm, actually. Now he works for his brother, driving visitors around town. When he got settled here, he noised it about that he was a Union man like his brother. But I didn't credit that story."

"He was so friendly, such a gentleman. Did you really think he had kidnapped me?"

"It's his job to be polite," D.R. replied. Heat crept up his neck as he remembered the smirks and whispers from bystanders when Annie said she'd asked Bauer for a ride. Had they thought him a jealous fool? Perhaps he had overreacted. He sighed, the evening air cooling his flushed skin.

He halted and pivoted toward her. Their eyes met, his gaze intense and unwavering. More than anything, he needed her to believe him. What good were words if she couldn't see the truth burning in his eyes?

"But I may have jumped the gun. Men don't usually go after each other's wives. I wouldn't have brought you here if that were the case—truly, Annie."

This town had its dangers, yes, but he'd never knowingly put her in harm's way. The very thought made his chest tighten. He slipped his arm around her, loving the curve of her waist under his hand. Maybe it was a good thing he was such an excellent shot. Nothing would harm her while he was alive.

Chapter Four

Annie

February 24, 1864

Over the next week, Lydia and Annie fell into a routine of morning strolls together; Annie got further acquainted with the shops in her adopted town. On one such walk, Annie grabbed Lydia's sleeve as they passed a secondhand furniture store. "Look at that desk! It's just like the one I had in Edgartown. Let's go in and see."

"Wouldn't you rather get something new at Abernathy's? You don't know where these pieces have been—they might even be scavenged from the side of the road."

"I don't care, it reminds me of home!" Annie said, pulling Lydia into the store.

Moments later, she stood stroking the desk's tiger maple top with its characteristic pattern of dark and light stripes. "This would be just the thing for an empty corner of our parlor, or bedroom, or even the guest room," she said.

"You don't even have a house yet, much less a guest room," objected Lydia, reaching for the drawer pull. "Isn't it a little soon to be shopping for furnishings?" She tugged at the drawer and grimaced when it wouldn't budge.

"Fiddlesticks! This is exactly what I want. I'd die if someone else bought it."

As the shop owner approached to greet them, Lydia told him, "This desk drawer's locked."

"Do you have the key?" Annie asked him.

"I'm not sure," he said. "I'll check and be right back."

Moments later, he returned empty-handed. "I'm sorry, madam, but we don't have it. That being the case, I could reduce the price for you. You think about it and just let me know." He walked away to wait on another customer.

"Maybe there's another desk you would like here," said Lydia. "Want to look more?" Strolling around the sales floor, she put her hand on an oak rolltop with many pigeonholes. "Look, Annie. You can stash lots of notes in these slots and when company comes you can close the lid to make it neat."

"No, I like this tiger maple," replied Annie. "I bet Daniel could get the drawer open. He has plenty of tools."□

That Saturday, when the desk arrived at their hotel sitting room, Daniel set to work on the drawer. It took until after dinner, but he was finally able to lever it open.

"Oh!" Annie gasped. "There are papers inside!"

"Have fun," said Daniel, rising and brushing off his trousers and turning to leave. "I need to talk to somebody downstairs."

Lifting the papers out, Annie found drawings, scraps of a poetry book, and a baby-fine curl of hair tied with a blue ribbon. None of it looked particularly valuable, and she wondered why someone had locked the drawer. But when she reached the bottom of the pile, she understood.

Putting aside the detritus she had already examined, she lifted out a leather notebook embossed with the word "Diary" and took it to the parlor to read.

Journal of Veronia Naughton
Shady Grove, Cass County, Missouri

Annie frowned, trying to remember the counties along the Kansas-Missouri border. Cass County was well south of Leavenworth in an area of Missouri known for raising tobacco and hemp with slave labor. Was Shady Grove in the region Daniel called "Little Dixie"? Noting that the journal's starting date was four years earlier, she read on.

Wednesday, May 2, 1860

Today we made strawberry jam. I asked Mama why I had to help and she said it's important for a young lady to have homemaking skills. I think that's silly. What are servants for, after all? But she said the lady of the house has to oversee the servants, and the best way is to know how to do things herself.

Can't I just watch Cassie do it? Why do I have to sit there all morning hulling and mashing and boiling fruit?

When I told Mama the heat under the kettle made me feel faint, she advised me to loosen my stays. Never! Suppose Martin Bauer should stop over and see me looking like a servant?

Mama is so contrary. Tomorrow I have to help bake strawberry pies. She also taught me to make cheese. "I was a farm girl who learned how to do everything," she told me. "No daughter of mine is going to grow up to be a household ornament."

Please, God, don't ever put it into her head to teach me to kill a hog and make bacon!

We are having a strawberry social tomorrow, and I hope Martin will come. I figure he's the only boy tall enough to look me in the eye when he kisses me. I hate being tall. But Mama told both Iris and me that a tall woman carries her weight better, especially when a baby is on the way.

Iris went with Papa to Kansas City, where they plan to visit a library and stay in a hotel. I can't wait to hear all about it.

Friday, June 1, 1860

Iris came back just before noon. She saw an entire building full of books—imagine! Wasn't she lucky to miss all that jam-making?

Martin was at the social yesterday, and so were his parents. His daddy and mine got into a kerfuffle over slaves—Papa wanted to permit them to visit more frequently between our two farms, but Mr. Bauer disagreed. It seems like a cruel practice to keep them from seeing their friends and family nearby.

Annie set the journal in her lap, her fingers brushing the worn cover as she stared at the gold-trimmed velvet drapes across the room. She didn't really see them, though. Her mind was overwhelmed with the significance of the book resting against her legs.

She wasn't sure how she felt about this diary. Unease twisted in her stomach. Did she even *want* to read about the life of a slaveholding family? The very thought made her skin crawl. She hated everything they stood for—the injustice, the cruelty.

And yet . . . the girl who wrote this was her age. That made it harder to push the curiosity aside. What would it be like, to live in a world so different from her own?

Her fingers tightened around the edges of the journal. And then there was that name: Martin Bauer. It had to be a coincidence . . . didn't it? But she couldn't shake the question: Was the man from the livery the same Martin Bauer mentioned in these pages?

The thought sent a prickle of disquiet through her. She wasn't sure she wanted to know the answer.

While she wavered, Daniel burst into the room.

"There's a bunch of Republicans downstairs," he said. "I'm going to have a few drinks with them. I won't stay late."

After nodding absently to Daniel, Annie resumed reading the journal. The word "died" bursting from the next paragraph. She sank back into the life of the young woman who had begun her story so innocently.

Friday, September 14, 1860

My dear mama died today at 3:00. A week ago she caught a chill and it went to her lungs. The very next day she got burning hot and Iris put wet cloths on her but there was nothing else we could do. Papa sat there with tears running down his cheeks, brother Tom took off to who-knows-where, and we watched the breaths rasp in and out of her until they were just a whisper and then no more.

Wednesday, January 2, 1861

It got so cold last night that Iris and I slept in the same bed for warmth. Since Mama left us, Iris has been giving orders to our house Negroes, which is fine; when she orders me and Tom about, that's a different matter.

I ache for Mama. Does she hear me from that far-off place? I braided a lock of her hair into a little wreath and tucked it inside my locket. When the missing gets too sharp, I press it to my chest, right over my heart, and pretend she can feel it.

A lump formed in Annie's throat as she recalled losing her own mother at a young age. Her heartache had softened with time, but never really left. At least Papa had married dear Aunt Eliza. Without her, life would've been so much harder.

She flipped back through the diary, growing accustomed to the handwriting, but the more she read, the more tangled everything felt.

The words were right there, plain as day—a Missouri slaveholding family. But Union supporters—how could that be? Weren't slaveholders always on the Confederate side? Apparently not.

Nothing about this was as simple as she'd thought. The next entry confirmed her new understanding.

Saturday, November 3, 1861

S. Carolina seceded from the Union. Papa is very unhappy. I don't see how politics so far east can affect us here?

Wednesday, November 7, 1861

We went to the Bauers' for dinner last night, and there was much talk about the election. Mr. Bauer does not like Abraham Lincoln, but Papa said he heard him speak several years ago and thought he had some good points. Bauers have a lot more slaves than we ever did. When the men went off to smoke after dinner, I was glad that Mrs. Bauer did not palaver on about the war. She shared a recipe with us and called us "poor lambs" for losing Mama.

Tuesday, February 5, 1861

Iris helped me make a new dress, the first I have had in a long time. I kept asking Cassie to make it, but she said she had too much to do. Iris is a much better seamstress than I and did most of it. It's fun to wear something different that wasn't hers first!

Seven states have seceded altogether. They call themselves the Confederate States of America. Papa frowned and shook his head as he read the newspaper. Also, Kansas officially became a free state last month. Papa says those two events happening in such a short time could cause serious trouble.

Sunday, March 3, 1861

Raiders from Kansas have attacked some of our neighbors. That's why Papa is making a secret closet behind a bookcase in his office. If any strangers come, he said, Iris and I should hide there so no one can take liberties with us. The Negroes have a way of blending into the woods when they want to, so we won't need to worry about them getting hurt. But if Shady Grove is attacked, he told Tom to take up his gun and defend his sisters.

Friday, March 15, 1861

Mr. Bauer warned us to watch out for a bunch of dangerous raiders from Kansas who call themselves "Jayhawkers." He says they claim to be abolitionists but they're just a pack of thieves. They sacked his farm. Now I understand why Papa is afraid for us.

Later, I heard that while the Jayhawkers were raising havoc, Martin B. galloped off to get some of his friends. From the woods the boys surrounded his family's farmhouse and began shooting to scare off the Jayhawkers. Martin shot some holes in the outhouse but didn't hit anybody. Before it was all over, the Jayhawkers made off with two of the Bauers' best horses and several barrels of food.

Annie frowned again, pausing to think. Daniel had been a member of Jennison's Jayhawkers. Had he been involved in raids like these? Picturing him on his horse, she could imagine how formidable he might look to an enemy.

Papa and Tom have been twitchy as squirrels, and yesterday I caught them whispering about something. When I got close enough, I heard them saying war will be declared soon.

Every time I hear horses outside, I worry the Jayhawkers are headed here. None of our neighbors have come by in a long time. Some of our colored people have left, including Cassie. Papa doesn't want to replace them.

With fewer of our field hands remaining, the rest are working longer days, clearing the fields for planting in a few weeks. Iris and Tom are working beside them. I do most of the cooking now and wish that I had paid better attention to Mama's instructions in the kitchen. I'm glad I have her recipe book.

Papa hopes to get a good price for his hemp this year. I am looking forward to fresh corn this summer. But that's a long way off.

Wednesday, March 27, 1861

This morning, Iris went to stay with cousin Felicity, who is almost ready to have her baby. I begged her not to go, but she said Felicity doesn't have any other womenfolk to help her.

I am scared to be here without my big sister. She always seems to know what to do.

In the time Annie had been reading, the sun had set. Daniel returned with political news; Annie welcomed a break from her reading. The diarist's notions of Union-sympathizing slaveholders and Jayhawkers-as-enemies turned her world on its axis. What had caused Veronia to leave the diary in the tiger maple desk?

Annie set the journal aside, Daniel's voice pulling her back to the present. As he spoke, laying out his clear, certain views, the knots of confusion inside her dissolved. The world slipped back into its familiar shape—good people on one side, bad ones on the other. Simple. Understandable.

And yet . . . not quite.

The journal's words lingered, unsettling and quiet, like a whisper she couldn't ignore. The world Daniel described felt comforting, but after everything she'd read, she wasn't sure she could believe in it as easily as she had before.

Chapter Five

Annie

February 26, 1864

After Daniel went to work the next morning, Annie could not leave the diary alone. No dime novel with its florid prose had ever engaged her like this bare-bones account. She couldn't help but recognize how Veronia's early life of ease mirrored her own New England upbringing as a shipbuilder's daughter. Even though the Naughtons had enslaved workers, the father's mixed feelings about that "peculiar institution" made Annie empathize with the sisters' plight as, by turns, they lost their mother, their neighbors, and their sense of security. Annie resumed reading, hoping the family had happened upon better times.

Sunday, April 21, 1861

Mr. Bauer came to tell us war was declared two days ago. Today, Iris tried to persuade Papa to leave Shady Grove for Kansas before we get sucked into the conflict alongside our neighbors. But Papa again refused.

If I were Tom, I would pack up and vanish tonight. But being a girl, I don't think I could survive on my own.

Oh, what will become of us?

Saturday, May 4, 1861

Jayhawkers came to Shady Grove. Several times I thought my heart would stop with fear, but everything turned out all right.

We were all in the house when five men arrived. Four of them spread out right away, searching the barn and other buildings while a man with a notebook stood in the yard. He hurried from one outbuilding to another.

"He looks like their leader," Papa said, and before we could object, he took his revolver and strode out to meet the man.

It seemed like ages till we heard Papa return and call us out of hiding. The Jayhawkers left empty-handed! The leader called off his men and said he was glad to find true Unionists in Missouri. As long as we keep flying Old Glory as proof we're loyal to the Union, no one else should bother us, he said.

Thank the heavens for another day of safety. I hope the leader makes good on his promise.

When the mantel clock chimed, Annie jumped to attention and gathered her things for her daily walk with Lydia.

⁂

Later, when she and Daniel had finished lunch, she mentioned the diary. "Were you ever at a place called Shady Grove in Cass County, Missouri?"

"Cass County, yes. Regarding a farm called Shady Grove, I don't remember. We policed lots of farms along the Missouri border."

"Well, the writer describes someone who sounds like you," she said, and described the Jayhawker who offered protection to the Naughton farm. "You wouldn't forget if you'd made such a promise, would you?"

Donning his suit jacket to return to the office, Daniel said, "Little Dixie's full of families like that. When we showed up, they all claimed to be Unionists. Sorting out the true loyalists was like picking dandelions out of spinach leaves."

Thinking of Veronia and Iris, Annie bristled at his dismissive tone.

On Daniel's departure, she was absorbed back into the diary.

Thursday, June 13, 1861

At dinner today, Tom told us about his visit to town and how Martin Bauer and some other boys hoisted the new Confederate flag over the mercantile. Papa frowned and growled, "You stay away from those troublemakers, son. We will not throw in our lot with a few ruffians who want to break with the Union over slavery."

Tom said he's seeing more Confederate flags lately. Some people prefer them to the Old Glory that continues to fly over Shady Grove.

Papa told Tom not to be deceived, that in our county a few people may want slavery, but most of Missouri wants to be quit of it. "We just have to figure out how to do it," he said. Maybe that's why he freed many of our slaves last year.

The appearance of the next entry troubled Annie. The handwriting was erratic, and the sentences were crossing over each other as if written by someone with poor eyesight.

Monday, August 19, 1861

Iris out for AM

Lantern too visible—writing by crack of light under door

Martin Bauer came to say Jayhawkers back—begged Papa & Tom to help defend their farm.

Papa told me to go to the secret closet.

His boots went out onto the porch.

I grabbed my journal and stepped in here.

Dead quiet for a long time. Safe to get out?

If Papa went to help B, Jayhawkers will think he's Confed.

Hope our Union flag is flying high—if no men to defend Shady Grove, Jayhawkers might

Annie scanned the unfinished page, piecing together the scattered phrases that tangled and overlapped and then just drifted off in midsentence. With each rereading, her frown deepened. The sentence cut off mid-thought—the writing simply stopped. What had interrupted Veronia?

She turned to the next entry; the writing was once again flowing and coherent. Annie's heart tightened, and she suddenly understood. The realization struck hard and cold.

Tuesday, October 15, 1861

The baby I'm carrying reminds me every day of that awful attack. I would throw myself down the stairs to end this pregnancy, but that would just make things harder for the rest of the family. If I died, that would mean another loss so soon after Mama. And if I simply hurt myself, they would have more work to do taking care of me.

I hope that disgusting brute drowns crossing a river. Or gets cholera. What I would give to lose this baby he put inside me! I hope his coattails catch fire and he burns up.

The mercantile won't sell to us anymore because we don't fly the Confed. flag. I wish we had grown more food instead of hemp and tobacco. Useless cash crops!

Tuesday, March 4, 1862

Martin Bauer called on Tom today. The moment his eyes dropped to my swollen belly, his face twisted in disgust. He turned away without a word, like he couldn't stand the sight of me.

As if I got this way on my own.

The shame burned hot in my throat, but underneath it was something colder. His lack of compassion chilled me to the bone. I used to think I cared for him—thank God I never told him.

Martin told Papa that Jennison's Jayhawkers became Union soldiers back in October and are torching Confed. households north of us. They are now an official Union regiment, the Kansas Seventh. Up north of here, they burned all but one home where a Union man lived.

Papa said, "See? The Union does take care of its own."

What a thing to say! Did he forget what they did to me? I pray they don't return to attack us again.

Annie chewed her lower lip. Veronia had already endured so much; the thought of a man forcing himself on her made Annie's stomach twist. But it wasn't just the horror of the past that would gnaw at Veronia. It was the looming fear that it could happen again. And what was this talk about the Kansas Seventh? Daniel's regiment? Anxiety shot through her like lightning. What did that mean about her husband?

Sunday, March 9, 1862

Papa, Iris, and Tom tilled and began planting a garden just big enough to feed our family. It's early for planting but we decided to risk it. On garden days, I fix them lunch and dinner since it's hard for me to bend over. I feel like a breeding cow. I am worn out from the baby's kicking, but Iris makes me eat enough to birth a healthy baby. I wonder what it's like to be a mother. I was the youngest of the family and won't know what to do with a baby of my own. How I miss Mama! But at least I have my older sister. She feels more like my mother at times, and I don't mind anymore.

Annie gazed out the window for a moment. Part of her wondering how it would feel to be pregnant with a child of such a terrible assault. She hoped to be a mother someday, but so far her monthly courses were continuing uninterrupted. Sometimes after church, Lydia let Annie hold Lily, her toddler, and nuzzle the child's soft hair beneath her chin.

Monday, April 14, 1862

Papa says the Union transferred the Kansas Seventh Regiment to Tennessee to stop them from tormenting people in Missouri. Rumor has it that their leaders were court-martialed. In my mind, that's the first good thing the Unionists have done for us.

Wednesday, May 21, 1862

My baby was born yesterday. I felt my very bones give way and my body feels bruised and broken. He is so little. I named him Robbie after Mama's father.

He studies me gravely as if to say, "Why did you bring me into this world of war?" I had no choice, tiny one, but I will care for you the best I can. No matter what the cost.

Monday, June 2, 1862

Robbie refuses to breastfeed and looks very skinny, so Iris feeds him a bottle of cow's milk. This makes him throw up, I think, but I cannot even do this most basic task of mothering. Why am I still alive?

Tuesday, August 25, 1863

Mercy me, all these months I've been too busy to write! My little Robbie seems small but toddles everywhere and is so easy to love—even considering who his daddy is. In truth, his hands and eyes resemble my own papa's. I wish Mama could see him. But he barely talks.

The war took another frightening turn today. A Union general issued General Order No. 11 saying all the Confed. sympathizers in several Missouri counties have to leave. Residents must leave their crops and anything they can't carry in their wagons. All this with only two weeks' notice!

The only way for us to get around the order is to present two signatures certifying we have always been loyal to the Union. Papa is determined to get them, but who in this area will vouch for us? Any neighbors who were Union sympathizers are long gone.

Sometimes, when I get up with Robbie at night, I hear Tom sneaking outside. I think he goes over to the Bauers'. Those boys brag that their lookouts have protected us from additional raids in these parts. Sometimes when we hear shooting, I wonder if they are driving away soldiers. Tom denies any knowledge of it.

I don't care which side of the war we're on—all I want is to keep my Robbie safe.

Tom posed a terrible question yesterday: What if Robbie cries while we're hiding? I used to give him paregoric to quiet him, but the rest of our medicine was stolen. T says next time we have to get in the closet we should smother R or we will all be attacked. Iris and I agreed that we would never kill R, even for our own safety. We will give him whiskey till it runs out.

Annie's breath caught as she recognized the chaotic words that covered the page of the next entry for what they were. She pushed herself to keep reading.

Wednesday, September 9, 1863

Writing by light under closet door.

Iris with me, & Robbie in drunken sleep. Hated dosing him that way.

Trespassers tore down Union flag. After Papa raised it again, Tom found holes shot through it.

Papa and T argued & T stormed off.

Past couple weeks, U soldiers harass us & steal food—flag or no flag.

Down to 1 meal/day—little food left. T will sell some of our furniture. Still Papa insists we stay & defend homestead.

Now I'm more worried than ever.

Annie's heart raced as her eyes reached the end of the entry. She quickly turned the page, needing to know what happened next. Nothing on the back, just blank space. Poor Veronia. The last time she'd penned such frantic thoughts, a Jayhawker had cruelly assaulted her. When had that been? She flipped back to August nineteenth, 1861, her fingers trembling as she traced the date. Three months of silence stretched out after that—a void that echoed Veronia's pain.

Annie's heart ached for the delicate girl whose life had been uprooted, forced to shed her innocence too soon. What had happened this time? Could Shady Grove have escaped the flames? Was Veronia safe? Was Iris still at her side? What of Robbie? She longed for answers, but they might never come.

Deep in thought, she laid the handwritten book aside, stood, and went to stroke the beautiful wood of the tiger maple desk. Perhaps the family had sold the beautiful piece of furniture to buy food. This desk had belonged to Veronia—she felt it in her bones.

Conflicting thoughts and emotions about the war swirled around inside Annie. When her father had first mentioned the conflict between the states at home, it sounded like a clear-cut political and economic struggle that men could settle with words. However, Veronia's journal had shown how decisions made on a purely philosophical level could cause unforeseen tragedy to women and children.

Thoughtfully, Annie fingered the assorted papers still inside the desk. So deep had been her connection to Veronia that Annie had easily pictured the light shining under the secret room's door and felt Robbie in her arms. The diary had allowed her to touch the young mother's soul in a way that transcended the labels of "slaveholder" and "abolitionist."

Now, with the Naughton story breaking off so abruptly, that bond had been severed, leaving Annie bereft. It hurt almost as much as leaving kin and friends on Martha's Vineyard.

Chapter Six

Daniel

That same day

D.R. spotted the man across the street, bent over a wagon wheel, broad shoulders straining as he worked. Seth Porter. D.R. hadn't seen him since the war, but there was no mistaking him—the steady, deliberate way he moved, the brown hair that always stuck up like he'd just yanked off his ha t.

D.R. adjusted his coat and crossed the road. He waited a second until Seth straightened, wiping his hands on a rag. Their eyes met . . . and after a beat . . . recognition flashed across Seth's face.

"Well, I'll be darned," Seth said, breaking into a grin. "Colonel Anthony."

"Not a colonel anymore," D.R. reminded him, extending his hand. "Just D.R.."

Seth's grip was as firm and callused as D.R. remembered. "Still feels like I oughta' call you 'sir,'" Seth said with a chuckle, "with your being mayor and all. What brings you to this part of town?"

"I heard you set up shop," D.R. said, his eyes sweeping the yard—neat stacks of lumber, a half-finished rocking chair by the workshop door, the wheel Seth had been fixing balanced on a sawhorse. "Looks like you've built yourself a good business."

"Better than I figured," Seth said, slinging the rag over his shoulder. "Get a fair bit of work from the fort—fixing wagons, repairing officers' quarters. And townsfolk've started coming around, too. Seems there's always someone needs a carpenter."

"Always will be," D.R. agreed. He let the words settle for a second, then glanced toward the shop. "I hear you bought this land after the fires."

Seth's smile thinned a little. "That's right. I figured it was too good a chance to pass up." He paused, his gaze steady. "Not sure everybody saw it that way."

D.R. met his eyes without flinching. "I don't regret burning the brothels." His voice was quiet but firm. "Those women were hiding bushwhackers. I'd do the same thing today."

"Oh, I know," Seth said, his tone light but his face serious. "Still remember the way those flames caught—fast and hot. And after the madams packed up and left, how men picked through what they left behind . . . like it was some kind of souvenir hunt."

D.R. laughed. "Well, the fires certainly increased my popularity with the church-going ladies around town."

A beat passed, the weight of memory lingering between them. Then he pushed forward. "I'll be building a house soon. Something solid. I'll need fine woodwork—good detail on the inside. I hear you do good work, and I'd like to see what you've got."

Seth's grin returned, slow and genuine this time. "You came to the right place. C'mon; let me show you some things I've made."

D.R. followed him toward the workshop, the scent of sawdust and fresh-cut wood filling the air. The war was behind them, so maybe this was a chance to build something good out of the ashes.

Seth's shop had a plain unvarnished floor and only a desk for furniture. In the corner stood two stout barrels on wheels—water for putting out fires, probably. Spare though the furnishings were, the shop boasted an ornate mantelpiece over the fireplace. D.R. crossed the room and felt the wood beneath his palm—smooth as a beaver hat. "Did you make this?"

"Sure did," said Seth.

From Seth's watchful attitude, D.R. sensed that the man was waiting for D.R.'s reaction, so he stood back to get a better look at the overall effect of the woodwork.

It had a plain firebox set in a brick arch and flanked by what D.R. would describe as flat Greek columns. Five horizontal sections above that featured carved branches and a wreath of leaves. To top it off, a heavily carved clock graced the surface of the mantel itself. "Beautiful! I bet you didn't carve this in a single piece," he said. "Is it all one kind of wood?"

Seth relaxed. Stroking the mantelpiece, he answered with enthusiasm, "Now this here is walnut. It's got a fine grain beautiful for carving." Then he indicated the clock case. "This is oak, stained to look like walnut. Just as good for carving, but you can see the grain."

D.R. stroked his beard while listening. Annie would love this, considering the kind of elegant home she'd had on the Vineyard. He could see himself in his private library smoking his pipe and reading, warming his feet before a hearth like this. Or sipping whiskey with Milton Clark. "Mind if I bring my wife by to take a look? We'd be wanting your work in a couple months."

Seth's smile broke out all over his face. "Heard you got married. Sure, bring her by." The two men walked out onto the porch, where D.R. pulled a cigar out of his pocket. "Care for a smoke?"

Seth put up a hand. "Not me, thanks. Occupational hazard, working in wood all day. But you go ahead—as long as you don't drop any flaming stubs. Don't want this place to go the way of its predecessor." While D.R. lit his cigar, Seth continued, "Hard to believe it's two years since I set up shop here."

"Well, I'm glad something good came of at least one of our fires. We ended with a nice controlled burn."

Seth shook his head, a faint grin tugging at his mouth. "You had us running like we were invading enemy territory."

"I was glad to have some men who knew fire and could work together."

"I never liked fire much. I was glad to get the job of policing the perimeter."

D.R. took a drag on his cigar. "You did it right, too. Kept that fire from jumping where it shouldn't."

"Wasn't easy," Seth said. "When that wind kicked up halfway through . . . I thought for sure we were gonna' lose the whole street. Had to shovel dirt over sparks more times than I can count." He took a long drink of his coffee. "Still . . . it was orderly, at least. We had a plan. Everyone knew their job."

D.R. gave him a sideways glance. "Not everyone thought we should've done it."

Seth shrugged. "Maybe not. Heck of a thing."

They stood in silence for a moment, Seth's face darkening as the moments went by. "Course, that was nothing compared to that farm we torched in Cass County."

D.R. frowned. "Don't remember any in Cass County."

"Maybe you weren't there," Seth said. "Anyway, it was chaos. We didn't have half the control we did with the brothels. No plan, no perimeter—just a bunch of angry boys with torches and guns."

Torches and guns. Those two words together brought back the stench of smoke and ashes.

"The neighbors said the family'd been passing information to Quantrill's raiders. Don't know if it was true, but the orders came down, and we did what we were told." He stared out into the street, his jaw tightening. "But it wasn't like the brothels. There, we kept it clean. Fast and controlled. That house . . ." Seth shook his head. "That was ugly."

"What happened?" D.R. asked quietly.

"Men went wild," Seth said. "They weren't just there to burn—they were there to steal. Stripped the place of anything valuable before the fire even started. I saw men carrying out silverware, clocks, dresses . . . even a cradle." His Adam's apple bobbed as he swallowed hard. "The owner and his son tried to resist but . . . became casualties. And when the fire got going, it spread too fast. Wind caught it, and before we knew it, the woods were burning. Neighbors came running, trying to save their own houses. I ended up spending half the night with a bucket, trying to keep the whole blasted county from going up in flames."

D.R. was silent for a long moment. "Sounds like a mess."

"It was. Wanna' know the worst part?"

D.R. wasn't sure he did. He had enough bad memories of his own without borrowing more. But he sensed this man needed to talk. "What?"

"I was the last to leave, and I saw—" he swallowed again "—two women with a baby running away from the house. I don't know how they made it out alive."

The lines of his face etched deep, D.R. clapped Seth on the shoulder. "Sometimes," he said slowly, "the boundary between right and wrong gets mighty thin in war."

"Ain't that the truth."

D.R. departed shortly after, glad to leave those memories behind. The sun was low in the sky and he was eager to get home for dinner. But on the way he passed Fanny Matthews walking toward Waverly House, which she operated as a restaurant and boarding house while her husband was away at war. When she beckoned to him, he pulled back on his reins and leaned down to greet her.

"Got a minute to talk, Colonel?"

When Annie's face flashed before his eyes, he wanted to say no. After twenty years of silent bachelor meals, he treasured every moment spent across the table from her, watching expressions move across her face as they talked. But if the people in Fanny's basement were discovered, she and her husband, Will, could lose their entire business and land in jail—the same risk Annie had taken.

Annie would understand. The memory of her gentle nod the last time he'd had to postpone still lingered. With a mixture of regret and resolve, he nodded.

"Meet me at the restaurant," Fanny said, and continued walking in that direction. By the time he had tied his horse to the hitching post, she strode up next to him and beckoned him into her office just inside the door.

"Something wrong?" D.R. said without preamble. He and Fanny had gotten to know each other well after he had put down good money to have a basement dug for runaway slaves under Waverly House.

Fanny leaned in, her eyes vivid in her dark face. "We just got some women who were house slaves and don't have decent winter clothing. They're mighty uncomfortable down there in this cold. I've given them blankets for now, but there aren't enough to go around. And they'll need something warmer when we move 'em on out of here."

Annie had collected clothing on the Vineyard. She would know what to do.

"I'll get right on it," he said. "I'll rustle up some more blankets tonight and get you some clothing as soon as I can."

"Thanks, Colonel. Oh, Will sends his regards."

"Where is he now, anyhow?"

"Tennessee. He says they have all different bugs down there and his troops don't like it much."

"How well I know. Thought I'd be eaten alive when I was in jail there."

Fanny cocked her head. "Is that when you refused to let contraband into your camp?"

D.R. nodded. "If you hadn't petitioned Lincoln to let me out, I'd probably still be there—unless the bugs carried me away."

Chapter Seven

Annie

February 28, 1864

Annie loved riding. On the Vineyard, it had been her remedy for restlessness. Letting Daniel go ahead of her this morning meant that she could focus on getting to know her new horse without worrying about where she was going.

Mounted higher on Bill than she had ever ridden before, Annie felt a little dizzy but willed herself to sit tall and proud. Daniel had helped her arrange the drape of her riding habit to its full advantage.

At first, he led the way at a slow pace among carriages and people walking or riding horseback. Annie's neck pricked with the sensation of someone watching her. Turning, she locked eyes with the beggar woman entering a cafe. As before, the woman had on a soiled dress and nothing but a ragged green shawl to protect her from the February wind.

Joining up with Daniel, she murmured, "Who's that poor woman in the green shawl?"

"Where?" said Daniel, his head swiveling around. But she had vanished.

Daniel muttered under his breath, "Well, if it isn't Doc Jennison. My commanding officer during the war."

Looking up at the man who had captured Daniel's attention, Annie could see that he gave the illusion of height because of his tall horse, but he was actually quite short. To her surprise, Daniel seemed ready to brush past him without a second glance. Just as Annie registered the slight tension, Jennison turned his horse to block their path.

"Anthony," he said, nodding. "Nice piece of horseflesh you have there." He eyed Annie's mount from bridle to tail, avoiding the rider entirely.

"Yeah, he's Bully Boy's—"

"I know. I bid on him, but you always did have a knack for stealing horses before anyone else could get 'em. So. You decided to tie the knot." His gaze then wandered over Annie, appraising her as frankly as he had sized up Bill. Despite the wintry chill, Annie felt her cheeks grew hot with embarrassment. She lowered her eyes.

"Annie, this is Colonel Charles Jennison."

She detected a sardonic note in Daniel's introduction. She faced the man and greeted him. "How do you do?"

Jennison nodded curtly. "I see you married the venerable commander." His voice dripped with sarcasm. Without another word, he flicked his reins and rode on.

"What sort of man is *that?*" Annie asked when he was out of earshot.

Daniel snorted. "Back in the days of the Jayhawkers, I was friendly with his wife. Used to help her with farm chores when he was too drunk to get up in the morning. Guess he still hasn't forgiven me for that or for beating him for mayor last spring."

"What is he doing now?"

"After he left the army, he started a freight company and a so-called restaurant. He was all settled back into civilian life when the governor asked him to raise another regiment to protect the Missouri border south of here. He must've come home on leave to see his wife."

"Having served under him for a long time, you must know him pretty well," she said. "Is he really a doctor?"

"He had some training but never practiced, far as I know. And I didn't know him as well as you'd think. Officially, he was our commander, but most of the time he dreamed up orders and sent me to enforce them." He paused. "I'm sorry he was so rude to you. He's a good man to avoid."

"Tell me the name of his restaurant so I don't patronize it. Is it in the circled area on your map?"

"Yup, it's called LeBonTon. They have cockfights there. And if the rumors are correct, it's a house of ill repute."

Giving her a level gaze, he repeated, "If you come across him, get away as soon as you can. The less he has to do with either of us, the better."

Chapter Eight

Daniel

March 19, 1864

D.R. shielded his eyes from the sun as he squinted at Annie trimming apple trees beside Ella. It was her second time helping at the farm, and she moved with more confidence now, her small hands gripping the pruning shears with determination.

"How was your visit to Ohio?" D.R. asked, lowering his hand. "I was afraid your vacation would give the criminals time to retake the town."

Chas smiled, but D.R. caught the hint of sadness behind it. "It was good to see relatives, but pretty sad to pass where we used to have our farm. Someone else is living there now."

"Sorry to hear it." The words felt inadequate, but what else could he say?

Chas surveyed the rolling fields beneath the blue Kansas sky. "Had somebody already farmed this land when you bought it?"

"No. When I first came here, all it had was tall grass and a few scraggly trees along this stream." The memory of that first day still made his chest swell with pride. Just weeds and potential then—now, the beginnings of something real.

"Figures."

"What do you mean?" Daniel peered at his friend.

"You like to start things. You're a pioneer."

Warmth spread through D.R.'s chest at the compliment. Coming from Chas, it meant something. "After I bought it, my brother and I cleared enough land to build the cabin, the horse corral, and plant the apple trees. We had apples in Rochester."

His gaze drifted to Annie as she reached for a sapling, her movements precise as she snipped away crossed branches. A laugh escaped his lips before he could stop it.

"What's so funny?" Chas wondered.

"Remember the first time I brought Annie here?" The memory tickled him still. "The day before, you should've seen her picking through my army duffle bag after I told her I had clothing suitable for work detail. Unfortunately, the first thing she came across was a pair of dirty old socks." He wrinkled his nose before returning to oiling a gear on the windmill. Thank God for Chas Goodman's help with the windmill. The blasted thing had been giving him trouble for weeks.

Chas gazed across the creek to where Ella worked beside Annie. "How's she doing?"

"She certainly took to the pruning lessons. I trust her with the trees now." Pride tinged his voice. She'd surprised him; the society girl wasn't afraid to get her hands dirty.

Chas turned back to stare at D.R. "Forget the trees. How's she liking Leavenworth? She's been here more than a month."

The question made D.R. pause. He hadn't really thought about it much. How hard had her transition been?

He thought aloud. "I married her knowing she was a society girl who had everything done for her, and I figured I could support her in that lifestyle. Even though she's got Lydia Clark and Ella for friends, she gets lonely while I'm gone. She even seems to resent it when I go to work."

"It is a long way from Massachusetts to Kansas," observed Chas.

A sigh escaped D.R. as he wiped his greasy hands on a rag and tossed it into the toolbox. "In the evenings, she's either reading or sticking to me like a burr. To tell you the truth, it's nice to have a little breathing room on weekends."

Small gestures of hers came to mind, glimpses of her strain to adapt. Those moments of uncertainty, the way her laughter sometimes faltered, the flicker of anxiety in her eyes—each detail he had brushed aside—came rushing back with new clarity. This wasn't just about change; it was about the choices she had undertaken to marry him, the silent battles she fought. His chest tightened as he understood that her journey had challenged her more than he realized.

They started walking toward the women, boots crunching on the uneven ground as they passed the cabin he now kept as a toolshed and temporary shelter.

"Doesn't she like going to lunch and sewing bees with other women?" Chas asked.

"Yeah, a little. When you met her that first day in the street, she was going to the Sanitary Relief Commission meeting with Lydia." It still needled him the way bystanders had snickered when he learned that Annie had asked Bauer for a ride. "But she's restless—needs to move. She used to roam all over Martha's Vineyard by herself. I can't keep her cooped up."

He shook his head, baffled all over again. "Unfortunately, she could get lost in a broom closet. I've never met anyone with so little sense of direction."

Chas frowned. "She ought to be careful where she roams, considering some of the characters around town."

The warning sent a familiar chill through D.R.'s spine. "I don't want to keep her like a hothouse flower—as she calls it—if she'd prefer otherwise. So I suggested the sections of town she should avoid." *Not that she always listened.*

Chas nodded and pushed back his cap. "Think you can teach her to use a gun?"

The image of Annie holding a pistol almost made him laugh out loud. "Not anytime soon. She's as gun-shy as a Quaker."

Chas chuckled as they reached the edge of the orchard. "Ella! Annie!" he called out to the women, who looked up from their work. D.R. surveyed the rows with satisfaction. They'd made good progress, leaving neat piles of skinny branches beneath each sapling.

"Let's eat," Chas called, miming in case they couldn't hear.

As the women approached, D.R. noticed how red Annie's nose and cheeks were, pinched with cold. The sight of her trudging toward him, determination in every step, stirred something deep in his chest.

⁂

She set her pruning tools on a barrel by the door before asking as they moved inside, "Where's the boundary of this farm?"

"On the other side of the creek," he replied, pointing.

"You were lucky to find water on your property," said Chas.

D.R. bristled slightly at the word "lucky."

"Not 'lucky.' Just *determined* to get this parcel with a creek. I slept in a cabin without a door near the Kickapoo land claims to buy it before any of the other homesteaders. I got plenty of chigger bites for souvenirs that night."

"Sounds miserable," said Annie, flexing her fingers and rubbing her hands together.

"Let's warm you up," D.R. said, reaching for her small hands with his large ones. Her fingers felt like icicles against his skin. "You amaze me," he murmured.

"What do you mean?" she asked.

"All the new things you're doing here in Kansas."

Her eyes flickered with surprise before softening into a warm glow of pleasure. "Why, thank you."

The moment passed as Chas knelt to light the kindling. "Dan, you got any small logs to warm our grub?"

The one-room building crowded around them, filled with firewood and implements. D.R. watched the small flame catch, its warmth barely enough to push back the chill. The two couples huddled in the one corner furnished with a few shelves, a bed, and a table—not much, but it was something.

As Ella unpacked the meat, cheese, and bread from the hotel kitchen, Annie's voice broke the silence. "What did you raise on your farm in Ohio?"

"Corn, wheat, and oats," replied Ella.

"You never said what brought you to Kansas," said Annie.

D.R. watched as the Goodmans exchanged glances. He already knew their story, but hearing it again never failed to stir his anger.

"You could say we were too devout for some of our neighbors," answered Chas, leaving a smudge of mud on his forehead when he reached up to remove his cap. The flare of the kindling reflected on his bald head. "You ever hear of Beecher's Bibles? We had a whole carton full of 'em."

Pride bloomed in D.R.'s chest when Annie replied without hesitation. "Oh, yes. Reverend Beecher, who said abolitionists might change more hearts with guns than with Bibles. There was quite a controversy about that in our church back home." She leaned forward. "So what happened after they discovered rifles on your property?"

Ella's voice dropped to a quiet murmur. "They stole the guns and all our animals, then burned our barn where we'd just taken in the harvest." Her pause sent a chill through the room. "The next day, I lost the baby I was carrying."

D.R. watched Annie's face as she received this news with appalled silence. This was the reality of the abolitionist fight—not just politics, but lives destroyed. Families shattered.

"We decided to come to Kansas where there are more like-minded people," Ella continued, her voice steadying. She held up a jar of home-canned applesauce. "D.R., if you have a pot, we can warm this."

D.R. took a swig from his canteen before handing it to Annie, who raised her eyebrows in mock disapproval. Her expression made him laugh. "No whiskey at this hour. It's just water from the stream." He watched as she drank, her throat moving delicately.

"How did you meet Daniel?" Annie asked as D.R. began heating the applesauce in his scratched mess kit.

Chas was the one who replied. "When Ella and I got off the steamboat, he was standing at the levee with a gun, guarding the mail sacks from the proslavery guys on board. As soon as we became acquainted, he offered *me* the guard job."

After dinner, D.R. grabbed his pruning shears and headed back outside with the others. Working alongside Annie, showing her the proper angle for each cut, he felt a strange contentment. When they finished by throwing the twigs into the kindling pile, exhaustion dogged his steps.

"Spring won't be far off now," said Ella, "and there's nothing so beautiful as apple blossoms."

D.R. caught Annie studying Ella—comparing herself, maybe, as his sisters sometimes did. Ella stood tall and confident, her abundant light hair caught back in a snood, her dark serviceable jacket and skirt fitting her perfectly. Annie, wrapped in his old greatcoat with her makeshift farm skirt, looked uncertain.

"We need to check on the pump before we leave," D.R. said to Chas. Then, struck by inspiration, he turned to the women. "Why don't you two take a ride while you wait?"

Annie shook her head sadly. "We forgot to bring my riding habit and saddle today."

A grin tugged at his lips. "That's where your 'farming costume' comes in handy." He stepped back to survey her from head to toe. "Looks sufficiently dirty to qualify as 'old' by now, don't you think? Ella can show you how to ride like a farm girl."

Understanding washed over Annie's face, followed by a deep blush. "Oh, no, I couldn't," she objected.

"Worried your sister Mary might criticize you for riding astride?" he teased, already knowing the answer.

As he expected, Annie bobbed her head.

"Side saddles are dangerous, you know," Chas chimed in. "I saw a woman slide down and get her foot caught. The horse dragged her upside down." He shook his head at the memory. "You're much safer riding astride."

"So I've been told," Annie replied, pausing a moment. Then a mischievous smile crept across her face. "Besides, I'm not on the Vineyard anymore, am I? So why shouldn't I?"

D.R. watched as Ella took Annie's arm.

"Come on, I haven't been for a good ride in weeks."

Drawing Annie aside, Ella helped her tuck the front and back hems of her skirt up into her waistband, fashioning makeshift pantaloons.

"That's the way!" D.R. said as Annie stepped into the stirrup and hoisted herself up onto his saddle without help.

"I can't believe I just did that," she exclaimed, a new light in her eyes. "Give me a crop, please."

D.R. patted the horse's neck, congratulating Annie with a look. "You won't need one now that you can grip with both your legs."

He watched as the women set off at a walk into the trackless field, then increased their pace to a trot beside the rushing stream. As the horses began to gallop, Annie's laugh rang out behind her—free and joyful in a way he'd never heard before.

A smile spread across his face as he turned to Chas. "Maybe Annie'll be all right after all."

Maybe they both would.

CHAPTER NINE

Annie

April 1, 1864

A couple of mornings later, Annie heard a scratching noise in the sitting room. Thinking she was about to encounter a Planters Hotel mouse, she went to investigate, and blinked with surprise. There, in front of the door that led to the hallway, lay an envelope addressed to her.

It probably wasn't an invitation because the size was wrong and the handwriting was messy. Someone must have delivered it personally after Daniel went to work, bypassing the post office. Turning it over, she found no return address. Inside, she found two old newspaper articles.

The most recent one, headlined "Anthony the Arsonist," described how her husband, "with his pants on fire," had approached Martin Bauer "with incendiary remarks," bringing a halt to that innocent citizen's hack trade. The article claimed that Daniel's Jayhawker past—and his notoriety for killing a proslavery publisher named R.C. Satterlee—had strained business relations with towns across the state line.

It concluded, "In these turbulent times, Leavenworth needs an impartial man as mayor. Fire the arsonist and vote for J. L. McDowell."

Next, Annie read a *Bulletin* article dated the week she had arrived:

Welcome to the West

Mrs. Daniel Anthony, wife of the mayor, was seen shopping in town today and, according to liveryman Martin Bauer, asked him for directions back to her lodgings at the Planters House, whereupon he offered her a ride. Mayor Anthony commanded Bauer to stop his carriage and implied that Bauer was kidnapping Mrs. Anthony. To back up his incendiary remarks, the mayor employed three lawmen to help rein in Bauer and escort Mrs. Anthony back to her hotel. We can only hope Mrs. Anthony soon comes to a clear understanding of Leavenworth, allowing city marshals to return to their pursuit of bona fide criminals.

Annie sighed. Despite the innuendo that Daniel was diverting town money to protect her, she could see the element of truth in the Bauer article. She wondered who had taken the time to send her the spiteful clippings. Some people just liked to stir up trouble.

All afternoon Annie looked forward to hearing Daniel's side of the newspaper stories. But she forgot all about the envelope when he breezed through the door and tossed a key onto the inlaid table in the sitting room.

"We're moving!" he said, smiling.

"What . . . when?"

"Tomorrow, if you can be ready. A small furnished house came vacant suddenly, and I grabbed it. It will be a lot quieter than the Planters." Removing his hat, he said, "Guess where it is . . . next door to Chas and Ella!"

"How perfect," said Annie with a smile. "But what about . . ."

". . . our house?" He took her hands and gazed into her eyes. "Just a little longer, Sunflower. I have to get through this election, and then we'll start building it."

"But it's early spring," she objected. "How long does it take to build a house? Don't they have to finish it before cold weather sets in?"

"As long as it's under roof by November or December, we'll be fine," he said. "They can work inside when the rains and snows come. But there will be plenty of dry weather between now and then." He paused. "More than you might wish."

She withdrew her hands and dropped her gaze. "Speaking of the election . . . someone wants you to lose." She pulled the offensive articles from her pocket and offered them to him. "These came today. Someone slipped them under the door."

She watched his face, waiting, while his eyes scanned the clippings. Would the writer in him enjoy the wordplay in the "pants on fire" article? How would he explain the stacked jury?

To her shock, his matter-of-fact expression collapsed, replaced by a flush of angry red.

"Not this again!" he snapped, slapping the articles onto the side table hard enough to jolt the lamp. He turned on his heel and stormed into the bedroom.

Annie followed, speechless, unsure of what to say. The only other time she'd seen him unravel like this was when he thought Bauer was trying to kidnap her. As he yanked off his jacket and threw it onto the bed, she faltered.

"What's the matter? No one would *believe* those, would they?"

"Oh, no, of course not," he responded, glowering. "Just the five hundred or so new voters in town who don't know the whole Satterlee story." She winced at his tone and scowl, even though he was not angry at her. "And that story about Bauer with its innuendoes. Disgusting!"

He dropped onto the bed to unlace his shoes, then raised his eyes to hers. His voice returning to normal, he said, "Annie, the truth is there are plenty of people who dislike my abolitionist stance and want a proslavery mayor, especially now."

Nervous about stirring the fearsome Daniel again, she spoke with caution. "Why now?"

"Because hundreds of contraband have escaped Missouri slave farms, and *certain people*"—he sneered—"want them to be even more miserable than they already are. I'm talking about the former slaves who live in the Contraband Camp, where conditions are unsanitary. *Healthy soldiers* sicken and die under such conditions, much less half-starved immigrants and former slaves."

Annie understood the source of his anger, because she too hated to see colored people mistreated. She had once risked her freedom on helping a Negro stowaway escape.

Changing his shirt, he continued, "As for the article about Bauer . . . I'm not ashamed of overreacting when I thought he'd kidnapped you. Nothing is more important to me than you."

Both his eyes and his voice softened as he stood and held his hands out to Annie, beckoning. Beholding again the honorable man she loved, she crossed the room into his arms to receive a warm kiss. The pressure of his hand on the back of her waist made her melt inside.

Releasing her after a moment, he said, "You ready for dinner? I'm starved."

"Speaking of dinner, who will cook for us in our rental house? You know my small skill in that department."

"Mary at the lunch counter will fix meals we can heat on our stove. Together, we can manage that, don't you think?"

Sitting across the table from Daniel at the restaurant, Annie watched him winding sauerkraut around his fork, an empty wineglass on the table before him. Again, she braved asking a question that troubled her.

Gently, so as not to upset him again, she asked, "If you lose the election, can we still afford to build the house?"

He waved her concern away with his fork. "Don't worry, I know some boys who will be glad to build it at a good price. I've had the money for it set aside for a year."

Annie removed a small volume from her purse. "I was looking at a book by Catherine Beecher called *The American Woman's Home*," she said tentatively, wondering if he would consider such interests beyond her womanly sphere. When he didn't object, she continued, "She suggests elements of house design that make homes more comfortable and easier to maintain."

"Oh, yeah? Tell me more." Though his words invited discussion, she saw him glancing at a couple behind her who had greeted him when they entered the restaurant.

Hoping to regain his attention, she responded to his question. "Homes should be designed with certain principles, Mrs. Beecher says, such as economy of labor, economy of health, and economy of comfort. A pretty home that is all for show is not good to live in, she maintains."

She was gratified when he asked, "And what does she say about economy of labor?"

"Make water-carrying more convenient by putting the kitchen, nursery, and sitting-parlor on the same floor. That way women are not always running up and down stairs with heavy pails."

"A dumbwaiter would accomplish most of those things," he said. "Still, I'd like to see her plans. She's an intelligent woman."

"How do you know?" she teased. "I've never seen you reading *The American Woman's Home*."

"No, but I've met all the Beechers. And the Stowes."

Annie's eyes widened as she leaned forward. "You have?" she breathed. "You must tell me about the writers among them." The day's tensions forgotten, they shared their love of books and dreamed about their future.

Later that evening, Annie wrote a letter to Catherine Beecher telling her how much she liked the chapter on homes.

By the first week in April, Daniel's term as mayor was coming to a close and he was finishing his campaign for a second term. This particular evening, Annie sensed his reluctance to go out and address the voters.

"Whether I win or lose, I'll be glad when all this mudslinging is over," he said, folding his speech. "Most of all, though, I hope it's a peaceful election. Oh—don't expect me back before ten o'clock."

Annie straightened his tie and stroked his shoulder. "I don't know what you're concerned about. This week people will demonstrate their gratitude for all the streets you've put macadam on this year, if nothing else. You'll win by a landslide."

He stepped out of her embrace and slid his remarks into his chest pocket. "I heard that McDowell has hired some bushwhackers to storm the polls." As her forehead creased in a frown, he added, "But don't worry. We've hired extra marshals for tonight and tomorrow. And we can have reinforcements from the army if we need 'em."

Annie invited Ella over to pass the evening of speeches together in the tiny Anthony rental home, a mirror image of the one Ella and Chas occupied next door. Without thinking, Annie poked a needle into a cross-stitch while Ella mended. It was a balmy spring evening, but they kept the windows closed as their husbands instructed.

"We've saved almost enough for our new house," said Ella. "Any progress on yours?"

Annie looked around at her trunks that served as tables and the packing barrel that doubled as kitchen workspace. There, Ella had taught her some rudimentary cooking.

"Still in the discussion stage," said Annie. "This election has taken so much time." Privately, she wondered if she would prefer that Daniel lost it so he wouldn't be mayor anymore. "I guess if his sister Susan were here, she would be asking why she's not allowed to vote in this election." Her tone was light.

Ella, however, gave her a look that was a mixture of disgust and disbelief. "No woman would be foolish enough to attempt to vote in Leavenworth," she said. "Haven't you heard about—" Her question was cut off by yelling from the street. A couple of voices at first and then an angry chorus.

Annie went cold. "I wonder what's going on," she murmured.

Ella bit off her thread, tied it in a knot, and picked up a simple shawl with a hole in it. "As I was saying, these campaign speeches sometimes turn into drunken shouting matches. Or worse. I heard a story about a past election when thousands of bushwhackers formed a mob and stormed the polls. Can you imagine?"

Annie's stomach clenched as the scene began to form in her mind.

As if to reassure both of them, Ella continued, "Chas promised me that he'd have extra marshals on watch to nip any problems in the bud."

As Annie recalled the civilians who had materialized with guns next to Martin Bauer's carriage, snatches of songs from the crowd invaded her thoughts. She crossed the room to look out the window while imagining several scenarios too gruesome to dwell on.

Seeing nothing amiss outside, she resumed her seat and said, "Here, give me that shawl. You can go back to your knitting."

"Are you sure?"

"I can mend," Annie retorted, shifting on the settee. "My stepmother taught me that much." Her voice softened. "You can work on that beautiful baby sweater."

Ella handed over her raveled shawl and pulled out a bag of soft, fine pastel yarn. Last week at the farm she had announced her pregnancy and ended her gallops with Annie. Gathering the yarn around the hole and beginning to stitch, Annie said, "At least this shawl can be repaired. Have you seen that poor woman in the tattered green shawl?"

"She's in a sorry state, isn't she?"

"I see some shopkeepers giving her food. What's her story?"

"Madame Collette told me she—the woman in the shawl—used to do laundry for the fort. But then she got kicked by a horse and it was several days before anyone found her." Ella shook her head. "Now she can't talk very well."

"How tragic," Annie said.

Ella leaned in, lowering her voice. "I heard she tries to talk, but it's just half-sounds and garbled words. Some say she babbles nonsense, others think she remembers everything but can't get it out." Her eyes sparkled. "Makes you wonder what secrets she might be carrying, doesn't it?"

Annie didn't care for Ella's gossipy tone. "I can't imagine losing my ability to speak," she demurred. Deciding to change the subject, she said, "Did you see the reference to Daniel in the *Evening Standard*? It called him 'Dead Rabbit Anthony.'"

"Pfft," said Ella. "Don't place any weight on things like that. They're just trying to be clever."

Despite the closed window, music from the street floated in. An amateur brass band was blaring a repetitive ditty while voices bellowed the tune. Interspersed with raucous cheers, the ersatz music continued for ten minutes in a nightmarish cacophony. As the din subsided, then rose again, her gaze flew to Ella, who pressed her lips together and drew a steadying breath. After several horses went by at a trot, two shots fired in rapid succession. The band fell silent in the middle of a phrase, and then a loud voice seemed to be giving orders. Without speaking, she inquired of Ella's eyes.

"Sounds like D.R.," her friend confirmed.

"I guess if we can hear him, he's still all right," Annie said with a weak smile. "Thank goodness for small blessings."

Half an hour later, both husbands came in, filling the small parlor with their tightly coiled energy. As Daniel banged the door shut and bolted it, she hurried to his side and wound her arms around his waist, pressing her cheek to his coat.

"I was so worried about you!" she breathed. "What happened?"

"There was an accident," he replied, holding her close. "One of the marshals got hurt bad."

Annie clung to him. "Oh, I'm so glad you're all right."

She watched Chas shoot a quelling look at Daniel before saying, "Did you hear the terrible music? But the chief attraction was when some of McDowell's boys got up some transparencies. Pretty clever, if you are of that political persuasion."

He crossed the room to sit on a folding chair next to Ella, who placed her hand in his. Since Annie had never seen transparencies, he described the large panes of glass decorated with paint. When the bonfire glowed behind them, they appeared like moving cartoons.

"What was the gist of the one with the black faces on it?" asked Daniel.

"Something about you using colored police to bully poor white farmers," replied Chas.

Daniel groaned and pulled up another folding chair next to Annie. "Guess they're referring to the colored deputies I used to disperse the crowd when Bauer had Annie in his carriage. Another nail in my political coffin."

Leaning his elbows on splayed knees, he punched his fist into his opposite hand and said, "They orchestrated the whole evening to make me look heavy-handed. First, they lit a bonfire to showcase those transparencies. My oath of office requires me to keep this city safe—and that open fire was dangerous. They knew I'd have to douse it, which would make me look like I was suppressing my opposition."

"They didn't have a parade permit, either," said Chas. "It's obvious they wanted you to shut everything down."

Daniel turned to Annie. "Did you hear the shots?"

She nodded, remembering the sound that made her fear for his life.

"I just fired off a couple overhead to get attention," he said, "and break up the crowd before they set the town ablaze. Restored the peace. And lost the chance to give my speech."

Chas rose, pulling Ella to her feet too. "We'll be going now," he said. He punched D.R.'s shoulder. "Sorry, Colonel. Sometimes doing the right thing feels mighty bad."

They shook hands.

The next morning, Annie and Ella set off for their marketing early in bright sunshine. She had calculated that spring came a week or two earlier here than on the Vineyard.

To prepare for making stew together that afternoon, Ella showed Annie how to select good cuts of beef at the butcher.

"Look for the fat marbled throughout the meat, rather than in thick chunks," she advised. "That way it's more tender."

On her way out the door, she encountered Miss Greenshawl, who followed Annie for a few paces before brushing by her, muttering, "Anthony. Homewrecker."

Annie froze mid-step, Miss Greenshawl's words hanging in the air like poisonous smoke. The accusation sliced through her, sharp and unexpected.

She glanced at Ella beside her, grateful her friend seemed not to have heard the venom in the ragged woman's voice. The boardwalk suddenly felt exposed, too public for the emotions roiling within her.

"Did you hear what she said?" Annie asked quietly, her voice steadier than she felt. Ella shook her head.

"Homewrecker." As the word turned over in Annie's mind, she returned to Mrs. Fisk's shop where she'd first heard that word on the modiste's lips. Her sunny morning darkened when she realized the woman had been referring to her and Daniel, but something didn't add up. They seemed critical of him for taking a young wife, but that didn't make him a homewrecker.

Miss Greenshawl had spat the word like it was personal. Had she lost a home to Anthony's regiment like the women in the diary? Was that ghostly smoke still burning in her memory after all these years? Or was it something completely different?

Three blocks away from the Planters they encountered Maria Rice with a list in hand. After greeting Ella, she turned to Annie. "Did you hear about the fracas last night at the hotel?"

"No, but we heard the shots," said Annie.

Mrs. Rice scoffed. "Your Daniel has survived more fights than you have pins in your hair," she said. "But our poor saloon didn't fare so well." She gestured to the list in her hand. "I have to get some supplies replenished."

"Truly? What happened?"

"Your husband's supporters"—she gave Annie a pointed look—"and Jim McDowell's friends had a shouting match that escalated. They smashed a lot of our glassware and some good bottles of whiskey, and destroyed most of the chairs. Damaged the paneling, too."

Annie felt guilty by association. "Oh, I'm so sorry to hear it! Wait till the colonel finds out! He'll be mortified."

"He already knows. First thing this morning, my husband paid calls on both him and McDowell." She patted Annie's arm. "They both contributed handsomely to take care of the damages. If it isn't one thing with these boys, it's another."

"Who was hurt?" Annie asked.

Maria looked solemn. "Marshal Schott. I haven't heard a report on him yet. Good day."

Chapter Ten

Daniel

April 4, 1864

At dawn on Election Day, D.R. mounted Bully Boy to make his rounds at the polling places. By half-past eight, he'd completed his visits and settled in across the street from the Fourth Ward voting box outside Max Fielding's barbershop. There, men stood waiting in the sun, the line stretching into the shade formed by an alley perpendicular to the main street.

He positioned himself far enough away to avoid interfering with the polls, but close enough to nod at each new arrival. Some tipped their hats in acknowledgment while others, like Martin Bauer, avoided his gaze. Among the voters were men missing limbs or bearing scars, veterans from both sides of the war, mingling with the townsfolk.

At nine-thirty, Jim McDowell took up his post next to the barbershop and seemed to be asking a lot of questions. D.R. scowled at his rival with open dislike. McDowell was narrow-shouldered with an elongated neck, his head twitching like a nervous bird, his sharp black eyes scanning for supporters. D.R. couldn't help but smirk at the man's resemblance to a chicken; it reinforced his conviction that McDowell was ill-suited for the responsibilities of mayor. The care and management of freedmen would be the foremost challenge once this infernal war concluded.

Glancing across the street at Anthony, McDowell spoke briefly to several supporters before they dispersed into the crowd. D.R. observed that people weren't leaving the area after they voted. Instead, they were sticking around like they were waiting for something.

He shifted in his saddle and pulled out his pocket watch. In the thirty minutes he'd been sitting here, the sun had grown warmer and started him sweating, while across the street McDowell appeared comfortable in the shade. D.R. was hankering for a glass of sarsaparilla in the café, but something urged him to stay mounted.

As new voters arrived, the atmosphere grew increasingly raucous. Whiskey bottles passed among the throng, and when Chas Goodman rode up beside Bully Boy, he asked, "Are McDowell's boys stirring things up?"

"Yeah," D.R. replied. "I recognize quite a few of 'em."

"They're causing trouble at all the polling places. Hold on; I'll bring reinforcements, including the army." Chas trotted off.

Minutes after that, D.R. heard the ominous thrum of boots on the boardwalks and his pulse quickened at the rumble of angry voices. Violence was only a breath away.

Shouting to one another, the unruly mob poured into the intersection and converged on Fielding's Barbershop, nearly knocking down a man on crutches who was missing a leg just below the knee. D.R.'s fists curled in frustration at their callous disregard.

I don't remember seeing any of these men around town before, he thought as a red-faced man swaggered to the front of the voters' line, proclaiming, "We come to post our ballots. Ain't got all day."

"Yeah, we're workin' men," added another voice. "Diggin' latrines up at the colored camp. We can't stand here waitin' fer the cows to come home."

His companion, dusty from head to toe, elbowed him. "You don't mean cows, you mean pigs, right? Those pigs still in office? We gotta' vote them pigs out!"

"Now just a minute," interjected a man D.R. recognized as Amelia Bennett's husband, who worked at the general store. "You wait your turn like the rest of us. And they aren't pigs. Without their administration, you wouldn't even have your job!" He turned to the red-faced man. "Hey, I cashed you out at the mercantile—you said you're from Missouri, didn't you? You can't vote in this election!"

Redface thrust the neck of his flask under the clerk's chin, grinning as the man's eyes widened. His dusty companion grabbed the clerk's arms from behind.

"Now you wouldn't wanna' tamper with the voting, would ya? I hear that leads to some downright ugly feelin's."

D.R. felt a surge of adrenaline as the red-faced man swung a fist toward the clerk's groin. His body instinctively tensed, and he nearly sprang from his saddle. But no, he couldn't interfere—not now, not with the election in process. A rush of frustration coursed through him as the clerk doubled over, clutching himself and crumpling to the ground. The harsh laughter echoed against the close-set buildings, slicing through the tension in the air. D.R. clenched his jaw, fighting the anger bubbling up within him. He hated bullies.

Arguments erupted, fists flew, and the latest arrivals pushed through the line, crowding into the barbershop. From the corner of his eye, D.R. noticed McDowell slipping down the alley. Then, panic surged through him when he saw Annie making her way toward the intersection.

No, not now, not like this.

The world around him faded, heart pounding in his chest as dread coiled tightly in his gut. He had to act, had to protect her.

At that moment, the red-faced man pointed to D.R. and shouted, "Hey, look at Anthony sittin' on his high horse like he's got all day. We don't need a high-falutin' do-nothin' for mayor. Let's knock 'im down a peg, fellas!"

Anthony signaled Bully Boy to prance right and left. Wish I had a bayonet to shake at them, he thought. Where in tarnation is Chas?

D.R. lost sight of Annie just as Redface gathered his crew, a tide of malice surging toward the mayor. His heart constricted as the three marshals behind him faltered, their strength waning against the dozen thugs charging in—a roiling blend of snarls and shouts with raised clubs.

Bully Boy, usually a steadfast companion attuned to D.R.'s every move, abruptly froze when a man seized his bridle and held it in a vise-like grip. No help there.

The world shifted in a dizzying blur as hands yanked D.R.'s foot from the stirrup. He felt the hard earth rising to meet him, wrenching his body as he fought to land on his feet. A shove from behind sent him sprawling, the cacophony of grunts and laughter echoing in his ears—a dark symphony of violence that coiled hope into knots of terror.

All around him, the scent of sweat and adrenaline thickened the air, heavy with the promise of cruelty. He was lost now, swallowed by the storm, and dread clawed at his insides as he tumbled headfirst into the horror of the melee. Pain coursed through his gut and ribs as he struggled to shield his head from the barrage of blows.

Jeering, they hoisted him above their heads. "Hang 'im!" shouted a voice that D.R. half recognized.

Suddenly, the thunder of hoofbeats approached, and Bully Boy whinnied.

"Unhand the mayor! Stand back!" boomed a welcome voice just before he landed in the dirt. D.R. opened his eyes to see himself encircled by mounted police, their faces toward the crowd.

Chas leaned over him, asking, "Can you walk? We need to get you out of here. The city's gone wild."

D.R. struggled to his knees, every muscle protesting as his legs buckled under him.

"Healy, help me," Chas called to another officer. Strong arms lifted D.R. on either side, half-carrying him away from the chaos.

Suddenly, he planted his feet. "Wait. Where's Annie? I saw her . . ."

"Don't worry, boss. I told her to go home before she put you in danger."

Relief washed over D.R., but as he took a step, nausea threatened to pull him down again. He paused, glancing back at Fielding's. Coughing to clear his throat of dirt, he rasped, "I need to get the ballot box."

Marshal Healy protested, "But that would end the election early. It's not even noon yet!"

"The election's a bust," D.R. coughed out. "If I cancel it, maybe the mob'll disperse."

An hour later, D.R. sent a message to Annie: "I'm safe and sound, but the voting is canceled. Still, I have quite a bit of official business to attend to. I'll be late."

He returned home much later to find Annie unpinning her chignon at the mirror. Exclaiming with concern, she brought a basin and sponged off his face and hands before he resisted any more help. Instead, he collapsed into the bedroom chair and drifted off, dimly aware of her covering him with a blanket. When he woke again after she had retired, he thanked whatever god was listening that she hadn't had the chance to question him. She would have surely gotten herself into a stew.

Disturbing the bedclothes as little as possible, he climbed in beside her. Just before surrendering to sleep, the cry of "Hang 'im!" echoed in his mind, and he connected the voice with memories of his army days. His eyes popped open in the dark.

Jennison.

D.R. awoke with a start at eight o'clock the following morning, feeling bruised from fists and kicks, and followed his nose to the smell of coffee and biscuits.

"I decided to let you sleep," Annie said, slipping her arms around him. "Thank God you're safe. What happened?"

Still too tired to face her concern, he skirted the issue. "We decided to close the polls. There was no way I could win, and things were getting out of hand."

"Oh!" She paused. "That was a long day. I've never seen you so tired."

Late for work, he tried to disengage, but she nuzzled his neck and rubbed his back. After a moment, she stepped away and regarded him.

"So, will you have it declared illegal and call for another vote?"

He shook his head, his whole body sagging with defeat. "That would just cause more problems. We'll let McDowell have this round." Seeing her crestfallen expression, he assured her, "I'll get another chance in a few years."

It took considerable energy to stride as usual to City Hall rather than trudge. The damp April chill of the morning air pressed against his skin as he approached City Hall, its stern façade looming above him like a gavel ready to strike. He had always relished the hustle of politics, the thrill of speaking his mind, of rallying the crowd. Yet now, with the election behind him and the sound of the mob still echoing in his ears, his self-confidence felt frayed at the edges.

Yes, he had poured every ounce of himself into this campaign, stood before the people who had cheered his name, but today, they were a distant memory. Still, he refused to let that wear him down. Drawing a deep breath, he reminded himself that this wasn't the end but merely a chapter closed—nothing could extinguish that flicker of ambition that burned within him.

Sweat trailed down his back as he quickened his pace, each footfall resonating with the rhythm of determination. He was tired—soul-weary—but tiredness wouldn't be his downfall. It was a badge of honor, a testament to the fight he had put up. Striding through the looming doors of City Hall, he straightened his back, banishing doubts and exhaustion as he stepped into the still air of the building.

The scent of polished wood and bureaucracy filled his nostrils, a reminder of his battles won and lost within these walls. Today, he walked not as a defeated man, but as one who had tasted the heady flavor of ambition and intended to return for more. Despite the heaviness settling in his bones, he moved forward with renewed purpose. There was no telling what his next strategy would be and what new dreams awaited just beyond the grim horizon immediately before him.

Setting right to work, he neatened up the files on the outstanding macadam contracts and bridge work before filing them carefully for the new mayor. Next, he jotted down some pertinent facts about war refugees at the camp.

By mid-afternoon, he was sorting through his belongings and reading accounts of the previous day's chaos in various newspapers. One report claimed that McDowell had defeated him three to one. He scoffed—that hogwash didn't align with the reality that there were three hundred more ballots in the box than the total number of registered voters in Leavenworth.

His face flushed hot as he read an article in *The Bulletin* about his tenure as mayor.

Mayor Anthony's administration was a complete failure; its evil effects were felt not only in Leavenworth but in the whole country . . . Loyal persons from Missouri were arrested and imprisoned for no other reason than to gratify a personal spite of the mayor . . . A system of Negro police was inaugurated, and men were prosecuted as criminals because they dared to express themselves in opposition to the will of a tyrant.

Wadding up *The Bulletin's* pages helped to vent his anger enough to start his packing. Retrieving his dictionary from the shelves, D.R. stowed away the rest of his personal belongings. Finally, he rolled up the rug he had laid down on his first day as mayor. Half an hour later, a clerk assisted him in loading everything into a waiting wagon. Once he was sure the entire staff had left, D.R. allowed himself a malicious smile as he set the rest of his departure plan in motion.

His first order of business was to fill a sack with manure from the stables beneath City Hall. Then he returned to his office, where he crafted a note for his opponent:

Until the next election, all that will come out of this office is manure. I locked the files and put the keys in the sack.

With a sense of satisfaction, he tossed the keys into the foul-smelling bag, wiped his soiled hands on the upholstered chair, and left without a backward glance.

Chapter Eleven

Annie

April 6, 1864

Annie had dog-eared several pages in her stack of newspapers when Daniel arrived the next evening at their rental house for dinner. She noticed he looked nervous, which was unfortunate for him, as she had questions that needed answers.

Once he had taken off his coat and set down his belongings, she opened a newspaper and pointed to a specific line.

"When I left the polling place on voting day, you were sitting on your horse. What happened after that? *The Conservative* says you were 'knocked down and roughly handled.'"

"Yeah, well, some guys threw a couple of punches."

"Then you were locked up?"

He seemed to relax a bit. "That was quick thinking on Chas's part. It was for my own safety, really. Gave me some peace and quiet to write my close-the-polls speech."

She refused to let his smile disarm her. "What's this bit about Jennison? It says he was Commander of the Post, but it doesn't sound like he was on the scene."

"I can vouch for him bein' there," he said with disgust.

She continued reading aloud. "'When the army was called upon to quell the riot, they refused to come.' I can't believe that!" The paper rustled as she jerked it to her lap.

"A few years ago, when the army was investigating Jennison, I told them about some of his brutality toward the troops. He got court-martialed. But then they reinstated him to help them chase the secesh in Missouri. Guess being Commander of the Post yesterday gave him the opportunity to even the score with me."

Understanding washed over her.

"Yup. So Jennison not only abandoned his post yesterday, but he actively encouraged mob rule." Frowning, he shook his head. "I didn't know he would be commander during the election. That's like putting a fox in charge of the henhouse."

Reassured by his casual attitude, she felt tension drain away from her shoulders. "Yes. But I like this next part. 'Anthony was shortly released by his friends . . . was surrounded by an immense throng and preceded them down Shawnee Street . . . where the crowd halted and he made his speech.'"

As she continued reading, her heart swelled with admiration. "'He said the polls should be closed until a peaceable election could take place, and that with his consent they should not be opened again until such a time came.'

"I think you handled that with remarkable dignity." She paused, laying her hands on her bosom and feigning a swoon. "My hero."

D.R. laughed and dropped onto the settee next to her.

She changed to a matter-of-fact tone. "But they also said that many of your supporters were turned away from voting."

"Too true." He began unlacing his shoes.

Annie set the pages aside and scoffed. "That column in *The Bulletin* was another story altogether. Literally." Picking up another paper, she thumbed through to the article she wanted. "It says you seized the ballot box early in the morning without any provocation because you knew you were going to lose."

His jaw tightened. "McDowell's men beat up two police officers in the last several days. I closed the election so nobody else would get hurt, not because I was losing." And he would've been next in line for a thrashing if Chas hadn't returned.

He sighed, frustrated. "What other discrepancies did you see?"

"It says, 'At every polling place all around the city, utmost quiet prevailed.' Horsefeathers! I was there, and I've never heard so much commotion in all my life!"

He frowned at her. "So what were *you* doing out yesterday, risking your safety?"

She looked defiant. "At home we celebrate elections with bake sales for charity. I didn't know they were such dangerous events here. But"—she waved her hand as if displaying a magician's rabbit—"I have something to show for my errand. Beef stew."

Half an hour later, as D.R. was sopping up gravy with a flaky biscuit, Annie watched with a heavy heart.

"You worked so hard as mayor. What will you do now?"

He shrugged, a quick motion that felt like a dismissal, making her cheeks warm with embarrassment. For him to brush off her concern like that stung. Today, bruises bloomed on his face and arms, a stark reminder of the chaos that had unfolded. The slight hitch in his gait told her it was uncomfortable for him to walk. If she were in his shoes, having lost an election to a hate-filled mob, she'd be trembling with fear. She wanted to wrap her arms around him and let him know it was okay to let the walls down. He didn't need to wear a mask around her; she could handle the truth.

Daniel's voice was matter-of-fact. "With two-year terms, being mayor isn't a job you can bank on. I can just beef up my insurance business and we'll be fine." For the first time in days, his eyes gleamed. "*And* I have another plan."

As he described it to Annie, she laughed and then questioned the difference it would bring to their own affairs. "Can we still afford the house?"

"You keep asking me that. If it will make you feel better, see for yourself." He pulled the bankbook out of his pocket, opened it, and pushed it toward her.

Curious, she glanced at the figure he indicated—a sum that made her gasp. "That should be enough!"

"But I guess maybe I should tell you . . . While selling insurance, I may be too busy to start our house right away."

She rested her forehead in her palm and shook her head.

Chapter Twelve

Daniel

April 7, 1864

The next day, D.R. sat in his insurance office reviewing his accounts. Though he had built a thriving business before the war, fire and accident claims had been only a side interest during his days in City Hall. He would have to get some new policies to provide for his new business venture. His mouth quirked. He could always set a fire somewhere to scare people into buying insurance.

Perish the thought.

When the door jangled in the front office, he straightened his tie and went to see who was there. A bank messenger stood holding an envelope addressed in Milton Clark's handwriting. After giving the lad a generous tip, D.R. returned to his desk and opened it. Inside he found a check for a huge amount and a note that read, "From one of your disappointed supporters." D.R. furrowed his brow, put on his jacket, and set off for the Clark Gruber Bank.

When the clerk admitted him to Milton Clark's office, his friend sighed with feigned displeasure. "You're as predictable as chigger bites in the summer. But even so, I didn't expect you this soon. Sit down."

D.R. lowered himself into the leather chair and pushed the mysterious check across the desk blotter. Without preamble, he demanded, "Who sent this, and what do they want?"

Milton pursed his lips and glanced away. Then, meeting D.R.'s eyes again, he said, "The donor wishes to remain anonymous."

"Mighty peculiar time to make a campaign contribution—after the election is lost."

"Yes . . . there's no accounting for some people's timing."

"Is it a political bribe?"

"No. Definitely not."

The leather creaked as D.R. smiled and relaxed in his seat. "One less thing to worry about."

A game of cat and mouse ensued as he tried to pry the information out of his friend.

Finally, Milton said, "I will give you one clue. The donor expressed a wish to buy some time."

D.R. drummed his fingers on Milton's desk. "Buy some time . . . as in . . . time to repay a loan? No, they wouldn't *give* me money if they owed me." Milton steepled his fingers and listened with amusement as D.R. continued. "Buy some time, as in, time to go on living? Couldn't be that, 'cause I'm not holding a gun to anyone's head."

"I should hope not. Discuss it with Annie when you go home tonight. Maybe the name will come to you."

D.R. looked startled and then smiled. Pocketing the check, he rose and said, "Thanks, I'll do that."

He didn't mention the money until he was facing Annie across a table at Giacomini's restaurant. While they were waiting for their food, he brought out Milton's envelope and laid it on the table.

"I received this odd note today from the bank."

She didn't spare it even a glance. "What's so strange about it?"

"There's a check for the very amount of the annual mayor's salary."

She tsk'd. "My goodness. Was Milton offering a discount on money to good customers?"

Chuckling, he said, "No, but your personal bank account was down by that same sum."

She tapped the table. "Oh, fiddlesticks! I forgot you can see what I have in that account." Despite her tone of voice, she looked unperturbed. In fact, she looked like a fox that had just feasted on chicken.

"I told you we have enough money," he said. "You needn't worry. I started saving for the house when I first got to Leavenworth, in anticipation of meeting the woman of my dreams. Now it's time to spend it."

"Yes, but you said you wouldn't have time to oversee the construction because you'd be building the insurance business back up. So I thought I would make a business transaction."

He raised his eyebrows. "What do you mean?"

"I want to buy time, Daniel Anthony. *Your* time. Instead of increasing your insurance clients, you can pour all your energy into newspapers. Buy *The Bulletin*. But don't run it on a shoestring, hire expert help. That way you can come home earlier at night to supervise our construction. Will you do that for me?"

He shook his head. "I can't."

"Why not?" She cocked her head, accentuating her graceful neck.

"Well . . . husbands don't usually . . ."

She pursed her rosy lips. "Pish. If it makes you feel better, you can write me an IOU. I'll keep it in my lingerie drawer."

"We promised Susan to keep your money separate," he said, less intensely now. "She'd have my head."

She folded her arms over her bosom, holding his glance captive. "I've already written Susan a letter explaining it's in *my* best interest to move into our house sooner. And I stressed the fact that you never asked me for a penny. Want to read it before I mail it?"

He raised his hands in surrender. "You're one step ahead of me all the way. I give up."

She lifted her wine glass. "Here's to the new owner of *The Bulletin*," she said, clinking his glass, "whose revised editorial policy will put an end to that poor excuse for journalism. Now, when can we start our house?"

At three o'clock the following afternoon, D.R. gathered his closest friends in Milton's conference room. It was the first time he had seen some of them since before the election. As each man crossed the threshold, Anthony handed him a cigar and clapped him on the shoulder, thanking him for his political support. They filled all the seats at the table.

D.R. leaned forward to pour himself a whiskey and passed the bottle to his right. "Our administration gave McDowell's men a good fight on many fronts," he said. "We kept Tom Ewing from buying up all the best land in Leavenworth, helped make a halfway decent camp for the refugees, and nailed down some good railroad deals. We macadamized more roads in town and built good solid bridges over many of the creeks."

Milton proposed a toast to D.R., and several more followed.

When the mood had risen, D.R. placed his glass down firmly and commanded the room's attention. "I have an announcement to make." He looked at Milton. "This morning I completed the purchase of *The Bulletin.* I aim to make it the most radical paper in Leavenworth and hope you'll all subscribe—or renew your subscription—and advertise with us. Of course, we will always be interested in hearing your point of view on matters pertaining to life here in our fair city."

He raised his glass. "Here's to having our say—"

"I second that," chimed in Milton who, like D.R., had been cheated out of buying land parcels reserved for the wealthy Tom Ewing.

"—without having to tiptoe around the opinions of City Council!"

Chas raised his glass. "To the new *Bulletin!*"

A few evenings later, D.R. brought home his first edition of *The Bulletin* and laid it on the table for Annie to read. As he was polishing his shoes in the butler's pantry, she entered, tapping her palm with the rolled-up paper.

"Did you write this?" she asked, pointing to a three-inch article on page one entitled "He Knows No More of an Army Regiment Than a Spinster."

D.R. put on a smug face. "Mmm-hmm."

"If anyone ever had a doubt about you and Doc Jennison, this will clear things up. I can't believe you said the regiment is *cursed* by having him as their commander."

"Well, it's true. Ask any man who's ever served under him."

She frowned. "Nevertheless, is it wise to point that out in the paper?"

"Truth is truth, and I've never been one to shrink from it. By the way, there's a meeting of the Republican Party in Topeka next week. He hopes to run for Senate next term."

"God save us."

Chapter Thirteen

Annie

May 17, 1864

Annie dressed carefully in a lightweight skirt and blouse, for today was Tuesday, the day she usually attended the Sanitary Relief Commission meeting with Lydia.

Many soldiers had come back from battlefields scarred, broken, or missing limbs, while others had returned with infections. Through fundraisers and collections of clothing, the women's society provided relief to men on the field and in hospitals. In addition, they helped the formerly enslaved people who had seized freedom by going behind Union lines. Private inquiries to a few of them had quickly provided more than enough clothing for the freedwomen hiding in Fanny Matthews's basement.

Annie liked the way they rotated their meeting location because that provided her with invitations into many homes.

"Oh, what lovely green wallpaper," she exclaimed upon entering the parlor of Mary Gray, whose husband was a judge. "Did you get it here in Leavenworth?"

"Yes, from Drakes," replied Mary, whose jade earrings bobbed when she spoke. "I don't know whether to believe it or not, but they ran an ad yesterday saying they just got in three thousand rolls! That's more than enough for all the homes in Leavenworth, don't you think?"

Annie smiled at Mary, who folded her hair behind her head in a way that reminded Annie of Susan.

"Please rise for the Pledge of Allegiance," said President Rachel Stark when fifteen women had gathered. Then she led the group in prayer for a swift victory in the war.

When the women settled in their seats, Rachel's solemn tone changed to glee as she waved an announcement from the newspaper. "*The Times* mentioned us on the front page this morning, ladies. It starts off with our $1,600 contribution to the Sanitary Fair in St. Louis, and then there is this lovely tribute from the president of the whole Commission. I'll pass it around.

"Now that we have finished the Sanitary Fair project, it's time to address the next scheduled item on our calendar, the Contraband Camp," she continued. "I'm not quite sure why we voted to support it, since it's not really part of the war effort. How do we want to help them?"

Annie cleared her throat and ventured an opinion. "Not long ago, my husband visited the Contraband Camp and found that many of the escaped slaves are sick—especially the women. I once met someone who had just escaped. I couldn't believe his sores. Do they have enough medicine and healthy food?"

Henrietta Jellico spoke up. "The Freedmen's Commission is in charge of their medicines. I'm sure they're handling that part just fine. But the entry to that camp is a blight on Leavenworth. I think we should do something to brighten it up."

"We could show our community spirit by putting up a flagpole at the entrance," said treasurer Lavinia Roy. Several women nodded excitedly.

"How about a garden around the flagpole?" This came from Mrs. Kipling, whose husband owned the feed and seed store. "That would let the new arrivals know how welcome they are."

Rachel Stark fingered the gold chain around her neck as she said, "I wonder how much this will cost."

Annie sensed the president had no more enthusiasm for a beautification project than she had herself.

"Might be as much as a hundred dollars," Lavinia Roy said.

Mary Gray chimed in. "That would buy quite a bit of food instead, I think. Or we could help establish a vegetable garden within the camp itself."

Mrs. Roy tapped her pencil. "I'm sure the Freedmen's Bureau has the food situation well in hand, Mary. But that depressing entrance is not within the Bureau's jurisdiction, so it's a perfect project for us. I propose we take it to a vote. There's a benefit musical performance at Laing's Hall next week, and the Sanitary Relief Commission will receive half the proceeds. We could use that money for the Negroes."

Rachel Stark and Mary Gray looked satisfied. Annie wondered if the project would benefit the camp residents as much as it would the town.

After the meeting, Annie and Lydia parted company at Fourth Street to go to their respective homes. Annie decided to stop at a bakery and pick up some scones. She longed for the day when their house would be finished and she could hire her own cook to provide a steady supply of the foods she particularly liked. More fish, for one thing.

As she passed Corey's Fish and Fruit, she caught a delicious aroma. Fried fish! Hearing a church bell chime four, she realized it was still two hours till supper. The smell drew her inside. At the moment there were no customers, so she talked to Mr. Corey, who was frying bass behind the counter. Bass wasn't as good as the sea fish she loved, but it was still better than a steady diet of pork and beef.

After a few minutes, she bought a packet, assured that the merchant would wrap it so well it would arrive home still warm. "Just heat in the oven after you get home, and you'll have hot fish to put on your table at six," he assured her. Delighted, Annie was paying for her purchase when the bells above the door jangled behind her and she detected a less-welcome smell. Body odor.

She turned to see the woman in the green shawl, who sidled off to the end of the counter. Almost immediately, the proprietress appeared from the workroom and told the new arrival, "Not now. Come back in an hour." The strange woman shambled back outside.

But when Annie left the store and passed the alley to walk east, she heard her own name. At least it sounded like her name. "Miss . . . us-s-s An-n-n-ie . . . An-n-n-tho-n-ny. . . "

Puzzled, Annie turned around and saw Miss Greenshawl hurrying away down the alley.

How did she know Annie's name? Recalling that the fish store proprietor seemed to know Miss Greenshawl, she thought now of seeing the tattered woman removing rolls from a bakery's alley door her first week in town. Were many of the local merchants in the habit of feeding her? Maybe she wasn't a thief after all. But what could possibly interest her about Annie?

A few days later, she visited Drake Brothers to begin her selection of wallpaper. She wanted some for the parlor of their house, whose interior walls had been "roughed in," as Daniel called it, and would soon receive plaster. As she passed a bench in front of the bookstore, she was startled to see Miss Greenshawl, who observed her with a sneer and muttered, "Naïve . . . girl." Annie blushed and hastened by, relieved that no one else was around to hear.

Similar chance meetings with the mysterious woman occurred during the rest of May. Annie regarded her with a mixture of curiosity and dread because of her personal comments such as "child bride" and "heiress." The worst one was "married for money." What would Miss Greenshawl say next?

When Annie asked Daniel for his opinion about the woman, he said, "I've never seen her myself, but according to Chas, she's not dangerous. If she bothers you, try shopping with a friend."

That was no help.

As time went by, the woman who had been a stranger became strangely familiar. Annie responded to these encounters by raising her chin and hurrying by. She felt like a coward.

Miss Greenshawl's attentions reminded her of Richie, her unwanted suitor on the Vineyard. One day when he attempted to kiss her in a secluded spot, she fended him off with a pair of scissors. What could she do to discourage Miss Greenshawl?

Besides her shopping trips with Lydia, Annie also liked to walk with Ella Goodman.

"I want to be nice and strong when it's time to deliver this baby," said Ella the next afternoon, patting her increasing girth. "Even though I continue to get fat, walking helps me feel better about it," she said ruefully.

"Don't be silly," said Annie. "You're supposed to gain weight when you're expecting." She had been surprised the first time she heard "fat" as a compliment for pregnant women. Someday she hoped to be pregnant herself, but so far none of their lovemaking had proved fruitful, except to make her love her husband more. Remembering his kindness to his niece and nephew in Rochester, she just knew he would make a great father.

"Ella," Annie said during one of their excursions, "you know that woman in the green shawl?"

"Yes, you and I talked about her, remember? Why do you ask?" "She turns up in the oddest places."

"She certainly does," replied Ella. "One day I saw her sitting on the Methodist Church steps. Guess who she was talking to? Colonel Jennison."

"Where does she live? And why is she so . . . ratty-looking?"

Ella shrugged. "No one seems to know much about her."

Annie was tired of dodging the woman's verbal abuse. The next time Miss Greenshawl made a snide comment, Annie would confront her.

Chapter Fourteen

Daniel

May 23, 1864

"Visitor to see you, Colonel," said the clerk at D.R.'s newly acquired newspaper.

"I don't have any engagements on my calendar," said D.R., keeping his eyes on the police report in his hands. "Tell them to make an appointment."

After some hesitation, the clerk said, "Says he's a relative, sir. A Mr. John Osborn." D.R. searched his brain to link a face with the name before guessing his visitor was a brother of Annie's that he had never met. Wasn't he in the Navy?

"Well, I'll be darned." D.R. pushed back from his desk, stood up, and strode out of his inner sanctum. Reaching both his hands out in welcome, he exclaimed, "John Osborn! What a surprise! Let me lay eyes on you."

As Annie's brother rose from the wooden chair, D.R. recalled that John was twenty-one—only two years older than Annie. He read uncertainty on the younger man's face, and fancied he saw an almost desperate hope—akin to what he'd seen in the expression of troops following him into battle. Clapping John on the back, D.R. ushered him into his office, cleared a chair for his guest, and resumed his seat in his own chair.

When John remained silent, he probed, "We weren't expecting you. Did we miss a telegram?"

John gave a nervous laugh. "No, I wanted to surprise Annie. Hope you don't mind." D.R. kept quiet to draw John out. "I was discharged about six weeks ago and decided I'd had enough of the seafaring life for a while," he continued, his eyes traveling over the dark green walls, polished floor, and daguerreotype of Annie on the desk. "I looked for you at City Hall and then the post office. They directed me here . . ." He trailed off.

D.R. explained the lost election.

John digested this news in silence, shifting in his seat. "How's Annie?"

D.R. smiled. "Adjusting," he said. "She loves riding. You like horses, too?"

"Sure. I left behind a beautiful sorrel on the island."

"I'll have to show you the horse farm." Eyeing an inflamed scar on John's face, he added, "You ship engineers don't see much action on the ground, do you?"

"No. I spent my tour of duty in a sweaty, deafening compartment waging a battle with the ship's boiler. Infernal enemy of a special sort."

Fifteen minutes later, D.R. had gained a thorough understanding of a boiler's insatiable appetite for coal. The melted-wax appearance of skin on John's right hand came from scalding drips from steam pipes. John hadn't yet mentioned anything about why he had come and D. R. wondered if the scar on his face might be hiding more scars on the inside.

D.R.'s stomach growled, telling him it was time for dinner. They set out together for home. On the way, they passed Dexter's Saloon, its door and windows standing open to the warm May evening air.

John pointed at the sign. "Buy you a drink before we see Annie?"

D.R. agreed, though he wanted to get home to Annie, guessing John had not yet overcome his sailor's penchant for alcohol. He dispatched a messenger boy with a scrawled note for Annie advising her of an arrival at six-thirty. "I'm bringing a guest," he wrote, but kept the identity of the guest secret to surprise her.

John tossed back two whiskies to D. R.'s one, before finally getting around to asking for more details about his sister's experiences in Leavenworth. Eager to head home, D.R. promised to update John en route.

Annie erupted with joy at seeing her brother before the men could even hang up their hats.

"John!" She flew into his arms, pulling him close and resting her cheek against his chest. "Oh, thank God you're safe! You made it home alive and now you're a . . . a hero, like Daniel!"

Daniel watched a tear form in the corner of her eye and slide down her cheek.

Disengaging himself, John mumbled, "Hardly a hero. Just a sailor who had the good fortune to come back in one piece."

Looking at his scar, Annie touched her own face in the same place. "This must've hurt. What happened?"

"Got on the wrong end of a hot coal shovel," he said. In answer to her puzzled look, he said, "I tended the ship's boiler. It takes lots of coal to make steam."

D.R. laid his hand on the trim waist of Annie's burgundy gown and drew her to himself for a quick kiss. "Let's go to Giacomini's for dinner and you two can catch up on all the news. We'll give him the grand tour afterward," he said while locking the door.

When he turned, Annie was already a few yards down the street on John's arm, exclaiming at his thin, wan appearance and telling him the Kansas sunshine would do him good.

Over dinner, D.R. compared John's face with Annie's. Both had auburn hair, though Annie's was a lustrous strawberry blonde while her brother's was darker and dull. Annie's mouth curved in the same way as John's, but her brother had a chipped tooth in front, near the scar. They ended the tour in the summer twilight with their backs to the Missouri River, gazing at the progress of the new house on the street called North Esplanade.

With the roof overhead and the walls sealed tight, the place now felt like more than a shell. D.R. ran his hand along the smooth strip of hardwood baseboard Seth had leaned against the wall, appreciating the clean grain and solid heft of it. Quality work, he nodded to himself.

They stood in what would soon be the dining room, sunlight slanting through the open window frames and catching motes of sawdust in the air.

He pointed toward the yawning gap in the floorboards at the far end of the room. "Tomorrow they'll set the stairs here," he said, his voice low, full of quiet satisfaction. "That'll go down to the cellar." Already, he could picture the clink of canning jars on shelves, the sharp tang of pickles and apples stored for winter. It was coming together—his vision, his home with Annie.

Turning to John, Annie said, "Where are you staying tonight?"

Her brother reddened. "With you, I had imagined. Unless you don't have room . . . ?"

"If I'd known you were coming, I would have . . ."

D.R. took the opportunity to smooth things over. "At our current lodgings we have only the main room and one bedroom. And the kitchen, of course. You can stay with us tonight, but I'm afraid you won't be very comfortable on the settee. Tomorrow, we'll find you something else."

"I'll be fine on your floor," said John. "I have my bedroll."

"Planning to camp out on the prairie? Push on further west?" D.R. asked.

Annie touched her brother's arm, her voice concerned. "John, you aren't just passing through, are you? You must stay a week or more. We have months of catching up to do, and there's so much to show you!"

Her brother hesitated. "No, don't worry. I just wanted to see you—see how you're doing and all—and then figure out my next step." He looked tentatively at D.R. "Maybe work for a while."

Back in the yard, Annie paused to step over a pile of rocks unearthed while excavating the basement.

"You haven't given me much Vineyard news," she said. "How is Mary doing with her wedding plans? I imagine it's challenging for her with Peter away at sea." Peter Kitts, Mary's fiancé, was a ship's engineer on the same vessel as John.

John paused. "Mary's having a rather rough patch." Annie crooked an eyebrow, inviting him to explain, but he said no more.

"I hope you brought me some letters. Seeing you makes me homesick for news."

Her brother looked away. "I have one from Aunt Eliza."

The evening had stretched a little long, considering how early D. R. started his days. He turned to John, looking pointedly at his watch.

"Why don't you come with me tomorrow to the post office and I'll introduce you around? And since you plan to stay awhile, we'll see about a job. I leave the house each morning at five forty-five."

Annie shot him a dubious look.

John laughed, disbelieving. "Hey, I thought I was done with reveille. Why so early?"

"Have to make sure all those letters get in mailboxes before the start of business."

"I doubt anyone is interested in hiring me at that hour. How about if I meet you later?"

Shrugging, D.R. said, "You have a point. Eight o'clock, then. But don't go to the post office; I'll be at *The Bulletin* by that time."

Chapter Fifteen

Daniel

May 25, 1864

The next morning, D.R. checked on the mail sorting one last time before going to the newspaper. There, a quick tour of the newsroom convinced him that the reporters would deliver their articles in time for the typesetters to begin another edition.

Continuing on to his office, he transferred his revolver from his pocket into his top desk drawer. Then from a file drawer, he withdrew an article he had written some weeks ago and passed it on to a typesetter out on the floor. Though he preferred to write a fresh editorial every day, he had banked a couple for occasions when he was too busy or lacked inspiration. With that out of the way, he opened the City Directory and began making notes about Leavenworth businesses.

When John arrived five minutes late, D.R. pushed a list across the desk to him. "I'm assuming that, after a warship, you could handle a boiler on a riverboat. Here's the name and address of the dock master at the levee. Ask him if he knows anyone who needs a boiler man."

"Well, the thing is, I don't know if I'm ready to go back to steamships"—John averted his eyes—"so soon after the war. A sailing vessel would be more to my liking."

"You may not have noticed, but there aren't many sailboats on the river." Seeing John bite his lip, D.R. softened his tone. "But you never know what else the dock master might have for you to do. Tell him I sent you. I've written some other names and businesses on here, as well."

On the way to the bank that afternoon, D.R. paused at Dexter's Saloon for a brief visit with Noah, who was a one-man newspaper all by himself. The proprietor knew who had just arrived in town, who was planning to leave, who had racked up gambling debts, and who needed to steer clear of the law. Though Noah shared information pretty liberally, he was particularly happy to trade news for D.R.'s choice cigars. Maybe he could recommend something for John.

To his surprise, he found John there too, looking much more disheveled than when he had set off that morning. He was nearly asleep at a window table, where he had been drinking, alone.

"Afternoon, Noah," said D.R., nodding. "Hot enough to melt tar, ain't it?" He put coins on the bar for a sarsaparilla. He seldom drank liquor during the day, preferring to keep his wits under control that way. Jerking his thumb toward the figure slumped by the window, he asked, "How long's he been here?"

Noah brushed his sandy hair out of his eyes and shrugged before continuing to polish the bar. "An hour or two, maybe. Didn't I see him with you yesterday?"

"He's my brother-in-law," said D.R., "and needs a room. Heard of anybody with vacancies?" D.R. proffered a cigar, which disappeared into Noah's pocket.

"I think so," said Noah, scratching his beard while he thought. "Somebody mentioned a boarding house last night. Now who was that? It'll come to me in a few minutes."

Pointing to his drink, D.R. said, "I'll be back to finish that." Nodding to a table of men playing poker near the bar, D.R. made his way over to John and clapped a heavy hand on his shoulder.

"C'mon, sailor, time to shove off."

Startling awake, John pushed back his chair and clambered to his feet. "I'm still plenty tired after that train ride," he said, "so after I had a good talk with your dock master friend, I came in to take a load off my feet. Must've nodded off."

Passing the bar on his way to the door, D.R. paused when Noah pushed a piece of paper towards them.

"Here's the name of that landlord," said the proprietor. "Somebody moved out of an apartment this morning. Maybe nobody's rented it yet."

"Thanks," said D.R., downing the remaining sarsaparilla in two gulps. He herded John outside onto the porch before asking, "So did my friend know of a ship that needs an engineer?"

John rubbed the back of his neck. "Well, no, not right now. But he said he would keep his ears open." He gave D.R. a hopeful look. "That sounds promising, doesn't it?"

"Mmmm," said D.R. "Did you tell him about your work in the navy and ask him for suggestions? How 'bout the other names I gave you?"

John's vague response confirmed D.R.'s guess that his brother-in-law had made only one perfunctory visit. Undeterred, he hustled John off to inquire about the boarding house vacancy and, for Annie's sake, he put up the money for the first month's rent.

"That should tide you over till you get a job," he told John as they went home to eat.

That evening after dinner, while Annie retired to the bedroom, D.R. again handed John blankets and a pillow to sleep on the sitting room floor. Then he joined his wife in the tiny bedroom. Savoring the sight of Annie's hair loose on her shoulders, he took up her hairbrush and drew it gently through her hair. They talked about the possibility of hiring people from the refugee camp to do their laundry and cook when they settled into their house.

Then Annie asked, "Neither of you said anything about John getting a job. How did that go?"

"He doesn't seem to have much energy for that search right now. Too soon after the war, maybe."

Annie looked skeptical.

"Some soldiers need more time to adjust to civilian life than others. Some just need a rest," D.R. said.

"You could be right," Annie said. "But he never was too eager to work. He and Father often argued about that."

"Hmmm." D.R., who had had to quit school at age fourteen to work in his father's store, had no patience with deadbeats. But he knew better than to get between Annie and her brother. "You must be glad that John brought you a letter from Aunt Eliza. How was it?"

"I haven't seen it yet, but I hope she'll tell me about Mary's wedding plans. John was vague about the details. I must get my hands on her note tomorrow."

Still in her dressing gown and braid the next morning, Annie stepped carefully around her sleeping brother to light the cook stove and mix biscuit dough. D.R., up at dawn even on a Saturday, had already finished reading two morning papers. Now, as he measured oatmeal and coffee, he made sure to bang a few pots. Still, John slumbered.

"Shhh!" Annie said, gesturing for D.R. to stop the racket. "He probably needs rest, as you said. Can't you be quiet?"

D.R. frowned and stage-whispered, "It's eight-thirty. Morning's half-gone."

The oven began to smoke and emit an unmistakable odor.

"Oh, no!" cried Annie. "My biscuits are burned!"

Seeing Annie's dejected expression, D.R. relented and headed out to the bakery. As he was leaving, John turned over and threw his arm over his head. He started to snore.

When D.R. returned, he found Annie dressed and John sprawled in a different position. None too gently, he nudged his brother-in-law with the toe of his boot.

"Time to get up, sailor. Coffee's hot and there're pastries."

"Honey, come here for just a minute," said Annie, pulling him into the bedroom and shutting the door behind them. Lowering her voice, she said, "I happened to notice this letter in John's pack." After handing him some folded papers, she twirled the end of her braid, her eyes filled with concern.

D.R. raised his eyebrows and whispered, "Have you been snooping?"

"What's the difference? He said he'd give me Auntie's letter yesterday, and I was tired of waiting for it."

My dear Annie and Daniel,

By now you may have welcomed John into your home. I hope a visit with you will calm him and help him make a new way for himself. When John announced he was leaving the Vineyard, I thought it best. Your father found it difficult to accept the unfortunate circumstances of your brother's discharge, and our dear Mary will need some time to deal with her loss.

Dearest newlyweds, I pray that this visit will not cast too big a pall on the joy of building your own house and establishing married traditions to last you a lifetime. Please write and tell me all about how your new home progresses and know that I remain, as always, □

Your devoted Aunt Eliza

D.R. scowled, his suspicions about John growing. "What do you suppose happened?"

Annie shrugged, pressing her lips together. "I'm not sure."

Next, she handed D.R. an envelope with the return address of the U.S. Navy. After a quick scan, he recognized it as a dishonorable discharge with John's name on it.

Annie began to weep. "Oh, Daniel, I don't know what to do! I had no business reading it, but he should have told us, shouldn't he?" She moved toward him like a kitten seeking its mother and, instinctively, he gathered her in for comfort.

His mouth set in a grim line as he stroked her back. "We'll get to the bottom of this."

D.R. waited until John had breakfasted and dressed before he explained how Annie had discovered his papers. Then, leaning against the wall with folded arms while John sat on the horsehair settee, he said, "Suppose you tell us what happened in the navy and why you're really here."

As John began, D.R. sighed inwardly, beginning to recognize a tale as old as military service itself.

"It began one day with a game of poker. I was losing, and this sailor named Lyman rubbed my nose in it. He said I oughta' give up poker because even when I cheated I still lost. I took a swing at him. He knocked me into a cabinet and that's when I got this gash on my cheek. I stormed off to console myself with some whiskey I had in my bunk. By that time I was supposed to go on duty in the boiler room."

D.R. reflected on how harshly the service punished soldiers for possession of liquor.

Looking grim, John continued his tale, telling how he had asked his bunkmate Peter Kitt to maintain the boiler pressure for a few minutes while he patched himself up. When Annie gasped, D.R. realized it was the same man who was engaged to Annie's younger sister Mary.

"I told Pete to watch and keep the pressure between twenty-five and sixty-five. Then I dabbed some whiskey on my cut and drank some to take the edge off the pain from my cut.

"I didn't hurry back because I'd given Pete very clear instructions. There was nothing to it." John paused as if to gather courage to continue his tale.

"But Pete had trouble *finding* the pressure gauge. By the time he found it, a pipe had burst. I got there just in time to see steam"—his voice faltered— "scald the entire front of his body." He clenched and unclenched his jaw. "I was able to prevent the boiler from blowing, which could've killed everybody on the ship. But that didn't help Pete. He lived two more days in absolute agony." He fell silent and stared at the floor.

"Were you implicated?" asked D.R.

John nodded. "I was found guilty and dishonorably discharged." At these last words he glanced away, refusing to look at either of them.

D.R. whistled in dismay. He glanced at Annie, whose eyes had filled with tears.

"Oh, John," she murmured. "What happened when you got home? Had Mary heard about Pete?"

John continued to speak without expression. "The island received news of Pete's death while I was awaiting trial. 'Killed in the line of duty,' they said. No one linked Pete's death to me till his father talked to my superior officer." He looked at his hands. "The night before I left, Mr. and Mrs. Kitt already knew and had told Father."

Misery welled in John's eyes as he looked at Annie. "Father wouldn't talk to me at all, and I knew it was only a matter of time till Mary found out. I couldn't bear to face her. Or anybody else, including Pete's family. So I left the Vineyard. When Aunt Eliza found me packing the next morning, she wrote you that note."

D.R. kept his expression unreadable when John raised anguished eyes to his.

"Now that you know the story, you can decide whether you want me in Leavenworth or not. If you don't, I'll move on." He dropped his gaze to the ground.

The sight of tears pooling in Annie's eyes struck D.R. like a physical blow. The pain transported him to those memories he fought to keep locked away—the eternally still faces of two young cavalry men who had died under his command, casualties of his flawed judgment. Private Fisk and Private Walsh. His mind conjured Mary, her chestnut hair so like Annie's, two years younger with that defiant tilt to her chin, canceling her wedding plans because her groom would never return.

He reached out to his wife. "Sunflower, let's take a walk, shall we?" Over his shoulder he told John, "Don't leave. We'll discuss this more when we get back."

The last glimpse he had before shutting the door was of John sitting with his head in his hands.

While they strolled up the street, D.R. kept glancing back at the house, half expecting to see John sneak out. When he tucked Annie's arm underneath his, he could feel her trembling as if they faced a blizzard instead of a warm June morning.

"What do you want to do, Annie?" he inquired gently. "Do you want John to stay?"

"I don't know. What're your thoughts?"

"He got himself drunk and was derelict in his duty. By doing so, he caused your sister's intended to die a horrible death."

Annie's trembling increased. "Yes. That's why they discharged him without honor. It pains me to even *look* at him, much less to consider what he did to poor Mary. Should we also turn him out?"

Her searching gaze reminded him of her expression the day he confessed how he had killed R.C. Satterlee in a civilian fight. He felt guilty, even though it had been self-defense. Now, though he had not cracked a Bible in decades, a phrase drifted back to him: "Let him who is without blame cast the first stone."

They paused, looking east across the river to the state of Missouri. There D.R. noticed young tobacco shoots emerging after an ill-fated Union command had burned them off during the previous August. In retaliation for Quantrill's murderous invasion of Lawrence, General Tom Ewing had ordered Union troops to destroy the counties of Little Dixie—those closest to the Kansas border.

A familiar bitterness came over D.R. Though he had no love for Missouri's slaveholders, he knew that some truly loyal Union families—unlike the Bauers, who had pretended to be Unionists—had suffered the destruction of their farms.

Coming back to Annie's question, he said, "Innocent people die in war for all kinds of reasons. John's plenty sorry for what he did, and condemning him won't bring Pete back. I'll find some work for him at the post office till he lands a better job."

As Annie nodded, D.R. glanced toward their home. "Has Mary written anything about this to you?"

Annie shook her head. "I'm sure she will, by and by."

D.R. scratched his beard. "If you write her anything about John being here, will she hold it against you?"

She thought for a long moment before shaking her head. "We can't do anything for her right now, and word of his visit here won't reach her for a while. But maybe in the meantime we can help John. Maybe he can start life over here."

He patted her hand. "I agree."

Chapter Sixteen

Annie

May 30, 1864

Annie's footsteps slowed as she reached Madame Collette's couture on Shawnee Street. After her embarrassing first-week encounter at Fisk's, she still hadn't established a relationship with another dressmaker. But now, even her lightest-weight gown from the Vineyard was too warm for the Kansas heat. She must find someone.

The shop's deep street-side awning provided some measure of relief from the sun as she stepped inside. Bolts of fabric in every hue lined the walls, giving the shop a claustrophobic feel. Platforms raised above the bolts featured gowns with the ruching, tucks, lace, buttons, ruffles, and ribbons Annie had seen on women walking about town. But none so far featured the style of dress Annie wanted.

The dressmaker herself was a study in simplicity in a black gown that rustled like expensive silk. As she moved, the heady scent of jasmine trailed her like an invisible veil.

"I am Madame Collette," she said. "How may I assist you?"

Annie showed her a copy of a Paris fashion plate in a magazine she had brought with her. "I have a gown like this and want another one made up in a cooler fabric."

"*Oui, madame,*" replied Collette, looking at the magazine. "I can create any dress you desire, but bringing a sample to my boutique would help me better understand your needs."

The next afternoon Annie hired a hack to help her transport her dress to Collette's on a hanger. As she entered the shop, the modiste was pulling a scrap of flannel off the end of a bolt and folding it for Miss Greenshawl. Annie tensed at the sight of the vagrant woman, the sharp tang of unwashed body and musty clothes cutting through the shopkeeper's customary jasmine scent.

Waving away Miss Greenshawl's attempted thanks, Collette said, "Use it in good health," her voice kind but eyes drifting toward Annie with a silent apology.

Annie pressed herself against a display of ribbons as Miss Greenshawl shuffled past, clutching the flannel like a treasure. Once the door closed behind her, Annie placed her gown on the counter.

"That was generous of you. Is it true she was kicked by a horse?"

Collette sighed. "Yes, in the head. The army surgeon stitched her up—with little skill, if you ask me. She used to be so lovely." Brightening, she turned her attention to Annie's dress. "*Voici,* allow me to help you with that."

"What have we here?" called a woman from nearby, her voice carrying a nasal pitch that filled the small shop.

"Ah, *pardonnez-moi,* Mrs. Anthony. Before you came in, I was helping this customer with her selection of trims. I will return to you in a minute. Perhaps you two have already met? *Non?* Mrs. Colonel Mellick, may I present Mrs. Colonel Anthony."

The woman regarded Annie from beneath the elegant angle of her hat. "My husband is training new recruits at the fort. Are you the mayor's new wife?"

"Former mayor," corrected Annie with a polite smile.

Soon the three women were deep in conversation about the latest styles in *Godey's Lady's Book.* Mrs. Mellick displayed the diaphanous material she'd selected for the upcoming summer fete at Fort Leavenworth.

"Colonel Anthony had already left the service when I met him, so I have never attended a military ball. Are they as magnificent as people say?" Annie asked, unable to hide her wistfulness.

"Oh, yes!" Mrs. Mellick's face lit with genuine pleasure. "Almost worth all the hardships of having a husband away for weeks at a time. I would commission my entire wardrobe from Madame Collette if my accounts allowed it!"

"High praise from such a discerning lady," Collette acknowledged with a slight bow.

Pulling on her gloves, Mrs. Mellick nodded. "Thank you, Collette. Enjoy your new gown, Mrs. Anthony."

When the dress was finished two weeks later, Annie persuaded Daniel to accompany her to a church supper with Lydia and Milton, even though he said he never set foot in a sanctuary except for weddings and funerals. Her new dress helped to boost her confidence to spend time among so many strangers.

Lydia introduced Annie as an eastern bride who played the piano and was interested in furnishings for a new home.

A redheaded woman said, "I like your dress. Is that something you brought from Massachusetts?"

"No," said Annie. "I had it made up at Collette's Couture."

"How clever of Collette to come up with something so new and chic. Perhaps I'll ask her—oh, but of course, I wouldn't copy yours, Annie . . ."

Annie waved a graceful hand, enjoying the attention. "I'm sure she can make a dozen variations." Turning from the redhead back to a woman introduced to her as Pia Egersdorff, she asked, "Did you see the new styles in the latest edition of *Godey's*?"

"I never look at the fashion section. Was that the issue that included a new song by Stephen Foster?" asked Pia, who played the organ at St. Paul's. "Wasn't it a wonderful tune?"

Annie sighed. "I can't say. I don't sight read very well, nor do I have a piano here."

"Tomorrow, from two to four, I'll be practicing in the church," said Pia. Her lively eyes regarded Annie from behind spectacles. "Why don't you join me? If the sanctuary is empty, perhaps we could even try a secular song or two."

Daniel, who had been discussing the expansion of the railroad with Milton, suddenly homed in on the conversation. "I learned plenty of songs in the army," he said before humming a couple bars of a catchy tune. "Would you like me to sing one for you?"

Pia shrugged. "I know that one. It's 'Goober Peas.'"

Annie was amazed when Milton exchanged glances with Daniel and snickered. *What had gotten into Milton? He was usually so reserved!*

Milton explained, "The army has its own version of 'Goober Peas.'"

Annie remembered bawdy lyrics she had heard Daniel singing while polishing his boots. Blushing and shaking her head, she shot her husband a panicked look.

He gave her a teasing look and cocked his head. "Aren't you glad you invited me?"

She swatted his arm with her fan, laughing and protesting, "I don't think Pia meant music that is quite so secular!"

Chapter Seventeen

Annie

June 9, 1864

Annie drew a clean breath after she and Lydia Clark had put some distance between themselves and a team of odorous oxen in the street.

With the decrease in noise, Lydia asked, "How's your new house coming?"

"This week the carpenters are building all the fireplace mantels." Annie sighed with satisfaction. "I just love beautiful woodwork. It reminds me of home."

They had rounded the corner in front of the Thompson, Eames & Crow general store when through the passersby Annie caught sight of something lovely in the window.

"Oh, look at that dear salt cellar, Lydia! I wonder which china pattern it matches?"

"You said you're trying to fill out a set of dishes from your hope chest, right?" asked Lydia.

Patting the basket she carried, Annie said, "Yes, and I have one plate right here; it's the Blue Willow pattern." She laughed. "This is the *only* one I have. The other ones are on the island in my sister's hope chest."

They waited a moment for the crowd to thin on the sidewalk before entering the shop.

"No hope for Anthony," a disembodied whisper rasped.

Lydia looked quizzically at Annie. "I beg your pardon?"

"I didn't say anything," Annie replied, but she had an idea who did—glancing around for the woman wrapped in green.

Nowhere in sight.

She returned her gaze to Lydia as if nothing had happened. Annie knew that there must be a story, but she did not enjoy being the target of this woman's ire.

Brushing it aside, Lydia demanded, "Why on earth would you leave behind an entire set of dishes for your sister?"

"Aunt Eliza said that most wouldn't survive the trip west. So she and Father gave me money to buy a new set here instead."

Lydia's eyes twinkled as she opened the door. "Let's go inside! I love spending other people's money!"

An hour later Annie emerged with the plan to use Blue Willow for everyday and consider a new pattern from France for special occasions.

"We look forward to seeing you again," Mr. Thompson called as Annie left.

Several people passed behind the two friends as they said their good-byes on the sidewalk, and again Annie heard, "No hope for-r-r . . ."

She wheeled around to see the figure in the green shawl dart across a crowded street. Grabbing Lydia's arm, Annie lowered her voice to an urgent whisper. "I keep seeing that woman around town. Do you know her?"

"What woman?"

Two days later, Annie was pondering a purchase at the general store when the elusive woman came to stand behind her, murmuring just above a whisper, "Colonel . . . ba-a-a-a-by."

Annie spun around and grabbed her stalker's arm. "Come here."

It was Friday afternoon, near the close of business, and no one was nearby to see her force the wretched woman into the alley. Noticing the curve of the woman's spine, Annie realized that she was quite tall, something she had missed because of the woman's way of carrying herself curled up tight.

Face-to-face, the stranger's watery brown eyes focused on Annie's blue ones before sliding away. From her light-colored braids, strands of hair and pieces of hay brushed against an angry scar on her cheek. The smell of sweat and manure made Annie want to cover her nose.

She withdrew her hand while getting right to the point. "You seem to know who I am. But I don't know who you are or why you always follow me saying hateful things." Surprised by how much she wanted to shake the woman, Annie backed away instead. "What's your name?"

The woman gazed over Annie's shoulder. "I-I . . ."

Annie waited several beats for the woman to finish her sentence, then said, "You what?"

"You . . . Young. Li-i-ike her." The woman drew out some of her words like a confectioner pulling taffy.

"Like who? Who's young?"

The stranger started moving toward the main street, looking away from Annie. "Mrs. Anthony."

These cryptic utterances made Annie want to shout questions at the vagrant, but she decided to let her go now and hope to engage her again.

Struck by an idea, she called after the retreating form, "Miss . . . May I call you Miss Greenshawl? Do you like peppermints?"

The woman turned—hopeful, Annie thought.

She offered the candy from her palm as one might feed a horse, taking care not to recoil when ragged fingernails scraped her skin lightly. When she'd emptied Annie's hand of mints, she turned without a backward glance and skittered back toward the street.

For the rest of the day, Annie pondered this encounter. Daniel told her that vagrants often talked nonsense, but what she couldn't understand is why the woman seemed determined to tell her something.

·»·—·•·—·«·

Later that week, Annie went to complete her wallpaper choices at Drake Brothers. Wine-colored flowers for the dining room and a complementary stripe for the parlor; blue medallions for the guest room.

When Annie emerged from the store into the heat of the afternoon, Miss Greenshawl was sitting alone on a bench in front of the stationers.

Forearmed with a bag of sweets, her heart pounding, Annie approached her stalker and demanded, "Who is young like me and knows Colonel Anthony?"

Miss Greenshawl regarded her silently for such a long time that Annie wondered whether she would reply at all. Finally, she stumbled out, "Long time. Missou-u-u-ri."

"She lived a long time ago in Missouri?"

"Number eleven. Gone." She made a slashing motion.

Annie shook her head, stymied. "I don't know what 'number eleven' means. Help me."

Miss Greenshawl gestured as if taking in a wide panorama. "Burnt. Al-l-l-l burnt."

"Was she in a fire? Dear God, was she burnt?"

But the other woman rose and turned to leave. Annie caught her shoulder. "I forgot to ask you, would you like a lemon drop? I got some at the confectioners' today."

Her companion frowned. "Peppermint."

"All right. Just a minute." As Annie rummaged through the small bags, she murmured, "What did you say about a baby the other day?"

"Anthony. Jayhawker."

As Annie doled out a peppermint, she concentrated to steady the trembling of her hand. Her insides quaked as these fragments swirled around in her head: Daniel had ridden with the Jayhawkers. He had cleared secesh out of Missouri. And now this woman spoke of a child—safe, and connected to her husband somehow.

Annie's free hand moved to her own abdomen, a protective gesture as her mind filled with questions about the man she thought she knew.

Chapter Eighteen

Daniel

July 24, 1864

On their last morning in the rental house, D.R. nodded to Chas Goodman and shut the door behind himself. Chas and Ella were sweeping out the empty rooms and would soon follow him and Annie to their new home on North Esplanade.

D.R. climbed into the wagon and headed toward their new house facing the river. He congratulated himself on the efficient way their move was unfolding. In little less than an hour yesterday, John Osborn and two of his soldier friends had trooped out of the rental with Annie's many trunks and D.R.'s few possessions and fit them into the back of a wagon bound for the new house.

Glad that the morning was still cool, he watched the horse strain a little going uphill towards number 417. Annie put her hand on his sleeve and squeezed his arm.

"To think it was just a bare field when I came to town," she marveled. "And now we have a brand-new house! I will love waking up facing east, just like I did in Edgartown."

"I was lucky to get a plot next to the park," he said, eyeing the neatly spaced saplings that would someday shield the river from view.

Between the back of the house and the alley, he could already envision his fine carriage house where Bully Boy and Bill would be at their disposal in a few shakes of a lamb's tail. No more trips to the livery every time they wanted to go somewhere. He still had to narrow down his choice of carriages to buy.

Annie interrupted his reverie. "Whose hack is that in our front yard?"

D.R. strained his eyes, focusing on the small vehicle parked between two homes. "That's someone else's yard."

"No, it's not. What time are the store deliveries to start?"

"In about forty-five minutes." He frowned and flicked the reins, signaling the horse to pick up the pace.

"That looks like Sam Cochran," said Annie, referring to a neighbor who had recently moved in. "But what's he looking at?"

As they got closer, D.R. recognized Nettie Cochran standing next to her husband and two other men on the lawn of number 417. They were talking quietly, glancing down and gesturing toward something at their feet.

A cold hand began to squeeze D.R.'s heart as he guessed what it was. "I think something bad's happened, Annie. You might want to stay in the wagon while I find out," he said.

When her hand tightened on his arm, he figured she too had made out the form of a man in a blue suit lying near the hack, face up in the dirt. A nondescript horse stood drinking water from a pail that someone had provided.

"Oh, no!"

He patted the hand clutching his arm. "I'll be back in a minute." He jumped down from the wagon while nodding to the people gathered in front of his house. Sam, in his shirtsleeves and vest, met him on the brick walk that led up to D.R.'s front door.

Cochran said, "I looked outside about an hour ago and saw this hack in your yard with the horse just standing there. At first, I thought it was you arriving early on your big day."

D.R. listened while striding toward the still figure. Something about him was familiar.

"Is he alive?"

Another neighbor approached the men who encircled the motionless form and said, "When we first got here, he had a faint pulse. Ten minutes ago, someone went for the police and the doctor. But I think he's beyond help now."

"Who is it?" asked D.R., still too far away to make out the man's face. Then he froze as if the truth had physically hit him. There lay Martin Bauer, who had offered Annie a ride on the day of her first solitary excursion in Leavenworth.

D.R. bent down to feel the man's carotid artery. Nothing.

"I can't tell whether there's been any foul play," said Cochran.

D.R. inhaled sharply. "We'll find out soon," he said with more equanimity than he felt.

Next to the presence of death and his worrisome connection with Bauer, the new house suddenly seemed insignificant. He peered across the yard at the wagon where Nettie had gone to sit with Annie, whose distress he could well imagine. A moment later he leaned into the wagon to tell her what he knew.

"Someone died here. Why don't you and Nettie take a little drive over to the store and ask them to wait about an hour before they deliver our stuff here."

After the women left, two deputy marshals and Dr. Tiffin Sinks approached on horseback via a side street. One marshal surveyed the scene and inspected the vehicle before driving it away. D.R. exchanged handshakes with Deputy Tom Healy and the doctor. As the former mayor, he was well-acquainted with both men, but having them call at his home to inspect a dead body made him uncomfortable.

Standing in a circle with Cochran and a couple of other neighbors, he watched as Healy and Sinks examined the corpse.

"No sign of violence," Healy reported to the bystanders. "Looks like a heart attack, plain and simple, even though he's fairly young."

Dr. Sinks nodded. "It happens now and then." He left after telling D.R. he would send the undertaker for the body.

The neighbors drifted away, leaving D.R. with Deputy Healy. As Healy wiped his brow, D.R. realized that he, too, was a ball of sweat. He longed for a drink of water.

"Colonel, I just need to ask you a few questions about your whereabouts in the last twenty-four hours."

D.R. tamped his anxiety down before he began. "Yesterday I left the newspaper early and spent the afternoon and evening here at the new house."

"Was anyone else with you?"

D.R. knew the question was routine, and he took care to answer it thoroughly since he had nothing to hide. "Yes, I was with my wife from that time until the moment I laid eyes on Bauer here this morning. And with Chas Goodman on and off last evening and this morning." D.R. saw Healy relax at the mention of Goodman's name. Sometimes it helped to have the chief marshal as your good friend.

"Did anyone else see you yesterday or earlier this morning?"

"Yeah. I've been in and out of our rental house for the last two hours loading boxes. Our neighbors in town and our movers can tell you all about it."

"Good. I'm sure your story will agree with theirs." Clasping D.R.'s hand, he said, "Bad business on your moving day."

He left. The undertaker came and went.

Thirty minutes elapsed before Chas and Ella arrived, followed by Annie and Nettie, and then the store deliveries. The women began directing the stream of movers while Chas took D.R. aside.

"Healy found plenty of bystanders who verified where you've been. I don't think you have anything to worry about from Sinks's report, either. But it's too bad you had such a public quarrel with Bauer a couple months ago. Someone may try to make a case against you because of that."

"Yeah," D.R. said, scuffing his boot on the dirt in the driveway, again regretting his knee-jerk reaction to seeing Annie in Bauer's carriage. "I can already see the headlines."

Together, they went inside to place furniture as Annie directed. Nettie supplied the workers with lemonade and fed them lunch. The heavy lifting finished, D.R. thanked his buddies and sent them home. Then he set up the bed so Annie could make it with new sheets and went to survey the boxes of French porcelain filling the dining room table.

After sharing a dinner that Ella prepared, the Goodmans left him and Annie in the cool of the basement kitchen.

D.R. looked around at the shelves where utensils and bowls awaited the hired cook.

"You did a lot of work down here," he said.

"I don't know how I would have done it without Ella," Annie replied.

Looking closely at his wife for the first time in hours, he observed how sharply her current haggardness contrasted with her joyful expression first thing that morning.

He reached across the table to tuck her hair into her snood. "Tired?"

"Very."

D.R. didn't believe in dodging unpleasant facts. "Are you okay about Bauer?"

Annie's voice sounded heavy with sadness. "I—we—have looked forward to being in our house for so many months. It's all we've talked about. I was so happy last night, thinking about starting to live here today. But what's the chance of someone having a heart attack on our lawn this very day? Life seems so . . ." She grasped for the word.

"Fragile?" he suggested.

"Yes, and someday you will . . ." Her trembling lip registered a future grief that he could only guess. He stood and drew her to him. As dusk gathered in the corners of their new home, they rocked each other for comfort.

Two mornings later, a clerk brought D.R.'s usual stack of competing newspapers to his desk at *The Bulletin's* offices. In *The Times,* halfway down the first page, he caught his own name in a headline.

Man Found Dead on Anthony Property

At eight o'clock Saturday morning, Martin Bauer, a driver for Bauer Brothers Livery, was found dead at 417 North Esplanade, where former mayor D.R. Anthony has recently raised a new house. David Bauer, brother of the deceased, said that the enmity between Martin and the former mayor has run high ever since Anthony forcibly evacuated the carriage driver from his plantation in Missouri last year.

Earlier this year, their quarrel flared again when Anthony recruited police to stop traffic and harass Martin in the middle of the street. Grieving brother David noted that the former mayor is known for his sudden rages, having killed another man for insulting him. The family considers it an odd coincidence that Martin Bauer met his end on Anthony's property.

Please contact the police if you have information about this deadly incident.

After pounding his fist on the desk, D.R. spun his chair to gaze out into the street where Chas was just striding toward the newspaper building. His powerful legs were rapidly closing the distance.

D.R. slipped his gun into its holster and met his friend in *The Bulletin's* lobby. "Have you seen the latest about Bauer?" he barked.

"That's why I'm here. Let's go into your room." Chas took D.R.'s elbow and steered him toward the office.

"No," said D.R., trying to shake him off. "I'm on my way to—"

"I've already been there," Chas assured D.R., holding fast to his struggling friend.

D.R. noticed the receptionist watching with interest. "Let me go, Chas," he muttered. "You're making a scene."

"Well, then, let's just walk along friendly like." As soon as D.R. stopped resisting, Chas released his arm and adjusted his hand to a more sociable pressure on D.R.'s shoulder.

"You mean you've already talked to David Bauer this morning?" D.R. asked as they crossed the threshold of his office.

"Sure did." Chas closed the door and pushed D.R. into his own chair. "I wanted to know how that article got into *The Times.* It wasn't from David Bauer, nor from police headquarters."

D.R. felt a mixture of puzzlement and hope. Regretting how he'd treated Martin, he hated to think of any further quarrel with the man's family.

"Then who?"

Chas leaned against the door with his hands in his pockets. "Doc Jennison visited David Bauer on Saturday afternoon. Dave said he was surprised because he hardly knew Doc and had never heard Martin mention him, either. Jennison paid his respects and poked around for details about your showdown in the street this past winter. Dave didn't particularly want to recall it, so Jennison soon took his leave."

D.R. jumped to his feet. "That snake, planting half-truths and innuendo!" He bolted toward the door where Chas still lounged.

"Where you going?" demanded Chas.

"To see Jennison, of course. Out of my way."

"Not on your life," Chas growled.

D.R. attempted to shoulder him aside until Chas planted a palm against D.R.'s chest and held him at arm's length. "You're not going anywhere with that head of steam and a revolver. Think of Annie and go take a seat." He gave D.R. a shove.

Glaring, D.R. did as he was told.

"Thank you. Now, as we speak, Doc Sinks and Tom Healy are making statements to *The Commercial,* and I helped Jennison realize he has urgent business in Lawrence for the rest of the week." He leaned over to gaze directly into his friend's gray eyes, his expression both crafty and sympathetic. "I've got this situation in hand, pal. But you have to cooperate by keeping your peace."

"You don't know what you're asking."

After Chas left, D.R. stared at the newspaper he'd crumpled, then retrieved his gun from the desk drawer. Minutes later, he stood outside LeBonTon during the lunchtime rush, the saloon's noise spilling onto the street. His hand hovered over the door handle as his mind painted the satisfying image of Jennison's face shattering beneath his knuckles, blood spraying across the bar.

Then Annie's disappointed eyes flashed through his thoughts, cooling his rage just enough. No, there were smarter ways to destroy a man than with fists. He would get Jennison another way—one that wouldn't cost himself everything he'd built.

Chapter Nineteen

Daniel

August 2, 1864

Birds called to each other in a desultory manner on a sultry Sunday evening while John Osborn sprawled in a parlor chair and D.R. sat reading. Looking around the edges of his new spectacles, he marveled at how they improved his vision. Near the open window, Annie's lemonade tumbler sweated on a glass tabletop as she sat writing a letter to Aunt Eliza. Without tall trees to block the sun, the new house felt stuffy.

John fanned himself and took a sip of whiskey. He was between jobs at the moment, having lasted only a few weeks at each of the ones he'd tried.

Angling his head to see the title of D.R.'s book, he read aloud, "'Breeding for Beginners?' What are you planning to breed?"

"Cattle," said D.R. "I need to buy a bull for my Huron farm."

"We didn't have many cows on the Vineyard."

"Your island, from what I recall, doesn't have much grazing land," said D.R. "Cattle need a lot of open space, and here in the West, there's plenty."

John fiddled with a deck of cards on the round table in the center of the room. "I'd like to see that farm," he said. "I've always liked horses. Maybe I'd like cows, too."

Presently, the men had a smoke outdoors and John left for his own lodgings. When D.R. came back into the house, he found Annie upstairs seated at her dressing table removing pins from her coiffure. As her hair cascaded down her back, it reflected light from a small lamp above the tiled fireplace.

He ran his fingers through her hair, and she stilled, content. "Horses are the first thing that's interested John since the war," he said. "I was thinking of taking him out to Huron this weekend."

"That might be good for him," she said, starting to braid her hair. "I've never seen Huron. If it's a good place for riding, I'll come along."

He dropped his hand to his knee, then bent to his boots, working at a tight knot. Too tight. Just like this situation.

"That'd be great," he said. "We're shorthanded—think you could help muck out some stalls?"

She wrinkled her nose. "No thanks. Maybe I'll play duets with Pia while you're gone."

He nodded, feigning disappointment. "Oh, all right. I won't force you."

Close call. But she'd taken the bait. Huron could stay his business—for now.

Days later, when John and D.R. returned from Huron, a gust of wind slammed the door behind them.

"Storm's coming," announced D.R. as Annie looked up from her copy of *Harper's Weekly.*

"How was your visit?" Annie asked.

D.R. slung his jacket over a chair while John went to the sideboard and poured himself four fingers of whiskey. D.R. frowned but said nothing.

D.R. replied, "Good, till I fell off my horse. Bully Boy hates jackrabbits, and the farm is full of 'em." He recalled that Annie had seen the ungainly creatures from the train that had brought her to Kansas.

Annie gasped. "Are you all right?"

D.R. shrugged. "No more than a bruise or two." He paused before adding, "Warm weather brings out snakes, too."

Her eyes widened. "You shouldn't be around snakes," she fretted.

He patted his hip. "That's what guns are for. Right, John?"

Annie's brother nodded.

She shook her head in frustration at D.R.'s blasé attitude about his own safety. "I saved you some dinner," she said.

"Thanks, but we already stopped at Dexters," D.R. replied. "John's going to start working at Huron." He'd never mentioned to Annie what an indifferent employee John had been at the post office. This was his brother-in-law's final chance to prove himself.

Annie put down her magazine and turned to her brother. "How could you do that? It's so far from Leavenworth."

"That's why I'll bunk at the farm most of the time." John tossed back his drink and then leaned against the mantel. When rain began pelting the house, D.R. dashed from window to window, slamming them shut. The room darkened along with the cloud-laden sky.

Annie bit her lip before saying, "But . . . this is so sudden! Is there a comfortable place to live at Huron?"

D.R. sat in his Morris chair and leaned back. "I've already finished part of the barn, so John will be comfortable enough. He'll spend some time working with the horses—and cattle—and also serve as my business agent."

Annie persisted. "But aren't you ready to settle down a bit, John? Maybe meet a nice girl and provide us with a niece or nephew?"

John shook his head. "Not yet. After being aboard the ship, I still hate being cooped up. With its wide-open spaces, Huron will suit me fine."

As John returned to the sideboard to refill his whiskey, D.R. intercepted him. "Better hold off on that for tonight, brother. You'll need to look sharp the next couple days while we make the final arrangements."

John smiled. "I guess that's good enough reason to abstain this once," he agreed, saluting with his empty glass.

At *The Bulletin* office the next morning, two experienced horse breeders named McMahon and Peck strode in, still dusty from the barn. D.R. quickly closed the door, shook hands, and introduced them to John. The leather on their holsters creaked as they settled into wooden chairs. After weaving his way through their sprawling legs to reach his own seat, D.R. swiveled his chair to face them.

A serious discussion ended with all parties signing a contract. D.R. then passed cash across the desk to each of his three guests. After another round of handshakes, the cowhands took their leave. D.R. spent an additional thirty minutes discussing his expectations with John before the younger man finally departed, duffel bag in hand.

His hiring session complete, D.R. laced his hands behind his head, leaned back in his chair, and smiled to himself. He was going to become a rich man, with jackrabbits and snakes to guard him from Annie's oversight.

CHAPTER TWENTY

Annie

December 14, 1864

Annie opened her eyes and noticed the bed beside her was empty. She squinted at the pale light filtering through the curtains. In the dreary month of December, it was difficult to determine the hour just by the brightness outside. Turning to the clock on her nightstand, she jolted upright. Nine-thirty!

But there was still plenty of time to prepare for her morning drive into town in her cabriolet—a one-horse cart with a hood that Daniel had recently gifted her for her birthday.

Lowering her legs over the side of the four-poster, she felt the first stirring of the queasiness that had dogged her steps recently. Not enough to stop for, just enough to slow her down.

Shivering in her nightgown, she surveyed herself in the mirror. Her slim figure still disguised the reality of the new life that was taking shape inside her. And now it was time to confirm her private suspicions with the midwife's examination.

She thought of her friend Cora on the Vineyard, a recent bride who had miscarried her first child in the second month of pregnancy. Annie had kept silent about her intuition that she was in a family way. But now that she had skipped her courses for three months, she was certain enough to tell Daniel.

Turning this way and that in the mirror, she hoped the changes of pregnancy and childbirth would not lessen Daniel's desire for her. A smile bloomed on her lips as she began layering on her lace-trimmed undergarments. Then she went downstairs and put enough money in her purse for a steak-and-potatoes dinner for Daniel and some peppermints for Miss Greenshawl.

That evening, Annie lingered over her dinner while Daniel made quick work of his favorite meal. When the cook finally left them alone, she sat back and watched her husband in the soft glow. His hair was curling again at the edges, unfashionably long. She liked it best that way. It gave him the air of a man who had better things to think about than his appearance. Her rough and tumble hero.

He looked content, fingers curved easily around his wineglass, the lines in his face softened by the light. She tried to hold that moment still in her mind, but memories slipped in—his face at their wedding, his patience the first time they made love, his interest in her viewpoint when they laid out plans for the house, the way he had encouraged her to ride astride, even though it wasn't proper. They had a life together. Real and flawed, perhaps, but theirs.

Her heart felt too full. She leaned forward, hands suddenly damp in her lap. "Honey, I have something to tell you."

He looked up quickly, set down his glass. His smile was slow, curious. "Ye-s-s-s?" he teased, drawing it out.

She took a breath, felt her pulse everywhere. "I'm with child."

The words sounded fragile in the air—real and not real all at once. Her throat tightened as tears pressed forward, soft and joyful.

"Annie!" His voice caught, and he reached for her hand. "My darling." He looked stunned, breathless, the way he had on their wedding day. "Are you sure? When?"

"Next May." She managed a watery smile.

He laughed—genuinely, richly—when she confessed how she'd started refusing gallops at the farm.

"You sly one," he said, eyes gleaming. "That explains a lot. Time to switch you to the cabriolet."

Then he was standing, pulling her gently to him. She went gladly, folding into his arms as he kissed her forehead.

"We'll get more help around here," he said, his voice thick with tenderness. "You'll need to rest, save your strength—for our little Anthony." He placed a warm hand on her belly.

She covered it with her own, pressing closer. "Mmm," she murmured. "That feels so good. Would you rub it a little? And my back? My shoulders?" She gave a sheepish little laugh. "Everything aches tonight."

Without a word, he blew out the candles and rang the bell to signal Mrs. Maguire.

"It's getting late," he said softly, lips near her ear. "How about we turn in, and you show me what you need?"

Upstairs, he added a log to the bedroom fire. The flickering light danced on the walls as he came to her, brushing a kiss against her neck before his fingers went to her stays.

"You mustn't lace too tightly these next months," he murmured. "I've heard it can be dangerous."

She tilted her head back. "There's hardly anything to lace around yet."

"Oh?" His voice dropped. "Then I'll need to inspect that myself."

His hands moved with reverence and care, easing the aches from her back and shoulders, his lips following like promises. She closed her eyes, melting into the comfort of his touch, and the new life quietly growing inside her.

The next afternoon he sent her a news clipping from *The Commercial* in an envelope.

Good Workers for Hire

General Curtis of the Sanitary Relief Commission announces that the refugee camp has catalogued the skills of many able-bodied workers who desire employment. Giving lie to recent charges of licentiousness and idleness in the camp, he said scores of camp residents, both `white and Black, are offering their skills for fair wages.`

A note in Daniel's scrawl accompanied the article:

It's time to hire more household help. Let's see if we can find someone at the camp to help with housekeeping. I'll come home at four o'clock today so we can interview people together.

Later, as they sat in the camp office reading over cards with names and qualifications, Daniel said, "This is a good selection process. Very efficient."

The clerk behind the desk gave a polite nod. "We want to help potential employers review our residents' abilities objectively before meeting them in person." He cleared his throat. "For the colored folk, in particular, it seems less like a slave market and more like applying for a real job with wages—which it is."

D.R. inclined his head. That was exactly the point, wasn't it? Let a man or woman stand on their own merit, and pay them for honest work. Not as someone's property, not under threat, but as free people earning their w ay.

The clerk went on, "Now you understand that if you hire a colored person, you'll pay them in cash. And a fair wage."

"Understood," said D.R. "Of course."

Annie slid three index cards across the table to her husband. "These are the women I would like to consider for housekeepers," she said. "What do you think?"

Without looking at the cards, Daniel handed them to the clerk. "Can we interview them? Oh, and while we're waiting, do you have any men or boys who might want work as a groom for my horses?"

An hour later, they had hired a boy and his mother.

CHAPTER TWENTY-ONE

Daniel

December 15, 1864

D.R. tightened his grip on the reins as the Anthony wagon creaked along the muddy street, cold rain stinging his face. He glanced back at the two passengers sitting upright behind him—Emily Johnson and her ten-year-old son, Andrew, both once enslaved, now riding toward a new chapter in their lives.

For four years, he had fought to end slavery. Now, he was striking another blow against racial inequality by offering them fair wages and a respectable home—just as he would any white servants.

Memories of the war clung to him—faces worn by suffering, shattered lives in crumbling shacks, the echoes of desperate cries. The weight of oppression had pressed upon his conscience, but now, he was determined to be part of something different. Something just.

His thoughts were interrupted by a florid-faced man striding up toward his passengers, a leer twisting his mouth.

"Hey, baby, you leavin' the concubine camp? Where'm I gonna get my honey now?"

The man smirked and melted into the crowd before D.R. could react. Though D.R. focused his attention back on the road, disgust soured his stomach.

Stealing another glance at Emily, he saw her warm brown eyes scanning the passing landscape. He wondered how much she had endured in the contraband camp—a place that had barely been a refuge, riddled with disease and danger, for women most of all.

The wagon rattled over a bump, and Andrew bounced in his seat. D.R. shifted his gaze to the grand homes lining the Esplanade. What would they think of his house? He would not join the ranks of rich white men who used their power to trample the weak.

As the wagon rolled to a stop beside his white stucco house adorned with intricate fretwork, D.R. jumped down.

"We're home, lad," he said, motioning for Andrew to help his mother down. Respect—that was the foundation he wanted to lay from the very first moment.

"Now we begin again," Emily whispered. "Lord, give me strength."

D.R. led them down an outside stairway to the kitchen entrance. Their new life started here.

Inside, he was pleased to see the space filled with light from the basement door and small foundation windows. The kitchen boasted the latest conveniences—a large cookstove, shelves lined with utensils, and a sturdy worktable with kettles and soup pots grouped by size beneath.

"This is Mrs. Maguire, our cook," he said, introducing a freckled woman in a black dress and white bib apron. Her curly brown hair framed kind eyes that softened Emily's guarded expression just a little.

Mrs. Maguire gave a welcoming nod.

"While she handles the cooking, you'll take care of the housekeeping," D.R. explained. Turning to the cook, he added, "Why don't you show them around?"

He knew she would be thorough, but he lingered anyway, watching Emily and Andrew take it all in.

"How d'ya do?" Mrs. Maguire greeted them before pointing to a screened-off area. "That's where the family eats when it's too hot upstairs.

And we have a dumbwaiter for sending food up to the dining room—or even firewood to the bedrooms. Isn't that grand?"

Emily and Andrew exchanged wide-eyed glances.

Leading them into a small corner room, Mrs. Maguire gestured inside. "These are your quarters." She nodded toward the bunk beds. "You can take the top bunk, young man. There's a ladder to climb up."

Andrew's face broke into a shy smile. Emily took in the washstand, the pitcher and bowl, and the small mirror above it—modest, but a space of their own.

As Emily's gaze roamed, Mrs. Maguire pointed to the inside of the bedroom door. "You and your son can lock it from the inside, see?"

Emily beheld the sliding bolt with the quiet wonder of someone witnessing an answered prayer. "Oh, Lordy," she breathed.

As Andrew hoisted their trunk onto the table and clambered onto the top bunk, Emily turned to Mrs. Maguire. "Where do you sleep?"

"I come in just to cook, six days a week," the woman replied. "Then I go home. You'll have the place to yourself till morning."

She pointed to the bottom bunk, where two neatly folded black-and-white uniforms lay. "Why don't you freshen up with some water from the pitcher? Then, after you change, I'll take you up to meet Mrs. Anthony."

Chapter Twenty-Two

Annie

January 24, 1865

Emily had taken to life with the Anthonys with such ease that Annie struggled to remember the house without her. A month had slipped by in a rush of days, and the once-weary woman now moved through the rooms with sure footing. Annie had wished for her comfort—had prayed for it. Yet at times, she wondered what thoughts stirred behind those warm brown eyes.

That morning, when the day's letters dropped through the slot, Emily brought them into the parlor. Annie dozed in the window near her new black piano, a Christmas gift from her husband. The sound of Emily's quiet steps stirred her.

As Emily placed the mail on the table, Annie sat up straight and murmured her thanks. A postcard caught her eye. After scanning the handwriting, she looked up with a smile.

"Miss Susan Anthony will be here in a week. I can't wait for her to meet you." She set the postcard aside and rose from her chair. "Speaking of that, let's go downstairs and work with Mrs. Maguire to make sure we have enough food for her stay. I expect that she'll have visitors."

Emily nodded, falling into step behind her as they made their way to the basement kitchen. The scent of fresh bread lingered in the air, and Mrs. Maguire had already left the ledger open on the worktable, her neat handwriting listing supplies to be replenished. Annie flipped through the pages, running a finger down the list.

"Emily, would you fetch the dried onion and the basil from the pantry?" she asked without looking up.

A brief hesitation. "The onion and—?"

"The basil," Annie repeated. "They're in small tins on the second shelf."

Emily wiped her hands on her apron and hurried to the pantry. A moment passed. Then another. Annie frowned, hearing the shuffle of tins being moved. After a long moment, Emily reappeared, holding out a small container.

"Is this it, ma'am?"

Annie read the label. "No, this is cinnamon."

Emily's lips pressed together, and she glanced away. Annie opened the tin, enjoying the delicious scent before handing it back.

"It's all right, I should have told you what the container looks like," she said.

But as Emily turned back to the pantry, Annie felt a prick of unease. How could she not recognize the label? The tin was clearly marked.

Then, as the pieces clicked into place, a quiet understanding stole over her.

Emily couldn't read.

The realization unsettled her more than she expected. She had taken for granted that anyone managing household tasks with such skill would have basic literacy. But why would Emily? Who would have ever taught her?

As Emily returned—this time with the right tin—Annie accepted it with a small nod, but her thoughts lingered. Emily had escaped slavery. She was earning wages, living as a freedwoman. But if she couldn't read, how much of the world was still closed to her?

Without a doubt, that needed to change.

Chapter Twenty-Three

Susan

January 28, 1865

When her train hit a bumpy section of track, Susan B. Anthony paused her letter-writing and gazed out the window. Thanks to D.R., she had lodged in St. Louis with comforts she could not have secured on her own. Soon she would have a chance to thank him in person for this kindness and other favors, as well.

As the ride smoothed out, she reread her letter:

Dear Clarina,

I am finishing the last leg of my journey to Leavenworth to visit my brother, D.R., and his wife, Annie. Sister Annie is three months along with her first child. Have you seen brother Daniel's newspaper, The Bulletin? They have just finished building a new house, so I think I will be comfortable. Once I get settled, I hope to call on you in person. For the meantime, write to me at 417 North Esplanade, Leavenworth.

Yours sincerely,

Susan B. Anthony

Satisfied, Susan pressed the envelope closed, running her fingers over the seal before affixing the stamp. Another letter sent, another connection strengthened.

Like D.R., Clarina had come to Kansas to keep it free from the grasp of slaveholders. But beyond that, she had been championing women's suffrage longer than almost anyone. If Leavenworth proved stifling—if she felt too much like an outsider in D.R. and Annie's world—she could always retreat to Clarina's.

The train rumbled steadily westward, Missouri's barren fields blurring past the window.

Soon, they reached the terminus at St. Joseph, where D.R. waited at the river's edge, ready to escort her and her trunks across the ice in a sleigh.

"How was your trip?" he asked as she stepped into the vehicle.

"Long but uneventful. New York had eighteen inches of snow, so I was glad to leave." Her gaze swept the frozen river, stretching wide and still in both directions, a silent world of ice and sky. "Are you certain this is safe? It feels too warm for January."

D.R. grinned. "I got across just fine, didn't I? Anyway, you don't need to worry—you never forget how to swim."

Once they reached the Planters House on the other shore, she set down her alligator purse. When no one was looking, she stretched to ease the stiffness in her limbs from hours of travel. D.R. went off to fetch the carriage, leaving her a moment to take in her surroundings.

Leavenworth.

It felt rough around the edges, raw in a way that both unsettled and invigorated her. But it was also a breath of fresh air—an open space where she could rest a soul worn thin from dubious audiences.

Here, the faces were unfamiliar. Open, maybe. Curious, she hoped. Minds she hadn't yet stirred.

They hadn't heard her voice yet. That alone made the miles worth it.

Susan watched Annie approach—poised, graceful, every bit the wife of an important man. By the time Annie reached her, Susan had already noted the powder blue cloak draped over Annie's shoulders, a color that spoke of luxury. Such a shade would never hold up to the miles of train soot and road dust that Susan's own black traveling coat had weathered.

Annie's cheek felt soft and warm as she pressed a kiss to each of Susan's cheeks. Arm in arm, they turned toward the unloading area, where D. R. and a stevedore wrestled her heavy trunks from the cart. Susan's gaze flicked to them for a moment before settling back on Annie. Travel-weary as she was, she could not help but wonder what kind of woman had marriage made of her young sister-in-law.

Nearby, mules waited to haul wagons laden with goods under tarps labeled *U.S. Army.*

Following Susan's glance, Annie said, "There's a fort here at Leavenworth. Among other things, they're in charge of the war refugees."

This made Susan think. Though she had spoken volumes about this war, she had never ventured this close to the action. "Weren't there battles in Missouri last summer?" she asked.

"Yeah, our boys made Price's troops turn tail and run out of there," said D.R.

Half an hour later, as he helped the women down from the carriage behind the house on North Esplanade, Susan looked at Annie.

"The house is just what you wished for, isn't it? White with green shutters. I like the two porticoes."

"I hope to start a vine growing on them this summer," replied Annie. "Before our trees get big, we'll need all the shade we can get. Just wait till you see how hot the summers can be."

D.R. slammed the carriage house door and strode up behind them, holding open the back door for them to enter. Following Annie along a hallway, Susan peeked into a butler's pantry on the left and the library on the right.

"Oh, my!" exclaimed Susan. "I've never seen a house without the kitchen at the back!" Her astonished eyes searched Annie's face for an explanation.

"It's not at the front, either," said D.R., motioning her toward the street side of the house, where the front parlor and formal dining room unfolded in polished splendor. The massive breakfront gleamed with glassware, and chestnut moldings lined the walls above thick Aubusson rugs.

"All right," said Susan, dropping her cloak into D.R.'s hand with a mock sigh. "Is there a hidden door, then? You've gone to great lengths to hide it."

Annie clasped her hands behind her back and walked ahead with an innocent air. "Oh, the kitchen is quite close—if you know where to look."

Susan narrowed her eyes. "I knew it. You've hidden it."

Laughing, Annie darted to a cabinet, yanked open the door, and stepped aside with a flourish. "Behold! The dumbwaiter. It carries food and dishes up from the basement without anyone having to clatter up and down the stairs."

Susan peered inside the empty shaft, shaking her head. "I suppose next you'll tell me the cook arrives by rope and pulley."

Annie grinned. "Not unless we're short-staffed."

The carved woodwork was so dark that Susan had overlooked the fact that it encompassed a small stairway leading down. She pointed to it and arched a questioning eyebrow. "This way?"

Annie nodded as D.R. wandered off to another part of the house.

"After you," Susan said, gathering her skirts in one hand and grasping the railing with the other. Annie introduced the colored housekeeper as Emily Robinson and then Mrs. Maguire, the cook, who busied herself peeling carrots for the night's meal.

"How do you do?" said Susan, bending to greet a Negro boy polishing the stove under a window.

"Susan, this is Emily's son, Andrew," said Annie. "He'll be making up the fire in your room in the mornings. He also turns the crank on our new rotary washer, which makes doing laundry much faster. After living at the hotel, I love not having to send it out anymore."

"I'll have to see that," said Susan.

Annie lifted her skirts and made her way up the stairs ahead of Susan, who said, "You don't seem slowed by your condition. How are you feeling?"

Back in the dining room, Annie turned to her sister-in-law. "The morning sickness has passed, thank goodness, and I'm feeling fine now." She put a protective hand on her midriff, which looked thicker than when Susan had met her as a bride. "Maybe you can help me prepare the layette." Annie hesitated. "That is, if you're not too busy with your antislavery campaign."

Half an hour later, conversation drifted upstairs to Susan as she unpacked her trunks in the spacious second floor bedroom allotted to her. Its four-poster was hung with royal blue curtains and, despite the modern bathroom down the hall, also contained a washstand with pitcher, bowl, and mirror.

Opening her work trunk, Susan removed two boxes of petitions from the Women's National Loyal League, whose offices she had left only days ago in New York City. She had promised to send out all of the letters this month and hoped Annie would help her. The League was petitioning Congress to abolish slavery.

Crossing to the large window, she ran her hand along the top of a beautiful tiger maple desk. Good, here was a convenient lamp. She loved a bedroom with enough light to read. There was even a small empty bookshelf awaiting her travel office that included file folders, a dictionary, a Bible, and portraits of her parents.

Her needs met, she decided to write a letter to share her first impressions of the West with Mrs. Stanton. But first she bounced lightly on the bed, something she always did in a new lodging. The eiderdown was welcoming, and it had been a long journey. On second thought, she might be able to address more petitions after a short nap.

Chapter Twenty-Four

Annie

February 8, 1865

Though it had been days since Susan had arrived, Annie was still getting used to her sister-in-law's high energy and curiosity. One afternoon, as they were having tea, Annie watched Susan's keen eyes scanning the room, taking in every detail.

As Emily placed a tray of fresh cookies on the table, Susan said, "Tell me, Emily, how did you come to be at the refugee camp?"

Emily hesitated, hands lingering over the tray as if steadying herself. Annie had seen that look before—the flicker of caution, the unspoken weight of a past not easily shared.

"It's a long story," Emily said, looking at the floor.

Susan waved a hand. "I've got time, and I want to hear it. Every story matters."

Emily glanced at Annie, as if asking permission. Annie gave a small nod, setting down her cup. "Only if you're willing to share," she added, realizing that she knew little of the freedwoman's history.

For a moment, Emily stood silent. Then, as if deciding she could trust them—at least a little—she spoke.

She started with the tobacco farm and losing her husband, Tobey, who had been sold to parts unknown. Annie's throat tightened as Emily described the moment she had given birth, only for her master to mark down the child's monetary value in his ledger.

"Oh, good, a boy!" Emily mimicked, her voice hard with memory. "Take good care of him so he'll grow into a strong young buck. Make me lots more money."

Across the table, Susan inhaled, her lips pressing into a thin line. "And people dare to call slavery a benevolent institution," she muttered. "How did you get away from there, Emily?"

Emily's expression shifted, something flickering in her eyes. Then she said, "Here's where the Lord comes in. In the form of a white man on a black horse."

Susan leaned forward, and Annie waited.

Emily nodded. The words came faster now, more alive. She spoke of how Jennison's Jayhawkers had freed some of the enslaved, but she had been left behind. How she had waited and watched, praying for another chance. And then, several months later—how a tall soldier had arrived, giving orders.

Susan's brows lifted. "Who was he?"

Emily met Annie's gaze before answering. "That's the confusing part. They said it was Jennison's Jayhawkers again, but a different man was leading them. It was Colonel Anthony."

Annie gasped. "No! You mean, my husband?"

"Yes, ma'am." A smile played at Emily's lips. "They had the master and his family tied up on the porch. Oh, what a sight it was! Mmm-mmm!"

Susan let out a low chuckle. "Now that's a scene I wish I could have witnessed."

Annie tried to picture it—the man she knew leading a raid, giving orders, setting people free. It was a side of him she had heard of but never seen, and it stirred a quiet thrill inside her.

Susan pressed on. "What happened next?"

Emily described how Daniel had ordered her people to take what they needed, how they had loaded the wagons with food.

"So then you came to the camp in Leavenworth?" Susan asked.

Emily nodded, detailing how the colonel had made sure the freed men and women rode in wagons instead of walking. How the owners had been forced to watch as their former slaves rode away. Annie laughed when Emily described how the soldiers had later dressed in women's clothes, drawing Daniel's wrath.

The mantel clock chimed, pulling Annie from the moment. "Oh, goodness, the colonel will be home for lunch any minute." She patted her hair as Emily turned to leave, but before the servant reached the basement stairs, Susan called after her.

"Emily, wait."

Emily turned back, her face expectant.

Susan studied her for a moment before asking, "Would you mind if we tell Colonel Anthony what you told us?"

Emily's answer came without hesitation. "No, ma'am. Like I said, them soldiers were a gift from the Lord."

Annie watched her disappear down the stairs, something settling deep in her chest.

An hour later, as they sat at the dining table, Daniel turned to Emily when she entered to remove the dishes. "Miss Susan told me what you said. I'm glad you survived the camp." He cleared his throat, something thoughtful in his expression. "I've heard of a woman who helps reunite families separated by the war. Would you like us to try to find your husband? Or has it been too long?"

Emily stilled. Then, slowly, a smile spread across her face.

"I would, yes!" she said, her voice trembling.

Then, more softly, like a promise to herself, she whispered, "Never too long."

An hour later, Susan and Annie were waiting for Daniel to bring the carriage to take them to Laing's Hall, where Susan would give a talk on reconstruction after the war.

"That's a thin shawl," said Annie. "Would you like to borrow something heavier?"

"I have warmer ones, but this is the one I always wear for speeches. I do hope this is the right topic for tonight," Susan fretted.

Annie hastened to reassure her. "You're onstage so much, I'm sure you know what people want to hear." Annie drew her cape across her growing belly. With the baby due in three months, she seldom went out in the evening, but since this was Susan's first week in Leavenworth, she made the extra effort. Besides, she did enjoy Laing's Hall, which was considered the most lavish theater for miles around.

That evening, from the first box in the theater, Annie surveyed the scene spread out before her—the glowing chandelier in the coffered ceiling, the colorful frieze around the proscenium arch, and the excited crowd waiting for the opening curtain.

The hall was not as crowded as Annie would have wished, nor was her seat as comfortable as she would have liked. However, these concerns faded away as Susan began to speak. Susan's voice seemed to fill the room without effort or strain despite the many eyes upon her. Her black gown with its white lace looked elegant and understated.

After lamenting the fact that colored men had been kept out of the war for so long, Susan turned her attention to the future of the United States. "We talk about returning to the Union as it was and the Constitution as it is—to the blessed conditions before the war. I ask you what sort of peace, what sort of prosperity, have we had? Since the first slave ship sailed up the James River with its human cargo, we have had nothing but war."

Puzzled, Annie looked at Daniel. *That's not true. We had plenty of peaceful years before this war.*

But Susan continued. "All these years, between the slave and master there has been war, and war only. This current conflict is but a new form of it. No, no, we ask for no return to the old conditions, but to something better. We want a union in spirit, not a sham. The Constitution, as it is, has stood pledged to protect slavery where it existed."

Annie nodded. Too bad the Emancipation Proclamation freed slaves in just the rebel states.

Hearing Susan's criticism of the Constitution, some listeners muttered dissent as she continued, "The politicians who protect slavery bow to the selfish interests of business."

Susan veered off onto a new track about how women needed to assume their rightful role as moral teachers. "Had the women of the North studied to know and to teach their sons the law of justice to the Black man, they would not now be called upon to offer their loved ones to the bloody god of war."

Laing's Hall hushed as both proslavery and abolitionists considered family members and friends lost to the war.

With her audience firmly in hand now, Susan launched into her concluding remarks: "Forget conventionalisms; forget what the world will say, whether you are in your place or out of it; think your best thoughts, speak your best words, do your best works, looking to your own consciences for approval."

Daniel jumped to his feet, applauding. By the time Annie had levered herself to stand, thunderous clapping filled the room. Four rows ahead, however, Annie noticed two well-dressed men glowering with folded arms.

Susan surveyed her audience with a grave expression and bowed. If Annie had ever doubted the importance of women's role in society, her sister-in-law's first speech in Kansas made her think.

From that day on, Susan attracted notice wherever she went. Some women crossed the street rather than cross paths with her; others sought her out as if they were old friends. Within days of setting foot in Kansas, she started receiving lecture invitations—not only from Leavenworth, but also from Atchison and Kansas City.

When Susan was invited to Lawrence, Annie said, "I've lived in Kansas for more than a year and never gone there, but here you are traveling south your first week here!"

"Come to Lawrence with me," replied Susan. "I would love the company."

"No, thank you!" Annie said. "Baby and I don't relish the hardship of stagecoach travel."

"But you drive Bill in your cabriolet almost every day," objected Susan.

"That's different. I can come home whenever I want or stop to see a friend."

Later, Annie found herself turning over the conversation, wondering what kind of future she wanted for her child. As Susan prepared to take her message beyond Leavenworth, Annie sensed her sister-in-law's impact would linger—on the town, and perhaps on Annie herself.

Chapter Twenty-Five

Annie

February 10, 1865

Two days later, Annie asked Emily to make up another guest bed for Susan's friend Clarina Nichols. Having Susan's friends to tea was one thing, but housing such a prominent woman for an entire week was quite another.

Knowing about Clarina's newspaper work, Annie looked forward to meeting the articulate writer behind the thought-provoking commentaries. Alongside Emily, she had made sure every room was dust-free and all the fireplaces were swept; with female guests, one could never be too careful about housekeeping.

Clarina was nothing to look at. Older than Susan, she wore her gray hair parted in the middle and plaited over her ears. The term "horselike" crossed Annie's mind, but she dismissed it. Clarina dressed in plain attire.

At lunch, Annie noticed that her visitor's hands looked as work worn as Daniel's mother's had been when they visited her on the Anthony farm. Clarina's lifestyle came into focus when she said she lived alone without a maid and hauled her own coal, shoveled her own walks, and caulked her own windows.

"That's nothing compared to my life as a widow in Lawrence," Clarina said. "But those stories will wait for another day."

Annie could not picture herself as a frontier wife. Ever.

"What a delightful meal," Clarina said, sipping her tea after Emily had cleared the dishes. "And thank you for accommodating a stranger on such short notice . . ." Her gaze lingered on Annie's thickening waistline. ". . . especially when you might not have your usual energy." With that, Annie felt her heart warm toward her visitor, and all her previous trepidation melted away.

On the way into the parlor, Susan said, "Tell me about women voting in municipal elections where you live."

"There's not much to tell," said Clarina. "All we can vote for are the school board and other issues concerning education—even after a decade of work for women. That's why I wanted to talk to you, Susan. Next year is a big election year, and we need to see if we can get something going for women in Kansas."

Annie shook her head. "You don't mean to have *women vote here,* do you?"

Two pairs of eyes registered surprise. "Well, of course," said Susan.

"It's too dangerous for women to vote in Leavenworth," insisted Annie. "Good gracious, it's dangerous for *men* to vote here. Daniel got mobbed during the last election."

Susan tsk'd. "You can't mean that, Annie. When women vote, the polls will move from the male watering holes to more accessible places. The mere presence of women will have a civilizing effect on everyone concerned."

Annie set her jaw. Having seen the mob herself, she knew that even Susan couldn't disband a voting riot in Leavenworth. On the verge of a retort, she realized she lacked the energy to argue. Instead, she announced her need for a nap.

As she stood to take her leave, empty teacup in hand, the two old friends began discussing the refugee camp in Leavenworth. "Have you been there yet?" Clarina asked Susan.

"No."

"Let's go tomorrow. I've collected some money for them and would like to deliver it in person."

"I wonder if Emily would mind showing us around the camp. Do you think it would be too hard on her to go there, Annie? And could you spare her for a couple of hours?"

Still resenting Susan's dismissive comment about elections, Annie considered refusing. After all, *she* was mistress of this house—not Susan. But then she realized that their expedition would buy her some quiet time to read.

"It's fine with me. Why don't you ring for her to come upstairs so we can discuss it?"

Several days later, after Clarina had returned home, Susan revisited the refugee camp. Upon arriving at the house on North Esplanade, she dropped her cloth bag on the table, her words instantly evoking Annie's empathy.

"Those poor children!" she exclaimed. "Many of them have nothing to wear but rags! Half-naked, in this cold. They're skinny and sick. Emily says she never sent Andrew to the school there because she was afraid he'd catch something." She removed her hat and hung up her cloak.

Reaching into her bag, she said, "The refugee children need education, in particular the colored ones. So I'll be teaching over there one day a week. You can help, too." She offered an ingratiating smile.

Annie cringed and put her hand on her abdomen. "Oh, no—I can't go near all that sickness. What if the baby—"

"Not at the camp, no." From her satchel Susan withdrew a primer and set it beside a slate and chalk she had purchased before she reached the house. "But that boy Andrew downstairs—*there's* a good mind going to waste. I know you have no colored school in town yet, but you could teach him his letters right here at home. I'll show you how. And what about Emily. Shouldn't you be doing something to help her read?"

Did Susan think she had all the time in the world to take on another task? Her days were already filled to the brim—managing the household, tending to Daniel, preparing for the baby's arrival, accommodating guests who came to see Susan. And now Susan expected her to take up teaching, as if it were as simple as setting another place at the table.

"I already thought of that," she snapped, before she could stop herself.

Susan raised an eyebrow. "Well, what are you waiting for?"

Annie bit back a sharper retort. It was easy for Susan to dole out instructions—she had never kept house, never carried a child, never lain awake at night worrying about dozens of small things like making sure she purchased food and peppermints for Miss Greenshawl every time she went to town.

And yet, the next day when Annie sang the alphabet song to Andrew and Emily, something inside her softened. Their eagerness was undeniable. As Susan guided their hands over the slate, forming letters for the first time, Annie couldn't ignore the spark of excitement that flickered in her chest. By the end of the week, their new routine had taken shape, and Annie had to admit: Susan had been right.

During the lessons, Annie got to observe Emily closely.

One day, at the end of the lesson, Emily lingered after her son had drifted off. "Miss Annie, I'd like to ask you something."

When she first arrived, the black uniform had hung loose on her fragile frame, her braided hair tight against her scalp, her skin dry and patchy like a withered leaf. But after two months of regular meals and restful sleep, Emily was changing. Her figure had filled out, her skin glowed with new health, and she now wrapped bright scarves around her head—small acts of beauty and individuality.

The servant cleared her throat. "Mrs. Maguire told me when you first came here, a man died on your lawn."

Annie said, "That's right. He wasn't that old, but he died of a heart attack. He worked at a livery. Martin Bauer was his name."

"Well, glory be!" Emily covered her mouth as if the words had slipped off her tongue before she could help it.

"I beg your pardon? Why do you say that?"

"Oh, sorry, ma'am. It's just that I knew him from the tobacco farm. He was the master's son. All us women had to look out for him."

Annie paused, trying to digest Emily's inference. Then she sighed and gave the servant a thoughtful look. "Between you and me, the colonel didn't trust him either."

Emily nodded and left, her steps light and quick.

Chapter Twenty-Six

Daniel

February 17, 1865

"Daniel!" Annie shook his shoulder vigorously. "Wake up. You're kicking me!"

He startled awake in bed, his heart banging in his throat. "Mmmph?"

"You kicked me!" she accused. "And hit me, too. You must be dreaming."

Still drugged with sleep, he mumbled, "Sorry. Drunk secesh . . . attacking you . . . " He reached for her, but she shrank away.

"I don't feel safe sleeping next to you when you're dreaming like that." In the faint moonlight, she got out of bed and drew on her wrapper.

"Where you going?" he muttered, now fully awake and full of regret.

"To the kitchen for some warm milk. After that, I'll come back and try to fall asleep on the fainting chair." The white velvet lounge gleamed in the moonlight.

He threw back the covers and swung his legs over the side of the bed. "No. I'm the one who was kicking. I'll take the chair."

She paused, hugging the robe around herself and lamenting, "Oh, Daniel . . . I don't want to sleep in our bed without you."

"Nor I without you," he replied. "But I don't want to hurt you, either." He moved closer, wrapping his arms around her, his chin resting on her head as he pushed aside the unsettling image of the thief reaching for her. "Nothing is as important to me as you," he said, his voice gruff.

He savored her warmth and softness while stroking her back. "You need your sleep, Sunflower. For the baby. Please go back to bed while I try to get sleepy again." Gently he guided her back to bed and lowered himself to the mattress, inviting her to sit beside him and then lie back to sleep. After a few minutes, he padded down the stairs and outside for a cigar.

⁂

After dinner the following evening, Susan stayed in her room to work on her correspondence, leaving Annie alone with Daniel.

"I bought a new towel rack for under the sink," Annie said. "It has three separate rods that can swivel out or back against the wall."

"Sounds like the kind Ma had on the farm," he replied.

"That's what Susan said. Will you put it up for me?"

"Sure. Come show me where you want it."

In the months since they had moved into their new house, they'd added a host of new details. Mirrors on closet doors. Grates for fireplaces. Hooks for mops. Racks for hats and bonnets. And dozens of shelves. D.R. kept a screwdriver always handy in the kitchen drawer.

While she held the rack in place, he began screwing it in.

"You know that nightmare I had last night? It was about secesh breaking into our home. Except we lived in a farmhouse."

Annie cocked her head, inviting him to say more.

"Two men came in and tied me up. They smashed everything—even the picture of my parents. But the worst part was when you came downstairs. I was so afraid they'd hurt you." He shuddered as if to shake it off.

"That's terrible. Did you ever have anyone break into your home?" she asked, hanging towels on the new rack.

"No. Usually the dream is different and I'm the one breaking in."

She tsk'd. "Just as terrible. I wonder why you keep dreaming that?"

He sighed. "The thing is . . . I did a lot of that with the Kansas Seventh back when Jennison was commanding us."

Annie's eyes widened before she sank into a chair at the kitchen table.

Leaning against the stove, he began, "One of the worst times was Pleasant Hill." He hadn't meant to bring it up—but once the words were out, there was no reining them in. "Supply train got captured. We were camped in Kansas, waiting on it."

Annie looked up, her brow furrowed as she paid close attention.

"Jennison was at the fort, gambling. I was in charge. As usual." D.R. kept his tone level, willing the old resentment to stay buried. "He showed up just long enough to stir the men up—full of speeches and fire—and then passed it off to me. Told me to take eight companies and get the supplies back."

His hand raked through his hair. The memory came quick now, pressing to be told.

"Doc ordered us to burn the place after. Teach them a lesson, same as we'd done the week before in Dayton." He hesitated. "I didn't argue. Even though the smoke from Dayton still clung to my clothes."

He stood and crossed to the sideboard, opening a drawer and tossing in the screwdriver he'd been fiddling with. The small clang gave him something to listen to besides his own voice.

"Pleasant Hill was quiet when we arrived. Small place. A handful of shops, homes. A few farms out beyond." His voice dropped a notch. "Our scouts found rebels hiding in the woods. We caught 'em off guard and took 'em easy."

He waved a hand, dismissing it. "Found the wagons too. Got what we came for. Then—torched the town. As ordered."

From the corner of his eye, he saw Annie flinch. She said nothing, but her silence changed the feel of the room.

He tried to lift the tone. "We freed every colored person we could find—fifty-five in Pleasant Hill alone. That was the best part of the job. That made it worth doing."

"I guess so," she said softly. "But the people who lived there . . . it must've been horrible for them. Like in your dream. Even if they were harboring rebels."

He gave a small nod. "We ordered folks out before the fires. Some fought like wildcats. I would have too, in their shoes."

His voice grew quieter. "The worst part? Some of them were Union sympathizers. But we couldn't tell who was who, so we torched the whole place."

Annie's expression shifted—first pity, then something sharper. Her gaze slipped from his face, like she couldn't quite bear to look at him.

"Like the Shady Grove family," she murmured, staring into the distance. "In the diary upstairs."

He didn't answer. Just watched her. He should've known it would land this way—with her measuring it not by orders or outcomes, but by right and wrong.

She pushed herself upright and brushed the wrinkles from her skirt with trembling hands. "You'd defied orders before," she said, "when you thought they were wrong. I'm surprised you didn't at Pleasant Hill."

Her words cut deeply. D.R. held her gaze, his jaw tight. He hadn't wanted to tell her all of it—but now that it was out, he couldn't take it back.

"It was war, Annie," he said. "I was trying to keep my men fed and moving. I didn't order the fires. But I didn't stop them either. That's the truth."

She met his eyes then, and something in her face closed.

"I don't know what unsettles me more," she said, "that it happened . . . or that you can speak of it so calmly."

Then she turned toward the door. "I'm going for a walk. Alone."

The door clicked shut behind her.

D.R. stood frozen, staring at the space she'd just occupied. He'd carried those words for years—words that had burned like coals in his chest. Saying them should've brought relief. Instead, he felt gutted. Not because they weren't true. But because he'd finally spoken them . . . and they'd driven her away.

He waited a while before stepping onto the porch. Down the hill, her figure moved fast and tight, her stride rigid with fury. Then she stopped and looked up.

He followed her gaze. The moon hung high, remote and pitiless, casting the same hard light she'd turned on him. He felt exposed—stripped bare beneath its glare, and hers.

When he saw her return, he slipped into the library and shut the door. Maybe she'd knock. Maybe they'd talk. But she passed by in silence and climbed the stairs alone.

He waited an hour before heading up, bracing for more. But if she was still awake, she gave no sign.

That's how the silence began.

Chapter Twenty-Seven

Susan

February 20, 1865

Susan heard the front door shut and tensed a little. Annie hurried into the parlor, her eyes sweeping the room until they landed on the scissors. Without a word to Susan, she seized them and sliced through the brown paper covering a package. Susan braced herself for an emotional outburst, given Annie's touchiness these last few days. Instead, Annie murmured, "Hmmm," her brow furrowed.

Susan looked up from her newspaper. "You sound puzzled."

"I asked my sister Mary to send me the pattern she used for Priscilla's christening gown." Annie's fingers tapped against the paper. "She's our niece. But Prissie's dress looked nothing like what Mary sent." She thrust the illustration toward Susan with a sharp gesture—long and short baby dresses with plain or puff sleeves depicted on the page.

Susan welcomed this pleasant diversion. Perhaps it would replace the edge in Annie's voice that had been present for a few days now. D.R. seemed testy too, though Susan knew better than to mention it.

"I imagine Mary used that pattern and adapted it," Susan offered. "Maybe she added a ruffle and some lace."

Annie shook her head, lips pressed together. "No, Prissie's was much finer than that." She held her hands two feet apart, movements quick and precise. "It was this long and had lace insets, pearl buttons, and tiny tucks. I think Mary embroidered it, too."

"Oh, my!" Susan replied, trying to sound enthusiastic despite Annie's mounting irritation. "That must have been lovely."

"I'm going into town tomorrow." Annie folded the pattern with short, crisp movements. "I'll ask my dressmaker if she can make this up with some more elaborate details. She did a nice job copying a gown I brought from back East."

Susan nodded and returned to her correspondence, sensing it was better not to offer further opinions on the matter. Annie's stiff posture and clipped words told her everything she needed to know about her hostess's mood today.

After her excursion the next day, Annie swept into the parlor. "Madame Collette doesn't like making baby clothes because they're so tiny," she announced, dropping into a velvet side chair with a dejected sigh. "I don't know what to do. I should have asked Mary months ago to make the baptism gown. Now it's too late for her to finish it and mail it in time."

She looked expectantly at Susan, as if she had nothing better to do than solve Annie's domestic crisis. Susan barely glanced up from her book. She already saw where this was going.

"You've made quilts, haven't you?" Annie pressed before Susan could respond. "You must be able to make very fine stitches. Besides the christening gown, I need a whole layette!"

Susan clenched her jaw. She had, indeed, spent years making quilts, but since devoting herself to reform work, the last thing she wanted to do was strain her eyes over tiny stitches. Did Annie think she had endless hours to sit and fuss over baby clothes?

"Babies don't wear an outfit more than a few hours before they've outgrown it," she said, keeping her tone even. "I doubt you need that kind of quality for—"

"Oh, but this is our first baby!" Annie cut in. "I've always pictured soft little gowns with delicate details. That's what the Osborns always have for their babies. I hate to give up that tradition just because I've moved to Leavenworth."

Susan exhaled a long breath, pressing her lips together to keep from saying something biting. Annie was young, idealistic, and stubborn—especially when it came to things she barely understood.

And yet, she had no other womenfolk nearby.

Susan reminded herself of that before replying. "Such tiny stitches strain my eyes," she said at last. "But how about I teach you to make the layette yourself? If you take your time, you can produce the fine work you want."

Annie frowned. "So you're saying I should just do it myself?"

"I'm saying I will teach you. That way, you'll have exactly what you want, and I won't go blind in the process."

Annie's mouth pressed into a tight line. "I don't see why you won't just help me. You know how."

Oh, for heaven's sake. "Annie, sewing is an exercise in patience and humility. You will have to rip out stitches and start over more times than you'd like. I suspect you might despise me for pointing out your mistakes."

"I won't, I promise."

Susan gave her a knowing look. "We'll see about that."

Annie crossed her arms but didn't argue further.

"About that christening robe," Susan continued.

Annie narrowed her eyes. "You think I can't handle it?"

Susan smothered a laugh. "A christening gown requires the finest handwork. Wouldn't you rather have something from Martha's Vineyard to remind you of the baby's heritage? Could one of your relatives lend you one?"

Annie pursed her lips, but then her expression brightened. "Yes! Maybe I can borrow Prissie's!"

Susan unleashed her smile. "Why not? Young Priscilla won't be needing it any time soon."

The next day, Annie held the door as Susan stepped into the dry goods store. It was quiet, save for a woman's voice at the counter.

"I know that's what we agreed, but my clothing budget has been trimmed. If you could just give me another month . . ."

Next to Susan, Annie tensed. "Oh, dear, I know that woman," she whispered. "How embarrassing for her. Let's go to the other side of the store."

Before Susan could reply, Annie seized her arm and dragged her toward the ribbons and lace. "I wouldn't want anyone listening if it were me," she explained.

Susan watched as Annie fussed over the finest cottons and embellishments, selecting each with the utmost care. No doubt about it. This newest Anthony would have a perfect layette—whether it was practical or not.

Chapter Twenty-Eight

Daniel

February 21, 1865

The war was grinding to a halt. Good news, but nothing compared to the relief of hearing Annie's voice again. After their Pleasant Hill discussion, he hadn't been sure she'd speak to him any more. Her pique had resolved without explanation, but that was good enough for him.

D.R. scanned the latest telegrams at *The Bulletin*, absorbing the reports with practiced focus. Even with his chair turned toward the wall, he recognized the sound of boots in the outer office—quick but deliberate. Chas Goodman. The steps hesitated only a moment before the clerk waved him through the door marked "Publisher."

D.R. turned just as Chas stepped inside. "What's up, Marshal?"

Chas caught his breath. "Bad news from Indian country."

D.R. shut the door. "Shoot."

Chas gestured toward the newsroom. "It'll be all over town soon, so I've come to give you fair warning. John Osborn was arrested in Coffey County. Jim McDowell's men were involved."

D.R. felt the blood drain from his face. Arrested. Now what?

He had paid John for this job—and if Annie found out . . .

His hands curled into fists against his desk. She couldn't find out. At least not till he'd done all he could to fix the situation.

Keeping his voice steady, he asked, "Is John all right?"

"Almost got himself lynched," Chas said, grim-faced. "There was a big fracas till the army arrived. You owe the provost marshal a huge favor for saving that boy's skin."

Favors D.R. could do. But if he didn't get John safely out of jail, Annie wouldn't just be furious. She'd never look at him the same way again.

D.R. drew a deep breath. "How soon can we bring John home?"

"Couple days, I expect," said Chas. "And you better watch your own back. McDowell's got up a head of steam." He rose and turned toward the door, shedding disapproval like sunburned skin.

D.R. noticed that Chas did not offer police protection. Coming around the desk, he said, "Thanks. I'll—uh—post some guards. Who do you recommend?"

Chas suggested a few names.

"I'm going to the Indian country as soon as I can. Would you be able to look in on Annie sometime today?"

Chas's icy gaze conveyed his awareness that D.R. had put John in a precarious situation. Still, the marshal consented to look in on Annie.

The moment Chas left, D.R. swung into action, first sending couriers to assemble a team of strong men to guard *The Bulletin* and others to accompany him to Coffey County. Then, after giving a few instructions to employees, he set off with a heavy heart for home.

Annie was out. Good—he could just write her a note, even though that might just mean having her chastise him later rather than now. He pulled the small notebook from his chest pocket and scribbled, "Went to see John. I'll be gone for a few nights. Take care, my love. D." Grabbing some food and a bedroll, he slammed out the back door and hurried to mount his horse.

As D.R. rode west to meet his friends, he pictured Annie coming home, removing her gloves, and reading his note. She would frown with puzzlement and show it to Susan. Then worry would set in. Once she learned of

John's arrest from the newspaper, he wouldn't have to explain. If he was lucky, he would be able to tell her that he had saved John.

This thought gave him satisfaction on one hand, but made him feel like a coward on the other. She would be afraid, and he wouldn't be there to comfort her. But Susan would. Thank God for Susan. She was almost as good to have around as a man.

D.R. straddled a chair outside John's cell and observed the bruises and scrapes on his brother-in-law's face.

"My scouts are out now. They tell me McDowell's got about fifteen hundred stolen animals stashed in various places, so it may take a while to find them all. Unless he's already sold them to someone else, we should be able to get him to drop the charges of cattle rustling in return for not turning him in to the authorities."

John threw up his hands. "Hold on! You promised there would be no trouble in this assignment! 'Perfectly safe,' you said."

"Turns out it's a trickier thing than I realized. I thought forming McMahon, Peck, and Company as cowhands would keep your name out of acquiring the cattle. Did you stick to your end of the business?"

John looked away. "Mostly. They handled the rustling, compensated the natives when necessary, and I settled up with them as you instructed."

D.R. narrowed his eyes, his voice firm. "Mostly? What part of that plan didn't you follow?"

"Sometimes all hands were needed. The Indians seem to think they have some claim to cows that roam the free range. Didn't figure on that." John snorted. "Sometimes we had to fight off McDowell's men *besides* the Indians. Got pretty rough."

John described the standoff that had occurred a week earlier when nearby white residents had banded with the Indians to protect the stock. "They told me the Indians would retaliate against any and all white men if we didn't leave them alone. That no farm or homestead—or wife—would be safe."

D.R. leaned forward, jutting his chin at John. "What I heard is that you were reckless enough to go into the Indians' holding pens and untie the animals. Where did you get such a numbskull idea?"

John let the question sit a minute before skirting the issue. "When the Indians caught me, I thought they'd kick me to death," he said. "But then, for some reason, they stopped and tied me up. Even brought me something to eat and drink. For a while it seemed like they'd let me go, but in the morning they marched me out to face the men from Oskaloosa."

D.R. let out a heavy sigh as he pondered the situation. The Indians had more determination than he had anticipated; he hadn't expected them to catch on right away. It seemed wise to withdraw while they were still ahead.

"What can you tell me about the team working for McDowell?" he asked.

"For every steer we took, they took three," John said. "They had more men, y'see. We exchanged some shots at a distance, but it never amounted to much. But then some of them joined the mob that took me."

"You should've sent for more help last week," said D.R. "You've got to know your own strength. *And weakness.*" Then, remembering that John was Annie's brother, he said, "You all right? Need a doctor?"

After thinking for a moment, John said, "Nothing broken. Lots of bruises. McMahon and Peck got away, making me afraid the Indians would take out all their anger on me. And McDowell's men proposed sending a message to you by lynching me."

D.R.'s jaw tightened.

John gave a bitter laugh. "Lucky for me, there weren't any trees big enough to hang a man. But while they were discussing it, the marshal and his men rode up. He persuaded McDowell to let him take me by promising he would 'submit me to the full force of the law.'" He looked bleakly at D.R. "So maybe I'll hang anyway. That's the punishment for cattle theft, isn't it?"

"I doubt you'll hang. If I can prove McDowell's guilty of even larger theft himself, he won't follow through with this finger-pointing. We just have to get you back to Leavenworth safely." He patted John's arm in an almost fatherly way. "Don't worry. I'll take care of it." He went into the office to post John's bail and thank the provost marshal by pledging a few cases of whiskey. His reputation for keeping his promises made it easier to get a yes.

Back on North Esplanade, D.R. eased the bedroom door open just enough to see Annie, sitting upright in bed, eyes shut tight as if bracing for something. He paused, torn between entering and leaving her in peace. She hadn't dressed. Not even combed her hair. That wasn't like h er.

A bead of sweat slipped down his back.

"Daniel?" Her voice was cautious. She opened her eyes, wary of what might meet them. "Is that you?"

He stepped inside. "It's me."

She exhaled a sharp breath and pushed herself upright with effort, the weight of their child heavy in her belly. "Oh, honey—I was so afraid." Getting out of bed, she crossed the room on unsteady feet and wrapped her arms around him, but her body stayed tense. "Some men came asking for you last night. In the dark. They were loud."

His hand found her hair, trying to smooth her fear, though his gut twisted. He should've had someone watching the place.

"Did they get in the house?"

She shook her head. "No. Susan told them you weren't home." Her voice trembled. "While they were still out there, Chas came and made them leave." She led him to the bed, and they sat close, but not quite touching. "Where's John? Is he safe?"

He nodded, feeding her the calmest version he could manage—bail posted, John sent back to Huron.

"Is that the end of it?" she asked. Her voice was hopeful, but her eyes still searched his face as if looking for what he wasn't saying.

"For now, yes," he said, avoiding her gaze.

She nodded, but her fingers tightened around the edge of the quilt. She was holding herself together, but only just. He could feel it in the way she avoided his eyes, in the slight hesitation before answering. She was glad he was home—he knew that much—but there was distance in her, and it unsettled him. Maybe she wasn't sure what to believe. Maybe she wasn't sure about *him.*

He watched her movements—the slow way she changed into a dress, combed her hair, and nibbled at the bread Susan brought. She was trying. That counted for something.

When Susan stepped out for her meeting, he lingered a moment longer, then slipped away, heading for his office with secrets pressing down like wet wool on his back.

Upon reaching *The Bulletin,* D.R. told his clerk, "I don't want to be disturbed. Get me every area newspaper you can find."

Half an hour later the man returned, saying, "Here's everything I could find—*The Times, The Conservative,* one from Topeka, and one from Oskaloosa."

D.R. shut the door, sorted the papers into chronological order, and began scanning for news about John. His expression grew graver and graver as he read letters to the editor from an anonymous accuser who knew the inside story.

Among the revelations from that correspondent were that D.R. had provided a letter of recommendation for John to the Kansas region where the cattle were acquired; that the livestock were purchased at the low price of five dollars per head; and that D.R. had bribed an army provost to allow the cattle droves to pass without challenge.

It ended with this threatening comment: "I am told by settlers of the region that those outraged allies will make war and reprisals, reproducing the horrors imposed on Lawrence by Quantrill."

D.R. suppressed a shudder. Invoking the name of that vicious bandit could signal the end of his own career and—worse yet—a death sentence for John. After scooping the papers into a pile on the corner of his desk, he decided it was time for *The Bulletin* to highlight McDowell's prowess in the cattle trade.

CHAPTER TWENTY-NINE

Annie

March 25, 1865

As the days grew warmer and Annie's graceful stride changed to a waddle, her sphere narrowed to her own street and home where Daniel, Susan, and the servants brought her the daily news and gossip.

One day when Emily brought her peppermint tea, Annie asked her to sit down. "There's someone I want you to look after while I'm on bedrest," she began, and told Emily how to find Miss Greenshawl.

Daniel had used his clout as publisher of *The Bulletin* to deflect attention from John's arrest. For each article in which *The Times* hinted about him or John stealing livestock, *The Bulletin* retaliated with one of McDowell's indiscretions, such as an investigation into his default on a ten-thousand-dollar debt. When John expressed an interest in visiting parts further west, D.R. bankrolled a several-month stay and promised more as needed. Anything to get him out of town.

One day in mid-March after John's departure, Daniel came home all excited. Before he even took off his coat, he announced, "The city received McDowell's resignation today, and the Republicans have asked me to run again for mayor."

Annie sent him a skeptical look from where she was watering her plants. "And after the mob scene at the polls during the last election, I'm supposed to be happy about this?"

Daniel kissed her hello before dropping his coat on the settee and flopping onto it. "I can't see us having another riot. Since that last election, tempers have cooled a lot and people are in a better mood. Besides, McDowell is out of town, sick, and he was one of the chief mob instigators."

Annie lowered herself to sit beside him. "What would you hope to achieve by being mayor again?"

He didn't even pause before answering. "McDowell and his friend Carney have robbed the city blind. Today I discovered that McDowell's administration is in the red. When I left office, it was in the black."

Annie was surprised to hear Daniel describe Rebecca Carney's husband in such disparaging tones. Was every politician accused of underhandedness?

Mrs. Maguire was taking a day off to entertain a guest, so Emily came in to begin placing hot dishes on the table.

After Daniel repeated his news to his sister at supper, Annie tried to wear him down with practical objections. "Last time you ran for mayor, you didn't own *The Bulletin*." She ticked off her fingers. "Between your work at insurance, the paper and the post office, I don't see how you'd have time to campaign this time around. Besides, city elections take place in early April, don't they?"

His eyes gleamed. "It *is* a short time, which means a shorter campaign. And I have a great plan to get us through a campaign, depending on your involvement, Suse."

Susan cocked her head, curious. "My involvement?"

"You're a good writer and already have a clear grasp of the city. I would still oversee the paper but if you write some of the editorials, I think I'd have time to drum up votes." He grinned. "Just don't fill the whole paper with antislavery and women's suffrage." He paused for effect. "How would you like to publish a newspaper?"

"I'm busy the rest of this week, but next Monday I should be free to help you," she replied, sounding to Annie as if it were the most natural thing in the world.

Annie watched as Daniel tasted a forkful of lemon meringue pie, delight dancing in his eyes. "Emily, please tell Mrs. Maguire this is the best pie I've ever tasted."

Emily paused, her hands hovering over the teapot as she filled Annie's cup. "Um . . . it's my own special recipe from the tobacco farm. That's why you've never tasted it before."

"You could sell these, Emily. Set yourself up in business."

Annie couldn't help but admire how effortlessly Susan chimed in. She had to admit that it was a wonderful suggestion, but why did Susan always seem to have the first, brilliant idea?

The next evening, Susan strode into the parlor and thrust a copy of *The Times* into her brother's face. "This is revolting. Did you see it?"

Daniel read aloud. "'Government agencies and military policies alike have taken to petting Negroes.'" Snorting, he showed it to Annie.

"I can't believe they *published* such a thing!" said Annie.

"Typical canard from *The Times.* Someone needs to write a rebuttal." Glancing pointedly at Susan, he handed the paper back to her. "But I don't have time tomorrow."

Taking it, she huffed, "Oh, all right!" and swept out of the parlor. Susan was still bent over the tiger maple desk when Annie peeked into her room to say good night.

The next day, page one of *The Bulletin* featured a long article that said:

We have looked over the whole round of the advocates for the equal humanity of the Negro race and have failed to find the first word in favor of "petting"—which, if we rightly understand, means treating as children, incapable of taking care of themselves. Rev. Henry Ward Beecher says, "Make them full American citizens." Frederick Douglass says, "I am for the immediate, unconditional and universal enfranchisement of the Black man in every State in the Union."

Annie smiled. The article went on to quote five more of Susan's famous abolitionist friends. Even though it was unsigned, it bore the distinct tone of her sister-in-law's voice. Susan was in her element.

***

As the days passed, despite Susan's oversight at *The Bulletin,* many pages still contained contentious reports of the campaign for mayor. Annie shuddered when she learned that Rebecca Carney's husband, Thomas, having just retired as Kansas governor, had advanced his name as Daniel's opponent. He was one of McDowell's friends.

"He drummed up a lot of New York money to protect Leavenworth on the Missouri border," fretted Daniel, "and poured some of his own into it, too. That's something people aren't likely to forget."

Sometimes being Mrs. Colonel Anthony took more energy than Annie had. Over tea with Lydia that week, Annie asked her friend to convey her regrets to the Sanitary Relief Commission where she would have encountered Mrs. Carney. Instead of confiding her embarrassment to Lydia, however, she cited growing fatigue as her pregnancy advanced.

"It's good that you have Susan and the servants to help you through these last months," said Lydia. "Of course, you will still be able to read about everything in the newspaper, too." Inhaling from her fragrant cup, she said, "Oh, did you see that article about a colonel who was court-martialed at the fort?"

Feeling the baby kick against her abdomen, Annie paused to catch her breath. "No, what happened?" she inquired, adjusting her chair's cushion to relieve the strain on her back.

"Seems he gave some unpopular orders two years ago when his men were out on maneuvers in Missouri, and some of them still bore a grudge. When they threatened him in January at LeBonTon, he shot one of them. I told you LeBonTon was a bad place!"

"Did the soldier die?" Annie asked.

"No, but lots of people saw it happen. Even though the officer said it was self-defense, the judge ruled otherwise," Lydia said. "Now he's in jail after losing a lengthy court case. Milton says legal fees cost a lot of money when you don't win."

Lydia leaned in, voice hushed with the pleasure of knowing more than she ought. "I heard it on good authority that his wife can't pay her bills." She shook her head, her expression heavy with practiced sympathy. "Poor woman. No wife deserves such treatment."

Annie held her tongue, though her mind spun with the implications. Behind her composed expression, she recalled Mrs. Mellick's plea for the modiste to extend credit. "Do you know the officer's name?"

"James Mellick," Lydia replied, eyes alight. "He was an officer in the army, I hear. They had a nice house on the post. But not anymore."

Annie felt a pang of sympathy, followed by a fear that began worming into her contentment. She had enjoyed Mrs. Mellick's lighthearted banter at Madame Collette's and wondered how the officer's trendsetting wife would weather such disgrace. If it could happen to Colonel Mellick long after the incident, what tragedy might befall Daniel years after his service?

That night in bed, Annie's back throbbed, low and steady, making it impossible to get comfortable. She shifted onto her side, easing into the curve of Daniel's body. Sleep hovered just out of reach. Then came the snore—loud and sudden, right in her ear.

She opened her eyes to the darkness. The grandfather clock chimed three-thirty, slow and solemn, like it was keeping count of every minute she lay awake. She rolled to her other side with a grunt, then froze. Was that too much pressure on her belly? Could stomach sleeping actually hurt the baby?

A familiar burn crept up her throat. Sighing, she pushed back the covers, grabbed an extra pillow, and propped herself up before sliding back into bed.

And because the night hadn't tortured her enough, "Goober Peas" started playing in her head—over and over. Daniel's off-color version followed, and despite herself, she half-smiled. Her mind drifted to that lone ambrotype of him in his Union uniform, proud and composed. She could imagine that voice of his carrying over a whole field of men.

But not all those men had followed him by choice. She knew that now. Knew how often he spoke hard truths, how ready he was to confront what others overlooked. Like that time with the horses—the soldier he reprimanded for carelessness. If Jennison hadn't stepped in . . .

Her smile vanished. Colonel Mellick hadn't been so lucky. Attacked by his own men for something long past—who was to say old resentments didn't fester in others, too? Daniel wasn't a colonel anymore, but that didn't mean he was safe. Not from grudges. Not from someone who felt wronged and wanted to settle it their own way.

Her stomach clenched, tight and sour. She pressed a hand to it, trying to breathe deep, trying to settle the worry. Could this heartburn—this stress—be affecting the baby?

Chapter Thirty

Annie

March 30, 1865

By the end of March, *The Bulletin* was attacking Tom Carney's supporters with comments such as: "These men, the owners of vacant lots, who opposed street improvements and refused to pay taxes for advancements, supported Mayor McDowell last year. These same men support Carney for mayor this year."

The next day *The Bulletin* announced that Carney would speak at Laing's Hall on Monday night, and on Tuesday, Daniel would speak. In a one-inch column, Susan proposed that each man speak on both nights, alternating which one went first. To Annie's relief, the candidates adopted her suggestion.

The evenings of speeches passed peacefully, as did the election itself in early April.

Once again, however, Daniel lost. The next day, he excused Susan from her editorial writing and used venom when describing the newly-elected: "Gamblers . . . disappointed office-seekers . . . sympathizing traitors . . . well-known pimps who curse our city . . ."

"Pimps?" Annie exclaimed as she read the article that afternoon. "What is he thinking, accusing people so publicly? He's treading on thin ice."

When Susan saw it, she rolled her eyes. "This is what happens when the editor's big sister is not there to keep him in line."

Annie, however, did not think it was funny.

Soon enough, Daniel had begun to cheer up. Word of Union victories rippled through town like a fresh breeze, lifting everyone's spirits a little higher than their usual fretting over local politics and supply shortages.

On a warm April afternoon, sunlight filtered through the porch railings as Emily and Andrew Robinson practiced their reading, voices soft and hesitant as they worked through the first volume of the primer. Annie sewed nearby, listening, offering a correction here and there. Moments later, a breathless boy from *The Bulletin* came up the walk and thrust a folded slip of paper into her hands. The ink was still damp.

Annie scanned the scrawled note—and froze. A quiet gasp escaped before she could stop it, and her eyes burned. She blinked hard, but the tears came anyway.

Emily's face tightened. "What is it?"

Annie braced a hand on the arm of the chair and pushed herself up from the chair, heavy with emotion, determined to meet the moment with dignity. "Please call Miss Susan down," she said, the words catching in her throat. She rose and went into the parlor, motioning Andrew inside the room too.

By the time Susan entered the room, Annie was holding the note in both hands as if it were sacred. Her voice shook as she read aloud, "Telegram just arrived—Lee surrendered to Grant at Appomattox Court House—I will stay late working on Extra Edition to spread the news."

For a breathless moment, the room held only silence.

Andrew and Emily looked at one another, their slate forgotten. Then Susan's arms were around her, and Annie clung to her sister-in-law, both of them weeping without restraint. Relief. Grief. Disbelief. It all pressed in at once.

Susan stepped back, eyes shining, and reached out her hands to Emily and Andrew. Annie joined them, their small circle tight with shared hope and exhaustion.

Susan's voice trembled with awe. "The war is over," she whispered. "Now we can all begin again."

Before the words had settled, Emily drew Andrew into a fierce embrace, rocking him, her tears soaking into the boy's nappy hair. Annie's throat ached at the sight. How many years had been stolen from families like the Robinsons? How many futures reshaped?

She glanced at Susan, who nudged her arm, and together they stepped away, closing the parlor door to give Emily and her son a sliver of privacy.

Not long after, bells rang out across Leavenworth, their joyful clamor filling the air. Annie stood at the window, one hand resting on her belly as the baby gave a fluttering kick, as if sensing the shift in the world.

She turned to Susan, her smile wide despite the tears still drying on her cheeks.

"I'm going to tell Emily to take the rest of the day off," she murmured. "Then let's go share the news. Nettie's brother is still at war. She should hear it from a friend."

Less than a week later, up and down North Esplanade, jubilation still prevailed; Annie stood in the yard discussing the news with Nettie Cochran.

"Daniel said thousands are gathering at Fort Sumter today while Henry Ward Beecher gives an address."

From the next lawn over, a woman with a baby on her hip called, "Nettie, your brother should be home soon from the war. How wonderful!"

The voices around her were light, threaded with laughter and the hum of ordinary joy. For once, it felt like the world might really be mending. But then the church bells began again—not the jubilant melody from two days before. This was different. One solemn note, struck again and again, slow and heavy.

The sound hollowed something inside her.

All conversation faltered. Eyes met across the porch.

Annie's breath caught in her throat. That tone meant only one thing.

"I wonder who died," Nettie murmured, her voice tight.

"Must be somebody important," Annie said. Her heart had already leapt ahead. "A general, perhaps?"

They tried to keep talking, but the unease was thick, clinging. Then the rhythmic clop of hooves echoed down the road. A rider slowing. Dismounting in front of the Anthony walk.

Annie stepped forward before anyone else could. "Over here!" she called, lifting her arm. The others followed quickly, remembering how Daniel's notes had come straight to her before.

The paper was small, the handwriting hurried.

She didn't speak at first. Just stared. Then, after a deep breath, she read aloud, voice hollow and faint, "Last night, President Lincoln was shot dead, allegedly by the actor John Wilkes Booth."

Gasps broke the silence. Annie pressed her hand to her lips, as if she could shove the words back in. Erase them. Make them untrue.

"Lord have mercy, not the president!" Nettie cried, her voice trembling.

"One day after the war ended . . ." someone else whispered. "Poor man."

"What will become of our country now?" Annie asked, but even as she said it, a sharp cramp seized her middle. Her breath hitched. The sweat came fast, prickling at the back of her neck.

She grabbed at her belly. "Oh—" The pain tightened again. "I think I need to sit down. The baby . . ."

"Are you all right to walk?" Nettie was already beside her, steadying her with both hands. "Come on, I'll help you."

Annie leaned into her, each step to the porch heavier than the last. Susan stood there waiting. Annie didn't need to say much—her face was heavy with bad news.

After she relayed the message, the others slipped back to their own homes, the street hushed once more.

By late afternoon, North Esplanade was lined with black—ribbons on doorways, wreaths on gates. Flags dipped low. *The Bulletin's* hung at half-mast, and inside its walls, Daniel didn't rest. He worked day after day, barely sleeping, not until the month was nearly over and Booth was finally found and killed by Union soldiers.

But that moment in the yard—Annie would carry it with her. That sound of the bell. That single sentence. The ache in her belly and in her heart, entwined.

Chapter Thirty-One

Daniel

May 12, 1865

In his newspaper office, D.R. smirked as he read *The Times*:

Though D.R. Anthony no longer serves as mayor, he yet wields considerable influence among the weak-minded. Marshal John Schott, having only partially recovered from cracking his skull during Anthony's 1864 bid for re-election, is still addle-brained enough to carry out a vendetta on businessmen he perceived to have been his—and Anthony's—attackers. Anthony has noised it about that Colonel Jennison was the root of the election mob that year.

No doubt aided and abetted by Anthony, Schott promoted entertainments that were not the usual custom at certain establishments, induced citizens to take part, and then raided the businesses to round up patrons and publicans alike. As expected, *The Bulletin*, Anthony's

```
mouthpiece, published this scurrilous news,
casting unfounded shadows on the reputation of
many an upstanding citizen. So stealthily was
this grand scheme carried out, even Mayor Carney
was powerless to stop it.
```

Breathing a satisfied sigh, D.R. tossed *The Times* aside. For once he was pleased to be mentioned in the rival newspaper.

Both D.R. and Schott had made sure that Jennison's LeBonTon was among the investigated saloons, where ladies of the night frequently lounged at the bar. Rumor was that Jennison's wife, with their daughter in tow, had since left town and might never return.

On his way home to lunch that day, D.R. took a celebratory stroll past LeBonTon, which bore a sign saying, "Temporarily Closed." As Anthony stood pondering it, out came the owner himself. Jennison's unsteady gait testified that, even though it was barely noon, he was already drinking.

Rocking back and forth on his heels, D.R. said cheerily, "Well, Doc, looks like your business has taken a turn for the worse." Waving at the notice on the door, he couldn't resist gloating. "Kind of like my campaign did after you pumped up the voters."

"Hey!" Jennison strutted up to D.R. and poked him in the chest. "We had a legitimate lunchtime trade before you delivered your puritanical tirade on entertainments." He spat as he uttered the last word.

"Legitimate!" said D.R., wiping the spittle away from his beard. "Your real business is robbing gamblers through dishonest games."

Jennison spread his arms wide, shouting, "So what? They're *gamblers!*" He eyed D.R. craftily. "Don't forget—you don't have the power of the mayor's office behind you anymore."

"You tell 'im, Doc," called a voice from the other side of the street.

Swiveling around to glare at the eavesdropper, D.R. noticed a hostile crowd watching. When he turned back to Jennison, Doc's shaky hand was pointing a gun at his face. D.R.'s instincts kicked in.

Jennison cocked the revolver. "You blasted, self-righteous . . ."

Before Doc could finish, D.R. thrust aside Jennison's arm, drew his own pistol, and aimed for Doc's leg.

Moments later, D.R. tasted dirt as he lay face-down with his arms pinned behind his back.

"Now who's gonna' have hell to pay, Anthony?" said a voice above him.

"Call the doctor for Jennison," another voice yelled.

A few feet away, Jennison's voice sounded like it came through gritted teeth. "More important, call the marshal!"

CHAPTER THIRTY-TWO

Susan

That same day

In the privacy of the parlor, Susan and Annie sat with their collars loosened, seeking relief from the stifling heat. Outside, the world seemed to sweat beneath the sun, and even the birds had fallen silent.

When the doorbell shrilled, shattering the stillness, Susan's pen jerked and Annie rose partway from her chair to accept the sealed envelope Emily handed her before retreating.

Susan waited, knowing how agitated her sister-in-law had been since John's arrest. After reading the note, Annie closed her eyes momentarily, then clutched her abdomen and groaned.

"Annie! Be careful! Emily, help!" Susan tripped over her own skirt as she rushed to Annie, who was crumpling to the floor. Together, she and Emily managed to ease her onto the settee.

"Let me see that," Susan said, reaching for the telegram.

It bore D.R.'s hurried handwriting:

Annie, I got arrested for shooting Jennison. Please have Susan meet me at the jail to post $100 bail. D.R.A.

"Let's take her up to bed, Miss Susan," Emily suggested, but Annie would have none of it. She wanted to be downstairs to learn every detail as it unfolded.

⁂

When Susan returned an hour later, her shoes dusted with road grit, she found Annie seated by the hearth, stitching lace onto a baby nightgown with mechanical precision. Relief fluttered in Susan's chest, though she kept her tone matter-of-fact.

"Chas said there was a shouting match in the street," she began. "Between D.R. and Jennison."

At once, Annie stilled. Her needle paused midair, and for one long second, she stared at nothing. Then came the inhale—sharp and silent—and a flush of red climbed her neck. Susan saw it all: the composure giving way to something raw and trembling beneath. Not a tantrum. Not theatrics. Just the quiet collapse of someone who had held herself upright for too long.

Susan looked away, giving Annie the dignity of pretending not to notice.

"After all the vile things he's written about Jennison lately, why didn't he just avoid the man? He practically dared Jennison to shoot him! And here I am, about to give birth! When will Dan ever think before he acts?" Tears of exasperation streamed down her cheeks.

Placing a steady hand on Annie's shoulder, Susan said, "It won't help you or the baby to get more upset. Try to calm down. Let's get you settled in bed, and I'll fetch something for you to eat."

Annie nodded, taking Susan's arm as they made their way up the staircase, pausing for frequent rests.

It took Susan half an hour to help Annie change into a lightweight nightgown, serve her a small meal, prop pillows behind her back, and open the windows to catch any possible breeze.

Just as Annie's eyelids began to flutter shut, Susan tiptoed toward the hall, but then Annie spoke up. "I can't sleep. Not now, and not at night either."

Susan desperately wanted to finish the speech she was working on but recognized the exhaustion etched on Annie's face, which was now puffy from pregnancy. Part of her longed for a tranquil room in Rochester.

Drawing on her own inner strength, Susan said, "Just a few more weeks to go, Annie. You'll feel so much better after the baby is born. Just think—you'll be able to sleep in any position you want!"

"No, I still won't be able to sleep!" Annie cried. "Having the baby won't erase my worries about Dan." She pressed a fist to her mouth to stifle a sob. "I never know what he'll do next."

Susan moved to sit beside the bed, at a loss for words. If she were honest, she didn't know either.

Annie continued her lamentations. "What if Jennison dies? Dan could face murder charges. It might turn into a long, drawn-out trial. What if we lose our house to legal fees?" Annie's face became blotchy with emotion.

As Susan handed her a handkerchief, she mustered as reasonable a voice as she could. "I've found that most of the terrible things I worry about rarely come to pass."

"But the things I never thought to worry about do!" Annie sobbed.

Susan suddenly felt the door shut inside her—no more room for this spiral of dread. She stood, brushing invisible wrinkles from her skirt, and said with a finality she didn't quite intend, "Exactly. See? Either way, it does no good to worry. In fact, it only hurts you."

As Susan turned away, she didn't look back. If she did, she might lose her resolve. Better to leave Annie stunned into silence than to let herself be pulled under by fear she couldn't fix.

Chapter Thirty-Three

Annie

That same day

Less than an hour passed before Annie heard Daniel's footsteps cross the foyer and take the stairs two at a time. Bursting into the bedroom, he cried, "Susan said the midwife came! How are you? How's the baby?"

Annie glared. "The baby has moved into position to be born a month early," she said in glacial tones, "probably owing to a *recent shock,* according to the midwife." She pressed her lips together, giving him a flat stare. "I'm confined to bed for the duration, thanks to your habit of shooting people. Please do me a favor and take your snoring elsewhere tonight." She waved toward the door, and he left.

As the day wore on, the heat and the baby pressed on Annie like a blanket. Nevertheless, when evening fell, she tried to sleep. But that's when her flock of worries returned to roost. Dan was a hothead who shot people in the street. It was just a matter of time till he killed someone else or got killed. Why, oh why had she put her inheritance into *The Bulletin*? If she became a widow, she would have nothing to live on.

She considered the scores of slaves Dan had freed. He was a hero. But he was also a villain who burned towns and used John to steal cattle. At that moment, she and her baby needed peace. As she rested her hand on her growing midsection, the baby pressed back from inside. "Hello, little one," she murmured. "We've both been through a lot, but there's nothing to worry about. I'll keep you safe." With those words, she tucked away her concerns about Daniel, burying them so deep that she could no longer reach them.

All the next morning, anger still simmered beneath her skin like a low fever. If she let her thoughts circle to him—his temper, his arrogance, the way he stormed through life without looking back—she'd only spiral deeper. And the midwife had been clear: "You need rest. Let things go."

Pushing away her half-eaten lunch, she resolved to think of something else.

The borrowed christening gown came to mind—folded in tissue in the next bedroom, delicate and waiting. The nearly finished layette. Small things she could control. She willed her thoughts to settle there, until a sharp pang of guilt caused her to sit up straight in bed.

Miss Greenshawl.

Annie's stomach turned. How long had it been since she'd brought food to that poor woman? Too long. She'd meant to go—always meant to—but her pregnancy, the heat, the tension with Dan . . . she had let it slip. Miss Greenshawl could be starving.

She summoned Emily.

Annie had traced the route on her lap desk as her servant looked on, brow furrowed. S-E-N-E-C-A S-T-R-E-E-T. Emily had focused on every step as if committing them to heart—three blocks down, one to the right. Then the bench. That infernal bench.

Annie's brows had lifted when Emily refused to sit there. "Ain't safe," she'd said bluntly. White folks wouldn't want her nearby.

Annie had no argument—just frustration. "Do you mind leaning against the wall, then?"

Emily's nod had carried more dignity than any satin-draped society lady.

Annie had described the vagrant woman—unkempt, scarred, barely speaking.

"Something terrible must have happened to her," she said. She went over the food—cheese, bread, fruit—and asked her to try and arrange a regular meeting if the woman was willing.

Then came the note—embossed stationery with the Anthony name in elegant script. Not a banner of protection, but a seal of legitimacy.

"If anyone gives you trouble," Annie had told her sternly, "tell them you work for me."

And then, more softly, "Hold your head up and don't act like a slave . . . because you're not."

Now, propped in bed with her sewing after watching Emily go, she felt satisfied that the link to the homeless woman might be restored.

Next to the bench on Seneca Street, Emily would be scanning the crowd, waiting for a flash of green. Annie could see her weaving through carts and carriages, eyes fixed on the ragged hem of a shawl.

"Be safe," she whispered.

Her needle paused, and the baby gown slipped to the sheet on her lap. In her mind, the scene played out: Emily upright and composed, the green-shawled woman hunched and mute. A white woman, once the mistress—perhaps, in a well-appointed parlor—now diminished, dependent. And Emily, once the one who served, now stood as the stronger of the two.

Annie resumed stitching in bed, though her heart remained in town. Two women would meet—one rising, one fading. Between them, a quiet exchange. More than food, perhaps. Strange how hardship could blur the sharp lines drawn by class and color.

She leaned back, one hand on the swell of her belly. She wanted to stay awake, to be ready when Emily returned. But the mantel clock ticked steadily, and the sound of bees drifted in through the open window. The stillness was irresistible.

Half an hour at least, she reasoned. Just a short rest.

She let the quiet pull her under.

Just a few minutes. Then I'll be ready.

CHAPTER THIRTY-FOUR

Daniel

May 15, 1865

Owing to Annie's continued aloofness, D.R. took his dinners at Dexters more often than not. By taking his dinners at Dexters and coming in late, he could avoid both Susan's pointed glances and the heavy silence upstairs.

On the single evening that he dined with his sister at home, he announced that his trial for shooting Jennison was scheduled for July thirteenth.

She made no comment on this news. The next morning, however, she cornered him in the downstairs hallway, demanding, "Do you have any idea what it's like to be confined to bed?"

D.R. shrugged. "Just once when I had the grippe. I woke up one day and realized I hadn't been awake or stood on my own feet in a week."

"That's like falling unconscious. But can you imagine being fully conscious and unable to get up or even turn over? How slowly each moment would drag by? How lying still like that would make your whole body hurt?"

He sighed. "You're talking about Annie, aren't you? Yeah, I realize it's hard for her. That's why I'm putting up with her, um, temporary coldness."

Susan planted her feet and thrust out her chin. "I'm just a guest here, but it looks like she has good reason to be cold to you."

D.R. folded his arms, speaking slowly and forcibly. "Lemme guess—you're talking about my run-in with Jennison. I told you: I was just walking past his bar when he came out, spat on me, and pulled a gun. I shot in self-defense! If I'd wanted to kill him, I would have."

"That's how you got off on the Satterlee trial—self-defense. But now I'm beginning to wonder if I'm seeing a pattern. You provoke people and they retaliate; then you shoot them. Annie's terrified that the jury won't believe you this time and you'll go to jail."

Susan paused. When he didn't reply, she added, "When you attack somebody just for the fun of it, how can you fail to consider *her?* Do you want to spend the first few years of your child's life in prison?"

Ignoring the question, he stated, "Jennison is a lying cheat. Someone needs to stand up to him."

"Oh, I see. So you appointed yourself to taunt this lying cheat till he drew his gun. And even though your wife will be delivering soon, you stepped right up for this assignment. Really, this mission of yours is almost as heroic as freeing slaves!" She paused and took a breath. "When you first started publishing horrible things about Jennison, I thought it was a one-time instance. But then you kept it up! What were you doing in front of his bar, anyway? It's not even on your way home."

He averted his gaze. "Oh, you know . . . I'm always on the prowl for news."

"News my foot! I bet you went there to take another jab at him. You're like a boy playing with a snake. It was just a matter of time till he struck back. And he's not the only one you go after. You seem to love fights."

"Excuse me, I need to get to work," he said, trying to push past his sister.

She stood her ground. "My key point is this: Picking fights isn't good for your wife or baby. You need to stop before you get into such serious trouble your friends can't save you."

He made as if to pass her again, but she said, "I almost forgot. I saw Marshal Schott on his way to work this morning and he said to tell you that Jennison and his friends are just waiting to get their hands on you again."

"Yeah, I know," he said, cutting her off. "More hot air from ole Doc."

She put a hand on his arm, her tone softening. "Look how far you've come, Dan. You have a wife who adores you and a baby on the way, this beautiful house, and a good business—why are you risking it all just to taunt someone? Mother and Father would be—"

"Ashamed of me." He finished her sentence with sarcasm. "And *you* have such a great imagination that you should be writing dime novels. It didn't happen the way you imagine, I tell you. Mind your own business!" Gritting his teeth, he stomped out the front door.

Later that evening, when he had simmered down, he took a cup of peppermint tea to Annie and told her he was sorry she was confined to bed. After accepting the tea and listening politely, she turned to face the wall, grunting with the effort.

Next, he stopped by Susan's door and said, "Sorry about this morning. You may be right."

He kept up a good front until bedtime when he stretched out on the sofa and tried to get comfortable. Though he hardly ever got the best of Susan, it always smarted to admit she was right. And this was the worst disagreement he had had so far with Annie.

Chapter Thirty-Five

Susan

May 29, 1865

Susan turned away from the clock, no longer wanting to measure the time. As moments passed, Annie's grip on her hand tightened with each contraction, until the pressure grew fierce.

After what seemed like an eternity, Emily offered to take her place.

Though Emily clearly knew more about childbirth than Susan, it took less than half an hour before Susan returned—unable to stay away. Susan ached when she heard Annie's groans and cries, and prayed as the laboring woman's pains intensified and beads of sweat formed on her forehead. Assisting her sisters, Hannah and Guelma, during childbirth had been much the same—an intense storm of pain followed by stillness.

When the baby's cry rang out, thin and fierce, something inside Susan stirred—deep and ancient. She stood still, watching the miracle unfold just a few feet away, and felt the ache of it in her chest.

This is what it meant. To give everything. To bring forth life with nothing but blood, breath, and will.

She had no children of her own. Nor would she ever, now. At forty-five, that door had quietly closed behind her without ceremony, without even her full awareness. She had thought she'd be a mother once—had imagined it in some vague, untethered way—but her path had curved elsewhere.

And yet . . . she didn't feel empty.

Not as she watched the tiny, squalling newborn lifted into the light. Not as she glanced at Annie's flushed, exhausted face and saw something both broken and triumphant there.

No, her role as a reformer was different—but no less vital. She would pour herself into the women who still bore the weight of the world. She would lift them up, steady them, whisper truth to them when they forgot their own strength.

The midwife examined the baby with approval before passing her to Susan. "Wrap her up warm," she said.

Susan, filled with wonder, counted fingers and toes, brushing her fingers over the downy vernix covering the baby's shoulders before following the instruction. Then she invited Emily to help swaddle the baby for the first time, creating a tiny package as fresh as dawn.

Meanwhile, the midwife helped Annie change her nightgown and put a ribbon in her hair. The new mother's gaze urged Susan forward as she approached the bed with the swaddled bundle.

When Annie reached for the infant awkwardly, Susan coached her. "Relax, I'll place her in your arms. Just support her head."

The midwife adjusted the pillows behind Annie. "Now you can present baby to her papa. Do you have a name?"

"Not yet," Annie replied, her eyes fixed on the sleeping infant cradled in her arms. She began to croon softly.

"She's perfect, Annie. Should I go get D.R.?" Susan asked. Annie nodded.

Susan found her brother smoking on the porch. As he heard her at the screen door, he stood up. "I couldn't bear to hear her in pain," he said, a hint of apology in his tone, his arm gesturing vaguely. "How is she? Did she . . . ?"

Susan's face still reflected the sacredness of the event she had just witnessed. "You have a healthy daughter." When D.R.'s expression turned bewildered, she clarified. "A baby girl."

His face fell, revealing his secret longing for a son—one who could carry on the family legacy and follow in his footsteps. Susan's heart sank at his disappointment, recognizing another daughter who could never fulfill her father's wish for a boy.

She squeezed his arm. "This is why I campaign so hard; to help men recognize the gifts that girls truly are, rather than seeing them as mere property. Now, go up there and be the man they need." Her expression softened. "And congratulations."

Feeling like a plate forgotten after the feast, Susan took a walk, nodding to the doctor who was arriving to examine mother and baby.

An hour later, D.R. found her on the porch where she was penning a letter.

"Would you like to join us?" he asked and followed her inside to the bedroom upstairs.

The midwife sat in the corner, knitting, while D.R. and Annie looked as tranquil as if their recent quarrels had never occurred. D.R. took the baby from Annie and held the tiny bundle on his lap, the infant's fingers instinctively wrapping around his pinkie.

"We've decided to name her Maude," he announced.

Susan suppressed her surprise. In the Anthony family, names passed down like heirlooms, meant to honor previous generations and guide the next one. Only last February, Merritt and his wife, Mary, had named their newborn son after D.R. As far as she knew, no Maude had ever graced the Anthony lineage.

"Are you naming her after someone in Annie's family?" she asked.

"Maude means 'strength in battle,'" D.R. replied. "Strong, like the woman who bore her." He exchanged a wink with Susan. "And determined, like the Anthony women."

Unexpectedly, Susan's eyes filled with tears. Here, in the midst of so much travail, was a namesake of sorts.

Chapter Thirty-Six

Susan

August 5, 1865

In D.R.'s office, Susan sat absorbed in the newspaper when the color drained from her face.

"I don't believe it!" she said. "The House of Representatives is considering a new amendment that would grant voting rights to Black men while excluding all women." She lowered the paper to look at her brother. "They can't do that! Women have fought against slavery for twenty years! The Loyal League alone gathered four hundred thousand signatures against it. Now it's women's turn to get the vote!"

D.R. shook his head in sympathy as she continued her tirade. "The plan was always to secure rights for everyone under the same amendment. How dare they prioritize Black men over women?"

"People are more inclined to give Black men the vote because they fought in the war," D.R. pointed out.

Fuming, she shoved the article into her purse and flung open the door. "I'm heading back East as soon as I can. I can't let this go unchecked."

⁂

The next morning, Susan gazed out the train window as it sped toward her colleagues in the East. With Annie adept at bathing and feeding Maudie, and Emily proving to be a good mentor, Susan ventured further into Kansas. Meanwhile, her mother had used the time to transform space on the second floor into a bedroom and a spacious office for her.

Many Westerners had been receptive to Susan's message of universal suffrage—equality and votes for every person, regardless of race or gender—but her speaking engagements taxed her endurance. The sparseness of roads, bridges, and comfortable lodgings made her travels across the still-developing state quite challenging.

As the train wheels rhythmically moved along the tracks, Susan reflected on how she could have retorted to her brother when she first told him about the proposed amendment leaving women out. It seemed it wasn't enough that women had fought for the abolition of slavery, took on the burdens of men who went to war, raised children alone, and cared for wounded soldiers. Perhaps if women had enlisted in battle, Congress would regard them with more respect.

Overwhelmed by her emotions, she attempted to redirect her thoughts to the recent months she had spent with her family in Kansas. While she had crossed paths with Merritt and his family on a few occasions, her primary focus had been on D.R. and Annie. Most importantly, she treasured the chance to be part of Maudie's birth—a milestone she deeply valued.

Additionally, she was grateful for the consistent platform provided by *The Bulletin*, which allowed her to share her thoughts and ideas to a wide audience without setting foot outside of Leavenworth. How wonderful it would be to one day see a publication created by and for women!

Chapter Thirty-Seven

Annie

August 6, 1865

That first day, it took Annie a while to adjust to the absence of her high-energy sister-in-law. Gradually, the house settled into a gentler rhythm. Still, she caught herself reaching for a second teacup out of habit, or turning to share a passing thought—only to find the chair beside her empty. She used Maudie's naptime to catch up on letters to Auntie and Cora. Sighing, she ruminated on how much to relay about Dan's trial and eventual acquittal for shooting Jennison.

As she sat thinking, Emily approached and cleared her throat.

"Did you want something, Emily?" Annie said.

"Which days you want me to take food to Miss Naught—I mean, Miss Greenshawl." She paused. "I forgot to tell you, I knew her when I lived at the tobacco farm."

Annie stared, her mind reaching back to Emily's description of life at the Bauer plantation. "Do you actually know her name?"

"Yes, ma'am. She lived at the next farm. They raised hemp. Last name was Naughton."

"Naughton. Where have I heard that name before?" She fell silent, considering, as her mind reeled. "Oh, mercy me! I know." she said, her hand on her heart. "Oh, I know! That will be all, Emily."

Before her servant could repeat her question, Annie was hurrying up the grand staircase to the diary restored to its place in the tiger maple desk. As she reached the top step, however, Maudie began to cry. When Annie reached her, the baby had soiled her diaper and needed an immediate change. No amount of feeding, playing, or outside strolls would lull the baby to sleep after that. By the time Daniel came home for dinner, Annie was sagging with fatigue.

"They've published next season's entertainments for Laing's Hall," he said after Maudie had finally succumbed to sleep at her regular bedtime. "Would you like to get tickets for any plays? I have the schedule."

"That sounds wonderful," replied Annie, yawning. "But right now all I can think about is sleep. Leave it on the bureau and I'll look at it tomorrow."

By the beginning of September, Annie felt more like her old self and she looked forward to new routines in her role as a mother. At four months old, Maude was big enough to leave for an hour or two with Emily. Walks about town would help keep both of them healthy.

On her first excursion by herself, she decided to visit the bookseller. Even if her interest in clothing had temporarily waned, she still enjoyed the fiction in *Godey's.*

Later, leaving the bookshop, Annie thought of Miss Greenshawl—*Naughton,* she corrected herself—for the first time in weeks. *I hope she's fared well since I last saw her. I wonder which one of the sisters she is—Veronia or Iris?* A few moments later the woman materialized quietly beside her outside the fish market. Her shawl looked more frayed than ever.

"How have you been?" Annie said.

Miss Naughton looked away. "Sister . . . sick."

"You have a sister who is sick? Does she need help?"

"Hungry."

"Do you need more food?"

The strange woman looked Annie in the eyes for the first time, startling her with such direct contact.

"Hungry. Weak . . ."

"I could send her some food. Tell me the place, and I'll do it."

Miss Naughton patted her own chest. "I take."

Annie headed for the door of Corey's Fruit and Fish. "All right. Wait here and I'll get her something to eat. And some for you, too." Turning to go, Annie paused when she felt a clawlike touch on her arm—Miss Naughton.

"M-m-milk."

"Yes, milk. Good." *Heavens above, I'm lapsing into three-word messages myself!* Oh! Corey's doesn't sell milk.

After getting an extra packet of fish for the hungry women, she hurried to the lunch counter that she and Dan had patronized when they rented a house.

"Good day, Mrs. Kunkel."

"Hello, Mrs. Anthony. Haven't seen you in a while. I hear you had your baby. Congratulations!"

"Thank you," said Annie distractedly. "I need some milk. I'm sorry, but I'm in a rush."

Concerned that Miss Naughton would wander off during her absence, Annie sighed with relief when she saw the beggar talking to herself on a bench. Annie handed over her own basket full of fish plus a bottle of milk, a loaf of bread, and some carrots. The strange woman did not even look in the basket. She simply drew it next to her body and said with what sounded like gratitude, "Family. Eat."

"Wait," said Annie. Before the basket disappeared, she tucked four peppermints inside. "To share with your sister."

The following day, though Annie did not need to buy anything, she went to town anyway and visited the general store. There, when Miss Naughton began muttering behind her, the clerk looked horrified. "Out! This is no place for the likes of you!"

Feeling both embarrassed for herself and sympathetic towards her shabby companion, Annie quickly nodded to the shopkeeper and said, "Excuse me, I need to go." Then, she whispered to Miss Naughton, "Meet me in the alley."

Annie had done her best to prepare for this next encounter, filling her basket with a good-size hunk of cold roast, some applesauce, and another loaf of bread. And milk.

"I'm happy to talk to you outside, but you mustn't approach me in the shops. Understand?"

Keeping her eyes lowered to the ground beneath her men's shoes, Miss Naughton repeated, "Outside."

"How is your sister? Could she eat the food?"

"Some. Hot."

"Could she keep the milk down?" asked Annie anxiously, picturing the sister suffering from fever.

"Milk for Robbie."

"Robbie?" Annie asked blankly. "Who's Robbie?"

The woman extended her palm to the ground as if indicating a small child.

Realizing she had forgotten the boy in the diary, Annie said, "Oh, yes, of course. Do you all live together?"

Miss Naughton nodded.

Dear Lord, thought Annie, are a sick woman and child relying on this poor creature for food and drink?

"Did you . . . bring food today?"

Annie did not let on how surprised she was to hear Miss Naughton utter a complete sentence. "Yes." She brought out her provisions. "But I doubt it's enough for three."

Miss Naughton produced a string bag and motioned for Annie to put the foodstuffs inside. But Annie drew back.

"Before I give them to you, I have a question."

The beggar withdrew her hand, looking troubled.

"I want to bring food to help your sister get better. Maybe medicine, too. So I need to know more about her. You said she was hot. Was she burned?"

Miss Naughton shook her head. "House . . . burned." She paused to consider, then added, "Fever."

"Your house burned and now your sister's sick with fever. And she has a child. Is that right?"

"Yes. Anthony . . . sister . . ." The beggar stammered, then pondered before speaking again. "Order. Border." She placed a tentative hand on Annie's bag of provisions. "Take?"

"No!" Annie exclaimed, giving vent to her frustration. "You follow me around, whispering about me and my husband, speaking in riddles. I've only been here a little over a year—not nearly enough time to grasp everything that's happened!"

Miss Naughton recoiled as if Annie had struck her. Why doesn't she just leave? Annie wondered, before recognizing the desperation written across her face.

Miss Naughton met her gaze earnestly, her lips working silently before two words finally escaped. "Order. Eleven." She shrugged, as if the meaning were obvious.

Wishing she could frame a question that would yield more, Annie relented and handed over the food.

Later, as she sat nursing baby Maude at home, Annie reviewed every encounter with the beggar that she could remember. *Suppose she* doesn't *talk nonsense? Suppose she's telling a coherent story two or three words at a time?*

Fitting her breast back inside her bodice, she lifted Maude to her shoulder and patted her back. Tenderly she laid her daughter on the bed, cooed into the baby's face, and finger-combed her hair into fine curls. Out of nowhere came the memory of Rebecca Carney's voice when proposing an orphanage at a recent Sanitary Relief Commission meeting: "Each of those street urchins was once someone's beloved child."

The Naughton sisters must be as devoted to Robbie as she, Annie, was to Maude.

When Maude's eyelids drifted shut, Annie seized the moment to do something she had longed to for quite a while. Laying her baby in the cradle, she searched her desk drawer for some notes she had made of

Miss Greenshawl's utterances months earlier. Her expression grew more troubled as she read:

D.R. . . . baby

Woman like me

Lived in Missouri

Long time ago

To these she added today's cryptic statements:

Milk for Robbie.

House burned. Fever.

Order. Eleven.

Chapter Thirty-Eight

Annie

November 6, 1865

As autumn settled in and Maude's naptimes fell into a rhythm, Annie enjoyed her daily walks even more. She missed Daniel, who had been away overnight, so she planned to welcome him home with Mrs. Maguire's savory vegetable beef soup for dinner. This morning, as she made her way through town towards Corey's Fish and Fruit, she wished she had worn a lighter dress. It was unseasonably warm for November.

Spotting an acquaintance from the Sanitary Relief Commission, Annie raised her hand. "Good day, Mrs. Stark," she called.

Rachel Stark met her gaze without flinching, dipped her chin in a bare nod, and turned away, cutting Annie as cleanly as if with a blade. No greeting, no hesitation—only absence, as if Annie no longer existed.

The blow landed harder than words could have. Rachel had once stood beside her, working to help those most in need. Now she fled as if Annie carried some contagion.

Swallowing the sting, Annie moved on toward the fish market, her steps hollow on the stones.

She had never taken Rachel for a gossip, but someone had spoken. That much was clear. Whispers must have wound their way through parlor rooms and sewing circles, twisting her name into something unrecognizable. Annie searched her memory for an offense worth such a public dismissal. She had helped with the Contraband Camp garden project and advocated for hiring teachers for the colored children. If the fault was not hers, perhaps it was her connection to Daniel. Something from his past dredged up and laid at her feet? The questions offered no answers—only a steady hum of shame rising beneath her collar. Whatever goodwill she had earned, it had slipped through unseen hands.

At the corner, two men staggered from a saloon, the reek of spirits thick around them. She edged to the side, but not fast enough. One man's laughter burst out, raw and coarse, followed by a foul jest loud enough for the street to hear. Annie kept her head high and her hands tight at her sides, but the words followed her down the street like burrs clinging to her skirts.

The taller man scoffed, "Oh, don't buy into all that nonsense the papers churn out. Those newspaper hacks are always slinging mud at each other. It's all just a ploy to sell more trash."

To avoid hearing any more, Annie scanned the street for a safe way across, but a throng of horses and carriages prevented her passage.

The other man sneered, "Did you hear about him raiding Little Dixie to start a farm in Huron? Those animals were supposed to go to the army, but he kept 'em for himself."

"Yeah, but he was the commander, so rules don't apply to him, right?" the taller man said, his voice laced with contempt.

Annie knew instinctively that they were talking about Dan. Though life had been calm since Maudie's birth, something new must have happened. The thought tensed her stomach.

Finally, she reached the fish market and greeted the owner as she added garlic and carrots to her basket.

"Hello, Mrs. Anthony. How's the baby?" he asked.

"Fine. Taking her morning nap." She fanned herself. "I wish it would rain."

"If we're lucky, we'll get a thunderstorm this afternoon," he said.

Nodding, she said, "Do you have any more potatoes?"

"I know how the colonel likes them," he replied with a grin. "So I saved you some."

She met his eyes with a heartfelt smile, the kind that rose from someplace sore. His small kindness stood in quiet contrast to the cold shoulder Rachel had shown her.

Two shabbily dressed women burst through the shop door, their laughter slicing through the rows of produce.

One of them said, "I'm glad someone's taking issue with them Jayhawkers. If not for them, we wouldn't be overrun with people from Misery."

It took Annie a moment to realize they were mocking the state across the river.

"That woman who accused him is plumb crazy. I saw her throwing a fit. It's a wonder Anthony would ever be attracted to . . ."

"Shhh," interrupted the first woman, stifling a giggle. Annie's face turned crimson as, unable to meet Mr. Corey's gaze, she hastily finished her transaction and made her escape.

With each step toward home, the autumn air pressed around her—heavy with unshed rain—as she turned the conversation over in her mind. Her insides churned with disappointment from Rachel's insult, anxiety about discovering Dan's latest mishap, and a sense of shame at the probable connection between them.

An hour later, when the doorbell rang, Annie's breath caught in her throat. It was too early in the day for calls; who could it be? She smoothed her hair and opened the door.

"Lydia! What brings you here at this hour?" Grateful for a friendly face, Annie continued, "Come in. Can I interest you in some tea?"

Lydia shook her head, settling on the arm of a chair with an anxious sigh. "I hate to bring you this news, Annie, but I wanted you to hear it first from a friend. This morning's *Times* contains a very disturbing article about a mistress of D.R. from Missouri. It says she and her fatherless child are running homeless in the streets."

Annie could barely find her voice in her dry throat. "Who said that?"

"Colonel Jennison mentioned it in a speech he gave last night about running for senator." She leaned in. "On my way here I happened to see Ella, who saw him talking to that homeless woman earlier yesterday. In fact, she saw the whole thing happen with the boy!" She offered the front section of the newspaper.

The color drained from Annie's face as she struggled to process Lydia's words.

"What on earth does that have to do with running for office?" she managed to ask, recalling the gossip she'd heard in town.

Lydia shrugged. "I'm sorry I can't stay with you a while longer," Lydia said. "But don't worry; we'll figure out a way to defuse this."

Following her friend out onto the front porch, Annie devoured the story, catching the highlights first: A three-year-old boy ran into the road . . . two women ran after him—one a homeless woman frequently seen about town called Iris Naughton. She named Colonel Anthony as the father . . . women and child in police custody.

All the while, Miss Naughton's puzzling pronouncements clicked into a pattern. So the woman I've been talking to is Iris. She said there was another woman—who must be Veronia—with a child.

Was Daniel the father of Veronia's child?

He was late for lunch. Unable to sit still, Annie went into the backyard and traipsed from the hedgerow to the rose bushes to the carriage house, which had one side discolored by dirt.

Sinking into a garden chair, surrounded by dust and neglect, Annie gazed up at the gray sky that stubbornly withheld its rain. She felt as powerless to alter the weather as she was to prevent Dan from wreaking havoc in her life. Like a parched tree yearning for rain, she raised her arms in a silent plea for relief and strength.

Just then, Mrs. Maguire called out to her. "Mrs. Anthony, it's noon! I've fixed you and the Colonel a cold meal today, and lemonade."

Annie hastily lowered her arms and went inside. Even though she felt far from ready, she would have to confront Dan. She told the cook to take the rest of the afternoon off in order to gain privacy for the difficult conversation ahead.

As heat lightning flashed outside, Daniel hurried into the house.

"Maybe we'll get a thunderstorm this afternoon," he said, settling at the dining room table.

While Annie anxiously waited for him to bring up *The Times* article, he told her inconsequential things about his morning. Finally, she showed him the article, her voice quivering slightly as she asked, "What's this all about?"

He examined the piece in silence before responding. "I didn't see this."

Annie served the meal and sat down, her gaze sharp. "The news was everywhere this morning when I went to Corey's. I've never felt so humiliated in all my life!"

Daniel sighed deeply, rubbing the back of his neck and leaning away from her, avoiding her eyes. "What do you expect me to say? To apologize for not warning you?" He paused, running a hand through his hair. "I guess *The Times* learned of it before my reporters did. I'm as shocked as you are."

She watched him in silence.

"Okay. Chas informed me first thing, and I hoped this would all pass and you'd never be hurt by it."

"But I did get hurt," she whispered, her eyes full of pain. "Please, just tell me what's going on."

He picked up his sandwich and set it down again without taking a bite. "I don't even know these women."

At his cold response, her hurt turned to anger. "What do you mean, you don't know them? You were in Little Dixie three years ago when this woman was attacked! If they don't know you, why on earth would they pick you to gossip about?"

Daniel's face flushed as he threw up his hands, shouting, "I don't know, I swear!"

No one had ever spoken to Annie like that before. She recoiled, fearing to voice the question uppermost in her mind. But he must have seen it in her eyes, as he abruptly pushed back his chair and stood up.

"I've lost my appetite. I'm going back to work." Seeing her shaken expression, his tone softened. "I'll find out what I can and let you know. This will blow over, you'll see."

Sitting alone after he left, Annie tried a bite of sandwich and discovered she had no more appetite than Dan. Daniel had more of a shady past than she expected, and Miss Greenshawl had used it against him.

Chapter Thirty-Nine

Daniel

That afternoon

Blood beat in D.R.'s pulse and his boots pounded on the boardwalk outside the jail as he hurried after Chas. Dropping a heavy hand on the Chas's shoulder, he felt the marshal brace for a blow before he spun around.

"So nice to learn of my alleged indiscretions from the daily news," D.R. growled. The oppressive air made him feel bear-like, and his pent-up anger at Annie's distrust came out.

"Oh, it's you." said Chas. "Figured you'd be unhappy, but there was nothing I could do about it. *The Times* reporter followed me here and witnessed the whole thing before I had a chance to send you word. It happened right on the street, anyway."

He angled his head toward the marshal's office. "C'mon in."

Once inside the small, neat room in front of the jail, he offered a chair to D.R.

Chas swallowed hard. "It was Jennison who started the scheme with the Naughtons."

That name alone was enough to make the heat travel back up D.R.'s neck.

"He's the one who cooked it up. Quite some time ago, from what I can tell."

Braced for the worst, D.R. waited with gritted teeth.

"Some time ago he hired the two sisters to move into the back room of LeBonTon with their little boy—looked about three years old. But they complained about men trying to buy their other services." He gave D.R. a significant look. "So recently he made them a slimy offer—said he'd post a guard on their door if they'd help him with a little . . . task."

D.R. narrowed his eyes. "Task?"

"A walk through town, he told them. That was all."

"But with Jennison, it turned into more than that," D.R. said flatly. "He drives hard bargains."

Chas glanced away. "He told them to walk the boy between them down Delaware Avenue—one sister on one corner, the other sister at the other end of the street. Said all the boy had to do was cross the sidewalk to meet his mother. Seemed simple enough."

"So what was the catch?" D.R. muttered.

Chas's jaw tightened. "Jennison knelt down, like he was showing the boy something. Then—bam—the boy darted into the street. Fast, like something spooked him. A rider was coming through at a good clip. Nearly hit him."

D.R.'s breath hitched, and a heavy stillness settled in his chest.

"He could've been trampled," Chas said, voice low. "The crazy woman yanked him back just in time. Kid was screaming bloody murder. Folks started gathering, scolding them. I happened to be nearby, so I stopped."

"What do you mean, the crazy one?"

"You know. That woman in the green shawl who's been hanging around town. She really bothers some people. I've had complaints but found her harmless."

"And Jennison?" D.R. asked. "What became of him?"

"Gone. Slipped away the second the boy hit the dirt."

D.R. clenched his fists. "Figures."

"People were starting to say that the boy wasn't safe with the crazy lady. It was getting out of hand, so I brought them back here for a while." Chas shrugged. "Gave 'em something to eat."

Taking it all in, D.R. didn't move, even as heat lightning flashed outside.

"The woman who could talk straight—she made a point of saying that you were the boy's father." Chas held up his hands in innocence. "I had no reason to ask, believe me."

A slow breath hissed between D.R.'s teeth. "Did you get their name?"

"Nope. I left 'em for a couple minutes to eat, and the younger woman and boy climbed out that window."

D.R. shifted his eyes into the other room and back to the marshal's face. "You think that woman really is crazy?"

"No idea," Chas said. "But he set them up. That's clear enough now."

D.R. paced to the far wall and back, fury mounting in his gut like a storm rolling in off the prairie. Jennison had used a child—a three-year-old innocent—as a pawn. He'd put that boy in harm's way, apparently just to tarnish D.R.'s name.

Chapter Forty

Annie

That evening

From across the table, Annie felt Daniel's eyes upon her face. She usually looked forward to these intimate evening meals, but tonight the silence between them was tense.

"You know this homeless woman? How?" he asked.

Her fingers tensed against her napkin before she reminded herself she wasn't the one with accusations hanging over her head.

"I asked you about her a long time ago," she replied, her voice cool. "She began following me shortly after I first got here, so after several weeks I spoke to her." The woman's scarred face flashed in Annie's mind, along with a surge of anger at how Iris had manipulated her. "And I just remembered—I'm pretty sure her sister wrote the diary I found in the desk."

"I'll be darned. Why didn't you ever mention any of this?" Daniel leaned forward.

Annie's gaze hardened. "She said some terrible things, and I didn't want to . . . provoke you." A bitter taste filled her mouth. "But I couldn't ignore her need. I ended up giving her food." Food and sympathy and time—all wasted on a woman who'd been playing her like a fiddle.

"What terrible things did she say? About me?" Daniel's voice tightened.

"It was mostly rambling, mingled with talk about a farm on fire in Missouri," Annie said, remembering how she'd felt sorry for Iris, how she'd believed her scattered stories. Fool that she was. "But she seemed to have a fixation about the number eleven that I never understood."

Before he could comment, she blurted the question that had been burning in her throat, demanding release. "I need to know." Annie's eyes bore into his, searching for any flicker of guilt. "When we first married, you mentioned having had other women. Were any of them from Missouri during that time when you were . . . jayhawking?"

He folded his arms defensively. "No! Not even close."

The nerve of him, to dismiss this so easily when her world was crumbling around her. She'd been made a fool of—either by this desperate woman or by the very man she'd trusted with her life and heart.

"How can you be so sure it's not her? You don't even remember seeing this homeless woman."

Daniel shifted uncomfortably. "There were two other women before you, all right? One was from Leavenworth, and she died. I can introduce you to her parents if you want."

Annie narrowed her eyes. How convenient.

"The other—" he paused, and Annie braced herself "—was a secretary during the war. I shared her with General Lane."

His reply scorched her like heat off a forge—searing, sudden, impossible to ignore. "You *shared* a woman with General Lane? How could you!" Disgust knotted in her stomach, compounding her sense of betrayal.

"No!" Daniel looked appalled. "That's not what I meant. Lane and I shared her *secretarial work*. She and I had a mutual attraction—I never forced her." He paused, his words coming slower. "And Lane never gave her a second look. Regardless, all of this happened long before I met you. And none of it in Missouri." He shrugged as if the case was closed.

Annie stared at him, seething. Even if she did accept his tidy explanations, she was far from ready to nod and move on. He failed to apologize—or even acknowledge—the scandal that cut her so deeply.

As they parted ways after dinner, Annie felt twice betrayed. By Iris Naughton, who had preyed on her kindness and sympathy, worming her way into Annie's confidence only to cast this bomb into her marriage—after all Annie had done for her.

But Daniel's casual dismissal cut deeper. Did he understand so little of her feelings that her sense of shame didn't concern him? Why should she believe him over the woman who'd spun such detailed accusations?

After tucking Maude in for the night, Annie went in search of Dan and found him writing at his desk. She perched on a chair across from him, preparing to launch an attack. But he spoke before she could begin.

His eyes met hers. "You said Iris Naughton had a fixation on the number eleven. Remember I told you about General Order No. Eleven? That was General Ewing's fiasco when he evacuated some counties along Missouri's border."

She nodded, her eyes blazing with unspoken fury. How dare he give her a history lesson at a time like this?

Seemingly oblivious, he continued. "I'd left the army by then. He put Jennison's soldiers in charge, and they were brutal at times. Set fire to a lot of homes and even killed people." He toyed with his pen. "From what Ella said, Jennison knows these women from Missouri. Maybe that's how he met them."

"And you think he decided to use them against you, pretending there's a child." Her tone dared him to assert that they had no cause.

"Yeah. He's sore because I haven't supported him on the Republican ticket for Senate. I guess he's striking back." He looked at her with regret. "He's hitting me where it hurts most—where it involves you." He reached over to squeeze her hand, and though she kept her fingers limp, she allowed his sympathy to penetrate her frosty exterior. Just a little.

"Can you do anything?" she asked.

"Jennison's scheduled a series of rallies starting tomorrow night. I'll send a reporter to attend and take down every word. Doc gets pretty liquored up in the evening." He curled his lip. "He's such a fool. All the reporter has to do is quote him word-for-word and the public will realize that everything he says is a sham."

She picked her words with care. "But what if he keeps bringing up this so-called child of yours?"

Dan's mouth pressed into a line. "Then we endure. And we wait for the truth to drown out the noise."

Easy for him to say, she thought, slipping out of the room. Maybe he was used to being the subject of gossip—he had supplied the fuel for many a fire—but she wasn't. She had grown up as Abraham Osborn's daughter, raised to guard her name like a treasure. Her father's honor had never been questioned, and neither had hers. But now, yoked to Daniel Anthony, she might as well be guilty by association. In some people's eyes, she was already beyond the pale.

By now the entire Sanitary Relief Commission must be whispering about the Anthonys. Although Annie had returned to many of her pre-baby pursuits, she had lacked the courage to re-join her women's group ever since Dan antagonized Rebecca Carney's husband in town politics. Now, it seemed, she might never find the strength to go back.

Perhaps the journal in the tiger maple desk would shed light on the truth. Iris had been disfigured by something brutal—what, Annie still didn't know. But the scars weren't just on her face. They were stitched into everything she did, every half-muttered plea, every desperate gesture.

Hoping the journal might offer a clue, Annie flipped the journal pages back to 1861.

When she came to August 19, she got the same jarring sensation as the first time she'd read it.

The handwriting was jumpy, jagged—like someone writing in haste, or hiding. Likely scrawled from the dark hollow of that secret closet.

Two pages later, a troubled gap. Two whole months passed before Veronia wrote again—and this time, her words spilled despair. She was with child. Unwanted. Ashamed.

Annie stilled. Her mind raced ahead of her heart.

Robbie.

The name Iris had been whispering. The one she'd been scavenging milk for, coaxing bites of bread for. A child who had struggled to nurse, who'd been dosed with paregoric and liquor just to survive in hiding, and later ravaged by cholera.

Annie pressed her lips together. No wonder Iris wandered the streets, wild-eyed and clutching at scraps. Even now—ravaged, broken—she bore herself like a sister still trying to protect.

Setting the book down, Annie sat back. What if *she* had lived through that?

She flipped back through the entries. Hunger. Fear. Their mother gone. The girls alone. And then the attack—unspoken, unnamed—that left Veronia pregnant. A plantation lost, though the how remained unclear. Annie tried to picture it: two girls, as gently raised as she had been, scraping together food, shelter, dignity. No family left, no father to protect them. Just secrets. And survival.

Forgetting Iris's disfigurement for a moment, she searched again, heart thudding, for any hint of Robbie's father. A name. A face. Something to clear Dan's name once and for all. But the pages gave her nothing—only silence where she needed answers.

She closed the journal, staring at its worn leather cover. Reading the handwritten journal in the lamplight made Annie's eyes smart. As she was tucking the diary back into the desk, something fell out of it as Dan stepped into the doorway.

"C'mon. It's time for bed," he said. "Things always seem better in the morning."

She wasn't ready to lie beside him. Not with everything still churning inside her. Rising from the desk, she kept her voice even, though it faltered on the way out.

"Maybe people *will* see through Jennison—but that doesn't erase the way our name's been dragged through the mud." Her throat tightened. "You go on to bed. I'm going to read awhile."

Without waiting for his reply, she pivoted and headed downstairs, needing distance.

Behind her, she heard the quiet rasp of the bedroom door closing.

"Have it your way," Dan muttered—quiet, but not so quiet she couldn't hear.

She didn't look back.

In the parlor she sat before the unlit fire, listening until Dan's overhead footsteps ceased. Then she crept up the stairs to sleep on the large chair in the nursery.

Just as oppressive as the day before, an overcast sky greeted Annie the following morning when she awoke with firm resolve. Dan could stay in town waiting for gossip to calm down, but she didn't have to. By noon she had packed her farm costume and a few other outfits into a large suitcase for herself and Maudie. After writing Dan that she was visiting Clarina Nichols, she sent word for a carriage to take her and the baby to the stagecoach. If their absence came as a surprise to Dan, perhaps it would teach him to think about how he had shocked her time and time again.

Two hours later, Annie glanced uneasily at the one other person who was getting into the coach that afternoon. *I've never met a sister in habit before–what do you say to such a woman?*

They soon sat face-to-face in the airless compartment.

The woman in black, who introduced herself as Mother Xavier Ross, regarded Annie kindly with wide-set dark eyes from within her tunnel-like white bonnet.

"Would you like me to hold your little one while you settle in for the ride?"

"Oh, yes, thank you!"

Annie stowed her belongings and untwisted her skirt while Maude sat propped on the sister's lap, gazing with fascination at the woman's strange headdress.

When Annie had tidied herself, Mother Xavier handed Maude back, smiling into the infant's face. "Back to Mama." Then to Annie she said, "I think perhaps I recognize you from a reception for Susan B. Anthony. You're part of her family, aren't you?"

"My, what a good memory!" said Annie. While introducing herself and learning that Mother Xavier had helped to found three schools in Leavenworth, Annie gave Maude a rattle to shake.

Perhaps it was the intimacy of the small space, or maybe it was Annie's sense that her companion was devoted to kindness. Whatever the reason, Annie felt free enough to unburden herself about Dan and his activities.

She began, "Family can be so trying."

Mother Xavier's gray eyes looked thoughtful. "Yes, they can. Especially when they are well-known in the community. One might feel that everything they do reflects on oneself."

"Yes! That's it." As Maude played and then began drowsing in her mother's arms, Annie described what she understood of Dan's part in John's arrest, his own trial for shooting Jennison, and now the horrible accusations about getting a baby on an insane woman. "*The Times* prints terrible things, even when they're the direct opposite of truth!"

She gave a heartfelt sigh. "Dan suggested we just tough it out till it all blows over, but I hate being gossiped about."

Mother Xavier shook her head. "In the fifteen years I've been in Leavenworth, I've been confounded by the newspaper coverage. It seems there are a handful of powerful men who are always arguing in public." She gave a rueful laugh. "I've concluded that the general population will probably never know the truth. But I suppose that being family, you can't let issues rest there, can you?"

This clear summary of the situation comforted Annie, even though Mother Xavier offered no solution. "No. I suppose I can only go on what I know of Dan myself."

Annie lapsed into a thoughtful silence. As Maude dozed, Annie found herself lulled by the rhythm of the coach and let her eyes close. An hour later, she woke to find Maude beginning to fret and Mother Xavier reading a book of psalms. After Annie covered herself to nurse the baby, the sister closed her book.

"What do you find in that book? Why do you read it?" Annie asked.

"A reminder that God is with me. Companionship. Peace. Rest."

Annie considered this. "What do you mean by rest?"

"When I don't know which way to turn, how to proceed, or who to believe, I rest in God. And somehow that gives me strength to go on."

Who to believe. How to go on.

Annie said quietly, "I could use some of that."

"Have you ever considered asking God for peace?" asked Mother Xavier, looking out the window to check their progress.

"Well, no. I recite the prayers and sing at church, but I never thought of there being anything more to it than that."

"I would love to talk more, but it's almost time for me to get out," Mother Xavier said, putting her Psalter into her bag. "I'm visiting a benefactor in Kansas City."

Before stepping out of the coach, she handed Annie a card with her name and address. "If you want to get out of the fray sometime, come visit me in Leavenworth. We even have guest rooms." She turned the card over. "And here is the number of a psalm I think you would like, whenever you can get your hands on a Bible."

Chapter Forty-One

Daniel

November 7, 1865

While Annie had been packing suitcases, D.R. was at *The Bulletin*, receiving the routine update from a foreman. On his daily police rounds, Chas strode in and motioned for D.R. to meet him in the newspaper office.

"What's up?" asked D.R., shutting the door behind him.

"I let Iris Naughton go," he said. "It's pretty clear neither of those women did anything to harm that little boy. And neither one said anything more against you before they left, either. But even if they don't, everybody knows they named you as the father. They told me the younger one was assaulted on August nineteenth of sixty-one. Any idea what you were doing on that day?"

D.R. bristled and his voice rose. "In other words, was I in Little Dixie? Are you asking if I assaulted her?"

Chas hooked his thumbs in his belt. "Now, D.R., we've been friends a long time, and I saved your skin more than once. This is a nasty business, and I'm just sayin' . . . if you have any hard evidence that can prove you weren't involved, now's the time to produce it. No doubt Jennison will talk about you at Laing's Hall tonight."

As daylight faded outside his window, D.R. summoned *The Bulletin's* crack reporter, Bill Holden, to give him explicit instructions for covering Jennison's speech. "Quote him word-for-word and take down everything he does. Be sure to note his degree of sobriety, but don't exaggerate. I want everyone there to recognize the truth of what you've written. Oh, and observe how much beer is flowing around him before and after. There's usually plenty. Understand?"

Holden nodded.

"And if he produces the woman and child tonight, give me a complete description. If she's at all coherent, interview the woman herself. I want to monitor anything written about them." Hating to be indebted to an employee, D.R. twisted the button on his cuff. "I would consider it a special favor if you could drop over to my house as soon as the meeting lets out."

"Will do, sir."

Satisfied he had done all he could that day to clear his name, he went home early to share his progress with Annie. Except that she wasn't there. Her note was spare, containing little other than the location where she and Maudie had gone.

He laid it with care on the table, went to sit in a rocker, and leaned forward to put his face in his hands. Even though things between them had been tense lately, he had still hoped to catch a glimpse of the love for him that he was used to seeing in her eyes.

Gazing past the carved door casing into the darkened hall, he remembered the deep satisfaction he and Annie had shared when planning this house. For a short time, he had realized his dream of a cultured wife and family ensconced in a stately home.

But now, as he looked across the threshold, he marveled at how this rumor had destroyed his dream. The house felt as though the fireplaces had been swept clean of every lingering smile and shared laugh. The silence curled around him, more stifling than today's oppressive sky.

Staring into the depths of the shadows, he grappled with a prayer that felt both futile and desperate. Please bring her back, he pleaded silently, though he wasn't sure who he was asking. It was a surrender, a tiny piece of hope clinging to the edges of despair as he admitted, for the first time in memory, that perhaps he was not enough.

He ate a few bites of the dinner that Mrs. Maguire prepared, preferring liquid sustenance instead. But after three whiskeys, he stopped himself. Gotta' be presentable when Holden comes. Gotta' use the time to think, not drink.

"Think, not drink." The rhyme took on a life of its own, keeping time with the ticking grandfather clock. His mind paged through the story of his distant past, trying to recall any liaisons that could have resulted in a pregnancy. A thought twisted in his gut: If there had ever been a baby, would he have known? Memories blurred into his thirties, a haze of Wild West women and whiskey.

Suppose he was drunk and didn't remember? As the thought surfaced, he ceased his rhythmic rocking and sighed, regret settling on him like the cigar smoke thickening the air around him. Too late now.

At nine o'clock when Holden knocked on the front door, D.R. answered it with a frown. "I thought I told you to stay till the end of the meeting. Why'd you leave early?"

His question failed to intimidate Holden as D.R. intended. In fact, the man looked downright pleased with himself. The reporter said, "May I come in?"

D.R. grudgingly admitted the man, but without inviting him to sit.

"So? Let's have it," he growled

Holden planted his feet and got right to the point. "I arrived at Laing's Hall at six-thirty, only to find it locked and dark. A few others were with me, and we saw a note on the door saying the gas was out. When I went to check the meter, I discovered the entire thing was missing. One of Jennison's associates pretended to go look for the key and the meter, but the caretaker never showed up."

Holden smirked. "It looks to me like Colonel Jennison couldn't manage to get the woman and child to show up—if they even exist! No wonder he canceled his formal speech."

His worries assuaged, D.R. allowed a small smile. "What happened next?"

Holden continued in an upbeat tone. "Jennison invited all the would-be attendees to join him at Dexters. He didn't even make a speech, just rattled on for a while, stood everyone a round of drinks, and fell asleep in his beer." He gave a scornful laugh. "Eventually two guys had to walk him home."

At last, D.R. remembered his manners and gestured for Holden to sit in Annie's favorite chair. "Care for a drink? Cigar?" His relief made him generous. When Holden was settled with a glass of whiskey, D.R. asked, "Mind if I see your notes?"

The man handed them over, and D.R. took his time perusing them and wincing at Jennison's innuendoes.

Still, there was no substantial evidence about a woman and child. At length, he said, "Well done! Write them up verbatim for tomorrow's paper." He waved the whiskey bottle towards his reporter. "How do you like this brand? It's one of my favorites."

"Mmm, good," said Holden.

D.R. went to his liquor cabinet and returned. "Here's two for you to take home. That should keep you for a while."

The next day, the front page of *The Bulletin* quoted Jennison's speech at length:

There is a reporter for The Bulletin here as the tool of D.R. Anthony tonight to make a report of my speech for the paper tomorrow. But it is well known that the report of my last speech in The Times was humbug. How can we expect The Bulletin to do any better.

With this reporter tonight I am not here to make one of my speeches. But if I did, I'd tell him all about D.R. Anthony, and have his illegitimate child upon the stage with its insane mother—I ask the reporter to take that down. [Loud applause.] Yes, she has been begging in the streets and has to be supported as a charity of the City Council.

Give me a glass of beer now, gentlemen. Will the reporter put that down? I guess not. If he does, it will not be published tomorrow, gentlemen, you may be certain of it.

I've come to ask you for your votes, gentlemen. And I will tell you about how D.R. Anthony seduced the wives and daughters of the colored people. I don't go around and honey-fuggle with them and seduce their wives and leave them to go insane.

Honey-fuggle indeed, mused D.R, breaking into a full smile for the first time that day. Now there's new word for the dictionary.

CHAPTER FORTY-TWO

Annie

Quindaro, Kansas
November 8, 1865

On Annie's first morning in Quindaro, Clarina rose early to care for Maudie so Annie could sleep. Drawn to the kitchen by the aroma of warm oatmeal, Annie dared to broach the scandalous subject of the alleged mistress and child.

Clarina shook her head in sympathy. "How dreadful to learn of Jennison's accusations so on the street!"

"I was so humiliated," agreed Annie. "I went into town to buy dinner, and a friend from the Sanitary Relief Commission pretended she didn't even see me." Soon she found herself recounting episodes she had mentioned to Mother Xavier. "You know what else?"

"What?" Clarina asked, her eyes filled with warm concern.

"Dan was responsible for wiping out two towns in Missouri during the war. Burned them to the ground and left people no crops to live on. That's why so many people hate him." Her narrative ended on a cry of despair. "I had no idea when I agreed to marry this man and have children with him!"

Maudie whined and erupted into tears. Clarina scooped up the baby and held her close. "It sounds like your early years of marriage have been traumatic," she observed, putting a bowl of oatmeal in front of Annie. The words hung in the air, a stark summary of Annie's existence, yet something vital felt missing.

When Annie finished her breakfast, Clarina said, "Well, now that you're up and fed, I'm going to start my chores. I'll be pretty busy for several hours."

"I can take Maudie now. What do you have to do?" asked Annie.

Clarina folded a quilt into her laundry basket, reaching out for the baby once more. "Here, hand me that little chick," she said, propping Maudie into a sitting position against a pillow.

Annie marveled at the arrangement, a spark of inspiration energizing her. "With my hands free, I can lend you a hand!"

Soon Clarina was showing her how to gather eggs from the hens and pick the last quart of fall raspberries from thorny vines. Encouraged by the older woman's kind inquiries and quiet observations, Annie elaborated on the distressing events of the last several months.

"Dan's temper sounds fierce," Clarina remarked. "And I'd heard his name mentioned when towns were being burned in Missouri. But it *was* war." Annie gave her a dubious glance when she continued, "War makes monsters of men for a season, then they return to their normal lives. Even reasonable men do things as soldiers that they'd never dream of doing otherwise. But it's not usual for them to hurt their families." Studying Annie's face, she asked, "Has he ever threatened you? Struck you?"

"No, but his shouting frightens me."

"Maybe you can shout back."

Overnight, Annie saw lightning and wished for the hundredth time that it would rain.

By morning, the heat had let up a little and Clarina declared it a good day to make applesauce.

Annie decided to broach the subject of her relationship again. "You know, yesterday I told you all the bad things about our marriage. But there have been good things, too."

"Such as?"

Annie placed an apple on the table. "Before we were even married, Dan planned a welcome reception for me. And when he realized I couldn't find my way around town, he drew me a map of Leavenworth with all the landmarks circled. He bought me a horse. A piano." Her voice softened, "When he looks at me . . . I feel like the most desirable woman in the world."

She faltered then, her chin trembling. "But lately, he's too busy to look at me. He's totally caught up with other people. It no longer feels like a marriage."

Clarina moved to the cutting board and sliced apples, speaking with deliberation. "As I see it, you've got a couple of options."

Annie shifted Maudie from the blanket on the floor into her basket. "Yes?"

"You could choose the safety of divorce—free from gunfights and the ghosts of war. In Kansas, the law says you'd get equal custody of the baby."

The bluntness struck like a slap. Annie's breath caught. "But Maude needs both her parents." She hesitated, and before she could swallow it, the truth burst out. "And I love Daniel."

Clarina nodded slowly. "As you describe your marriage, it sounds like being yoked to a whirlwind. You can't predict where he'll choose to go." Her gaze met Annie's. "Even if you can tolerate that uncertainty yourself, it may get harder as Maudie grows. Is Daniel worth the cost?"

"God help me, but yes."

"Then you'll need something to sustain you when life gets hard again—a vision in here." Clarina pressed a hand to her chest.

Throughout the afternoon, the apples simmered and filled the kitchen with the scent of cinnamon while outside, the air grew heavy once more. After dinner, Clarina touched Annie's arm. "Why don't I watch Maudie while you step out onto the porch and see if you can catch a breeze? I think we're in for some rain."

Outside, the air felt thick, charged with something unsaid. The porch swing creaked beneath Annie as she leaned back and gazed into the pewter sky with its heavy clouds. The birds had gone quiet.

Setting the swing in motion with her foot, she pondered the idea of a vision to sustain her. What did she want?

It should've been easy to answer. Safety. Stability. A life where she and Maudie could live without fear of gunfire or newspaper scandals. A life without shame.

The swing rocked in slow arcs, forward and back, mirroring the pull of her thoughts—one moment reaching for stability, the next recoiling in boredom. Safety offered stillness, but not fulfillment. It wasn't all she craved.

She longed for meaning. A home filled with fierce love and shared laughter. A partner who saw her. A child who felt secure. That was her heart's desire. But longing and choosing the right path were not always the same.

Years ago, before she married Daniel, she had prayed for wisdom to do what was right. But now she sat with the weight of that decision—and the fear that she'd misunderstood God entirely.

She glared at the sky. "I asked You back then if Daniel was the one, if You were in it." She whispered. "You never answered me."

The clouds hovered overhead, silent. Was that a no? Was silence the answer all along?

Her chest tightened. "I tried to build something good," she said aloud, voice cracking. "To love wisely. To follow where You led. But now I'm lost."

"Say something," she pleaded. "Please. Just once. I need to know You're with me." A gust of wind swept dry leaves across the porch. Her heart beating wildly, Annie gripped the rail for balance. She did not have long to wait.

Thunder and lightning split the sky with power that left no doubt of its source. The first raindrop touched Annie's cheek like a fond greeting from a friend, gentle and familiar. She followed its invitation to stand on the lawn.

The heavens opened and rain fell in broad, steady sheets, washing the leaves and the roof above. The heat that had clung for days gave way, lifting from her chest like a burden laid down at last. A breeze followed, stirring the trees with a sound like breath returning to a weary body. It brushed her skirts and slipped through the loosened strands of hair at her neck, cool and kind.

And with it, her thoughts began to clear. For the first time in days, she felt space enough to breathe. Annie stepped forward, arms open, face lifted. It felt like being seen. Like being answered.

A message too deep for words sank into her soul. I see you. I have not forgotten you. You are not alone.

Her knees weakened, but she stood there in the yard, trembling, alive. A sob broke loose. "Thank You," she gasped. "Oh God—thank You."

The rain poured on, steady and cooling. Her tears mingled with the storm until she could no longer tell which were hers and which were heaven's. But it didn't matter.

She had been heard, answered. That presence would go with her no matter what path she chose.

Dripping wet, Annie entered the house with a renewed sense of peace. Clarina kissed her on the cheek and informed her that Maudie was already tucked in for the night.

Smiling her thanks, Annie said, "I'm going to go to bed early."

"Good sleeping tonight," said Clarina. It sounded like a blessing.

In the middle of the night Annie woke, chilled in her sleeveless nightdress. Getting up to wrap Maudie, she woke the baby and then nursed her back to sleep. The unseasonably warm weather had broken with the storm, leavin air that felt fresh as Annie's new perspective.

Clarina first words to her that day were, "Let's take a drive up into the hills so I can show you the view." After breakfast, they donned shawls and outfitted Maude in a soft woolen jacket before setting off in the wagon.

Beside her friend, Annie sat with Maudie on her lap as they left the small town and drove a few miles before pausing on a ridge overlooking the Missouri River. To the north of the waterway, the land spread out in an expanse of autumn-gold grasses waving in a cool breeze.

"I can just picture Lewis and Clark on their adventure along this great river," Clarina said. Watching a pair of ducks fly over and then land on the water, she said, "When I first met you, I got the sense that D.R. is the sun and you are a planet that orbits him."

"Hmmm. That sounds about right."

"It's a dangerous way to lead your life."

Annie bit her lip. "What do you mean? Isn't that what wives are supposed to do?"

"Many do that, yes. And then when they have babies, their children become their sun, displacing the husband. Such children become quite self-absorbed, used to being the center of the world. And after the children leave—"

Having never looked ahead to that stage in her own life, Annie interrupted. "What do mothers do then?"

"If the couple hasn't paid attention, usually she and her husband grow apart. The wife may develop a taste for sherry or laudanum, nap away her afternoons, and rouse herself every few years just long enough to redecorate her house." Clarina picked up a red leaf glistening with raindrops and handed it to Maudie. "No husband is ever enough for a woman to live through him. You must live your own life. After all, it was given to you and to no one else."

Annie looked down at Maudie, who was now holding the red leaf with quiet wonder. "What else is there to live for, if not them?"

Clarina held out her empty hands. "Where are my husband and children now? I'm basically alone, but all these years I've had my writing and speeches on behalf of women. My mission. What else do you care about?"

It took Annie a few moments to answer. "Well, I've always loved music. And I care about the people of Leavenworth. I'm starting to feel like I make a difference, even in small ways." She described how she had been teaching Emily and John. "I enjoy the Sanitary Relief Commission—at least when they're doing something substantial like helping families separated by war."

"Those are topics dear to me, too," said Clarina. "What does D.R. think about such families?"

Annie looked surprised. "I never asked him. Now that the war's over, though, maybe he feels the same way. After all, we hired Emily and John Robinson."

When Annie rose the following morning, she asked to go to town to buy a return coach ticket to Leavenworth. "I've decided to go back to Dan." She smiled. "But I'll try not to orbit him."

Clarina reached into a basket near the hearth. "I'm not surprised, so I put aside something that might help you." She held up a well-worn Psalter. "If I remember correctly, the sister in the coach told you to read Psalm 121, correct?" When Annie nodded, Clarina continued, "It's one of my favorites, also. It was especially important to me when my husband died shortly after we got to Kansas. Ever since that time, whenever I see hills, I remind myself to draw a breath of new air. Maybe a little like what you felt yesterday overlooking the river."

Annie smiled at this friend of Susan's who had become her own confidante. Being with Clarina *had* given her time to breathe.

"Read it to me," she quietly requested.

Clarina closed her eyes for a few moments before opening them to read and skipping a few lines here and there.

I lift up mine eyes unto the hills, from whence cometh my help.
My help cometh from the Lord, who made heaven and earth . . .
The Lord is thy keeper: the Lord is thy shade upon thy right hand.
The sun shall not smite thee by day, nor the moon by night . . .
The Lord shall preserve thy going out and thy coming in
from this time forth, and for evermore.

Annie smiled her thanks.

Clarina's voice brightened. "You have something going for you that I never had."

Annie shook her head, disbelieving. "You've been through such hardships and stayed so self-sufficient, whereas I totally depend on Dan."

Clarina's eyes crinkled at the corners. "No, you have something very valuable to both of you. You just have to learn how to use it."

That evening, as Annie tucked the psalm into her bag, her hand lingered. She thought of the storm she had weathered over Dan—the ache, the confusion, the sense of losing herself to his chaos.

Something had shifted. A quiet strength stirred in her, like a seed breaking open beneath the soil. Mother Xavier had planted it with her gentle insight, Clarina had tended it with truth and care, and the unseen hand had poured mercy over it. Now it reached for light—steady, alive, and growing.

Annie stepped outside and turned her face to the November moon. Despite the chill air, she considered her husband with unclouded warmth for the first time in months. She recalled the tickle of his beard against her cheek, the gentleness in his hands as he held newborn Maudie. His embrace had always felt more like home than any other place she'd known.

Daniel, my love. Soon.

Chapter Forty-Three

Daniel

Leavenworth, Kansas * November 12, 1865

Annie was coming home! D.R.'s pulse thrummed with the thought as he strode through the Planters House lobby to meet her stagecoach by the river. Tapping his foot on the pavement behind the building, he nodded as Mary Gray approached. But as he was about to speak to Annie's acquaintance from the Sanitary Relief Commission, the woman's large black hat blew off and sent him racing to retrieve it. After she thanked him and re-pinned it to her hair, he asked, "My wife's told me about the plans for the new orphanage. How is it going?"

"Very well. We are getting our facts in order so we can draw up a proposal," she replied.

"That's good," he said. "There's too many youngsters roaming the streets without parents."

"Yes, and the orphanage will need a lot of money. To build *and* to operate! All those little mouths to feed every day, you know." She paused. "Mrs. Anthony said you might be willing to contribute a generous amount to help set it up. Of course, we'll put the names of large donors on a memorial plaque inside the building."

"I'll be happy to," he replied. "Why don't you come by my office when you know how much you'll need?"

"Thank you." She paused a moment before adding, "I'm glad the marshal got that poor Naughton family sorted out." She looked at him intently and he nodded, understanding her unspoken conclusion that Jennison had fabricated the whole thing. "What a tragic life that boy's had, living with his mother and that strange aunt. Haven't seen her around in several days."

D.R. didn't want to get into any of it. "Oh, here comes the stage—right on time," he said. "Annie's got the baby, so I have to help her with her bags."

Excusing himself, he shifted from one foot to the other till the coach stopped and passengers began to disembark.

Dan shoved thoughts of Mary Gray into the farthest corner of his mind the instant he saw Annie step onto the sidewalk with Maude bundled against her shoulder. His breath caught. There they were. Flesh and blood. Safe. Real.

He closed the distance in a few quick strides and wrapped them both in his arms, holding tight—too tight maybe—but he couldn't help it. The lump in his throat surged upward, thick with the fear that he might've lost them for good.

"I want to hold you forever," he whispered, voice rasping against her hair. "I'm sorry—for everything. You're the only woman I've ever loved."

Her reply came soft and steady. "I'm sorry too . . . and I believe you."

Tears glistened on her cheeks. He hadn't realized his own were falling until he saw them mirrored there. Between them, Maude squirmed gently, her tiny face turned upward in trust.

Dan glanced down and blinked, startled by a hint of something new in the baby's expression. Had her face changed?

It had only been days, but still her eyes seemed a shade deeper, her brow a little rounder. Or maybe it was just him. Seeing her fresh through the fog of regret and relief.

He tightened his arms, breathing in the warm, familiar scent of Annie's hair, the soft weight of Maude between them.

Don't let them go, he told himself. Never again.

As they waited for the baggage, Dan caught sight of Mrs. Gray approaching, Rachel Stark at her side. He tensed instinctively, but her focus was on Annie.

With a gentle hand on Annie's arm, she said, "Mrs. Anthony, we've missed you the last few months at the Sanitary Relief Commission. I hope you'll be back soon. We need your vision to help work out plans for the orphanage."

D.R. studied Annie's face as she nodded, composed and gracious. Not just polite, genuine. That small tilt of her head, the promise in her voice—he knew it cost her something to make it after all the gossip.

They went straight home for lunch. As they made their way, she spoke about Clarina's well-stocked cellar and her new scheme to raise raspberries, he listened better than he had in weeks. Not just to her words, but to the energy behind them. Annie was dreaming again. Planning. Letting herself imagine another spring, with him. Here.

The front door slammed behind them as they stepped into number 417, the sound echoing with a finality that felt like crossing a threshold in more ways than one. He watched her unbutton her gloves, saw her pause at the hall table.

Her brows drew together. "Honey, what's all this?"

He followed her gaze to the porcelain bowl, overflowing with calling cards.

"I've been using the back door a couple days," he said, moving to the table. "Didn't notice." He picked up a handful of calling cards and began reading aloud, his voice growing quieter with each name. "Rachel Stark. Rebecca Carney. Madame Collette. Mary Gray. Lydia Clark. Lavinia Roy. Amanda Corey. Pia Egersdorff. Nettie Cochran. Ella Goodman." He glanced up. "Members of the Sanitary Relief Commission?"

The look on her face said everything—astonishment, disbelief, and something fragile beneath: hope.

"Maybe you're not as much of an outcast as you thought," he said, watching her eyes glisten.

She smiled then, small and tremulous, and he felt something in his chest loosen.

Outside, rain began to fall in earnest, slapping the windows in wild sheets. He stood beside her, both of them watching in silence for a moment, the noise oddly comforting.

Then he lifted Maudie into his arms and followed Annie upstairs. The warmth of their child against his chest, the soft sound of Annie singing, the quiet creak of the nursery rocking chair—each one stitched something back together inside him.

As they stepped out of the nursery and he pulled the door shut with a gentle click, he realized: The dream he thought he'd broken might not be lost after all. It was still here. Fragile, yes. But mending.

Thinking to celebrate with an outing, he said, "By the way, we have tickets for the play at Laing's tonight."

Her mood shifted. "I don't want to go. Everyone will be looking at us."

"But think of all those calling cards. You have plenty of friends to stand by you," he cajoled.

Annie made a face.

"Besides," he continued, "Lydia and Milton are supposed to meet us there. They'll be worried if we don't show up."

"Oh, all right," said Annie.

"I'd like to leave a little early and swing by the office to check on something. Won't take me long."

Annie sighed in a theatrical way. "Which office?"

"Insurance. I have an early meeting with a guy tomorrow at his house, and I want to look over some information before I go there. With the excitement of picking you up, I forgot to stop there on my way to lunch."

Chapter Forty-Four

Annie

That evening

Forty-five minutes before the opening curtain at Laing's Hall, the stench of stale cigars greeted Annie as she stepped through the door of the D.R. Anthony Insurance office. While Dan pulled together some pamphlets and forms, she roamed the room looking at photographs and etchings of Leavenworth on the walls.

She said, "I checked the Naughton diary, hoping to find some description of the man who attacked the mother of the little boy."

Dan looked up from the desk. "Did you find anything?"

"No. But I was wondering. Did you ever keep a journal of any sort?"

He scoffed. "Me? No."

"When did you start your insurance business?"

"Soon after I settled here—fifty-seven, maybe."

"Do you still have contracts going back that far?"

"Probably," he said. "What are you getting at, anyway?"

"Just a hunch. Are the policies filed according to the date you started them, by any chance? If so, then maybe you could find one dated August nineteenth?" Earlier, they had compared notes and realized that the date Chas mentioned to Dan matched the one in Veronia's diary.

"Nice thought, but they're filed A to Z, all eight years mixed together."

Despite the show of support at the theater that evening, Annie couldn't shake the feeling that people still whispered behind their backs. By the time she arrived home—worn out from travel and the effort of holding herself together—her composure was frayed thin. She kicked off her shoes at the bottom of the stairs and flung her wool cloak over the coat rack, then made her way to the butler's pantry for a cup of chamomile tea to calm her nerves.

If only there were a way to prove Dan's innocence.

Dan was in bed, almost asleep when she padded up the stairs in bare feet and climbed in beside him. Despite the tea, she still couldn't sleep, rehashing every frown, sidelong glance and whispered comment from strangers. Yes, her friends had rallied around her, but they could not constantly shield her from the glances of less compassionate townsfolk.

After forty-five minutes, she peeled back the covers and pushed her arms into her dressing gown. Intending to go downstairs for some warm milk, she was diverted by a band of moonlight beaming across the hall carpet.

As she followed the moonbeam to the guestroom window, her foot slipped across something: the sheet of paper that had dropped from the Naughton journal. The handwriting was smaller and neater than that in the diary. The date made her heart quicken because it was from the same timeframe as the alleged attack. As her gaze swept across the page, she realized this was Iris recalling events that Veronia wouldn't—or couldn't—express.

Monday, August 21, 1861

Two days ago, when I was coming home from the market, I found Jayhawkers ransacking Shady Grove. When I got close to the house, a man was hitching up our oxen as others loaded the hams from the smokehouse into our biggest wagon. I wanted to scream at them. But first, I had to find Veronia. I knew she'd be scared.

Someone on a horse was yelling at Papa, who ran inside and slammed the front door. Out of the corner of my eye, I saw the rider jump down and call out, "Take the house!"

I ran around to the back, hoping to find Veronia safe inside our closet there. Shots fired and then I heard heavy boots and shouts of excitement as they located our silverware in the front room.

My poor little sister. She had already been violated when I found her sitting just outside the closet, whimpering. While in hiding, she had sneezed—she does that a lot in late summer—and one of the Jayhawkers noticed the latch for our secret room and attacked her. When I asked her to describe him, she said the closet was so dark she couldn't see him. All she could remember was that he was short and smelled like tobacco.

Men were dragging casks of liquor out the front door, paying us no mind. I coaxed her back inside our hiding place and prayed they'd forget all about us. They caroused on the porch, and after a while the wagons and livestock rumbled off down the road.

Papa called to me and I left the closet to find him and Tom tied back-to-back. They had no idea what had happened to Veronia until I told them. Papa's face went red but he said nothing. Later I heard him whacking down a dead tree—for firewood, he said. But I knew that each blow of the axe meant his wish to fight back at the Jayhawkers.

Poor Veronia—she's not even seventeen. What will happen to her now?

The bandits took most of our farm wagons, hogs, and cows. The rest of our slaves left, even the old ones. They took bins of flour and nuts, jars of green beans, peaches and jam, and barrels of wine and beer. I did not see whether they ran into the woods or followed the raiders. Our big silver serving urns vanished, too. All we have left is a little cash and some jewelry. Ordinarily, we sell crops to buy food that we don't raise, but we have no help to harvest the crops. What will we do when the money runs out? Just thinking about it makes my stomach hurt.

Tuesday, August 22, 1861

Today, Papa went over to see how the Bauers made out. Jennison's Jayhawkers took most of their slaves and horses, too. Papa asked if Mr. Bauer could suggest who might have attacked Veronia. Mr. B said the group is named for a man named Jennison, but a Daniel Anthony is the day-to-day leader. "Shame on him, despoiling a girl," Mr. B told Papa.

One of the Jayhawkers called the Bauers "official enemies of the Union." Well, Papa has held fast to the Union, but I can't see what good it's done us.

If molesting a sixteen-year-old is how Unionists treat their friends, I shudder to think how they treat their enemies.

I guess those Union soldiers who came in May never told the rest of them to leave us alone.

Iris's written accusation of Dan burned into Annie's brain, making plain the thoughts of the woman who could no longer speak or write. The woman's belief that Dan had attacked Veronia certainly gave her ample reason to despise him. Now Annie understood her comments—connecting "Anthony" and "baby"—she was attempting to warn Annie that her husband had violated Veronia. Annie closed her eyes to erase that notion.

Recalling Dan's earnest gaze earlier when he denied any knowledge of the attack on Shady Grove, Annie believed him. But now, more than ever, she wanted him *proven* innocent. There had to be a way. A record, somewhere. If only the insurance policies had been filed by date.

But though Dan had filed them alphabetically by customer, surely he must have *dated* them individually! Looking out onto the moonlit lawn from the guestroom, she considered the number of file drawers she had seen in his office. Searching for a date through eight years of policies might take all night, but she wasn't getting any sleep anyway.

Dressing in the silence, she picked up the office keys from the dresser and pushed open Maudie's door as she passed, hoping that Dan would hear the baby if she cried. When she set foot on the cool tile of the front hall, she had to step with care because the windowless hall was pitch black.

Keeping one hand tight around Daniel's keys, she tucked her gloves under her arm and navigated around the shoes she'd kicked off a few hours earlier. As she reached for her cloak hanging from the hall tree, her sleeve snagged on a hook. The whole thing teetered.

She grabbed for it, but it was too late.

The wooden stand crashed sideways with a clatter, her heavy cloak tangling with hats and scarves.

Chapter Forty-Five

Annie

Later that night

Annie froze, her pulse thudding in her ears. The house fell silent again.

Then . . . a soft creak.

Her heart lurched. Dan? *If he was up, perhaps he would go along to the office.* She could wake Emily to listen for Maude—just till she and Dan got home.

But just as quickly, she remembered her frosty departure to Clarina's. The tears they'd both shed at the stagecoach. *No,* she thought. *This is something I need to do alone, to show him my support.*

Annie held her breath, staring toward the stairwell, ears straining.

Hearing nothing more, she crouched to sift through the heap of cloaks and scarves in search of the keys.

In a collision of knees and elbows, a body landed squarely against her with a muffled *whump.*

Both women screamed.

"Lord have mercy!" Emily gasped. "Mrs. Anthony?"

Annie clutched her chest. "You nearly scared me to death!"

Emily, panting in the dark, hissed, "You scared me! I thought someone was breakin' in! I heard a crash, then footsteps—and next thing I know, I'm wrestling ghosts in the coat pile!"

"I knocked over the coat stand," Annie said, catching her breath. "Sorry if I woke you."

She stood and turned up the gas lamp. The flickering light revealed Emily, her hair wild, shawl slipping off one shoulder, nightgown askew.

Annie blinked, then smiled. "Well. You don't look like a housebreaker."

Emily snorted. "And you don't look like a lady who ought to be creeping about in the dark. Honestly, Mrs. Anthony, if we keep carryin' on like this, we'll both be old women before morning."

Then her eyes narrowed. "You lookin for those?" She pointed to the keys peeking out of Annie's pocket.

Fingering them with relief, Annie said, "I couldn't sleep. I need air."

"At this hour? Open the window."

Annie moved to straighten the toppled coats. "Let it be, Emily."

Emily stepped closer, her voice hardening. "Not after what happened these last several days. You think it's smart to go out when half the town still believes your husband fathered that baby?"

Annie stilled.

Emily crossed her arms and gave a little shiver in her nightgown. "I heard tell that Jennison planned that little scene. A friend of mine heard 'em whispering earlier." Her voice dropped. "Made that woman name the colonel. Everybody still talking about it."

Annie straightened, her lips pressed thin. "He didn't do anything wrong."

"I know that," Emily said. "But the people who want to believe you did? They might be happy to cause you and the colonel more trouble."

"Yes, but I'm not going far."

"You don't have to. Jennison's the kind of man who sets traps in your own front yard."

Annie met her gaze. "I know how to fix it, Emily. I just need some time when there's no one at the insurance office." She explained her plan.

Emily nodded slowly. "If you're going out into the dark, I'm going, too. I'll keep watch outside while you search."

It was still dark at half past six by the time Annie had gathered everything she needed to produce three insurance policies dated August nineteenth. Lost in anticipation of Dan's happiness, she made it to the street before remembering that she had left the office door unlocked with the keys still inside. After a brief search through the room, she found them tucked away in her own skirt pocket. Just as she reached the half-open door leading outside, it swung wide, and a man stepped in, pointing a gun.

Annie screamed. "Don't shoot!"

When the hand holding the gun lowered, she beheld the astonished face of Doc Jennison.

He sputtered. "What the—Mrs. Anthony? What are you doing here? I thought it was a burglar! So I came to check." He cleared his throat. "I was just walkin' by."

Trembling inside, Annie forced herself to remain calm. "My husband needs some records for early clients today and since I couldn't sleep, I came to get them for him." Worried he would sense the documents' importance if she looked at them, she kept her eyes focused on the man in front of her.

Even so, Jennison crossed the room and picked up the folders. Her knees went weak with fear that he would read the policies and destroy them.

At least he had holstered his gun. Summoning all her courage, she stepped up and reclaimed the documents before he could inspect them.

"Thanks, but I can carry those. I'll be going now."

Acting on a flash of inspiration, she reached inside Dan's top desk drawer. As she'd hoped, he kept a gun there.

Picking up the pistol, she said, "Silly me! I almost forgot this." With exaggerated playfulness, she closed one eye and aimed at him while making for the door.

He ducked and laughed, keeping an eye on her hand holding the gun.

"Hey, you don't know how to use that. Leave it here so you don't hurt yourself."

Waving the gun past him, she said, "Oh, I won't get hurt. Please come out so I can lock the door." He did as she asked.

Once they were both on the stoop, she favored him with the most innocent expression her blue eyes could muster. "Do you really think Dan would let me to go wherever I want without the same protection he has? I keep it right here."

She slipped the revolver into her pocket and patted it affectionately, all the while praying that it wouldn't go off. "So you see, there's no need to worry about me," she said with feigned cheer. "Good night, now."

Suddenly she remembered Emily, who was nowhere in sight. "Where's Emily?"

Jennison straightened. "She's fine. Just stepped aside for a moment. Said she needed a rest."

Something in the way he said it turned her skin to ice.

"She wouldn't leave," Annie said to herself, eyes scanning the street, the doorways, the shadows. Leavenworth still slept. Only a milk cart rattled off in the distance.

"I insisted," he said. "Didn't seem right for her to be out here alone. And I didn't know who was in that office, you understand. Like I said, I thought it was bein' robbed. So I took precautions." He grinned that awful grin, pleased with himself.

"Now we have that all cleared up, I really must collect Emily and get home."

He stepped down from the stoop, blocking her view of the alley. "In a minute. You and I should talk first."

Her pulse thundered in her ears.

Jennison gave her a courtly little bow. "Allow me to walk you home."

She didn't move.

"Emily is safe, I promise. You'll have her back unharmed—if we arrive together. Calmly." He offered his arm. "I don't want a fuss, Mrs. Anthony. You wouldn't want that, either."

Annie set off beside him, refusing to take his arm.

Jennison smiled again, and they began to walk toward North Esplanade, she could smell his whiskey breath. What did he want from her?

"Wasn't expecting to see you out this morning," he said, his tone light, companionable. "All that business last week—what with the woman and the child and that outburst at the jail—must've shaken you up."

She said nothing.

"But then, maybe not," he mused. "You strike me as strong. Stronger than people think."

"I manage," she replied.

"Of course you do. Especially with a husband like yours." His voice darkened, turning soft and dangerous. "You ever wonder what it would be like to be married to someone . . . less pigheaded? Someone who doesn't draw fire everywhere he goes?"

She kept walking.

He leaned in. "You must've been disappointed. Finding out about the mistress. The boy."

Her breath caught—but she didn't stop.

He took that as encouragement. "It wouldn't be weakness to walk away from it all. You'd be right to. No one would blame you."

Annie's throat burned. He was trying to break her. But she wouldn't give him that. Not with Emily somewhere behind her, bound and waiting.

So she gave him something else: a smile.

"You're right," she simpered. "It would be easier. Safer."

He chuckled. "Glad you take it that way."

They turned onto North Esplanade. Almost home. Her heart beat faster with every step.

She could see number 417 now—and saw Dan's coat thrown across the porch rail. He was up.

Heartened by the thought of her husband, she decided to make one last bluff.

"Doc," she said, stopping just shy of the walk, "there's something I've been wondering."

He tilted his head. "Yeah?"

"How much oil and kindling would it take to burn down LeBon-Ton?"

His grin faltered.

She kept her smile in place, still holding the folder. "You remember how Dan handled those other houses of ill repute, don't you?"

Before he could answer, her voice turned bright and false and she called, "Good morning, husband!"

Dan had started off the porch, eyes narrowing at the sight of Jennison beside her. Annie raised one hand to stop him. Don't provoke him, she mouthed.

To Jennison, she said, "Thank you for the escort. It's been . . . enlightening."

He hesitated a moment longer, his posture tight, then tipped his hat and hastened off toward the Planters.

Only when he was halfway there did Annie turn to Dan and murmur, "Don't go after him. He's tied up Emily near the insurance office."

Daniel didn't wait for more.

Annie stood at the kitchen window, her hands wrapped around her teacup, eyes fixed on the street. The sun had risen on a morning cloudless and cold with an intensity that tightened the knot of dread in her chest.

Then she saw them.

Dan, striding along with fury still etched across his face.

And beside him—thank God—Emily.

Annie flew to the front door, throwing it open just as they reached the steps.

Emily looked exhausted. Her cloak hung crooked on her frame, and her eyes were glassy with fatigue, but her chin was high, her dignity intact.

Dan said nothing as he brushed past Annie into the house. He went straight to the library, the click of the door behind him tight with meaning. She would deal with him later.

Annie turned to Emily and opened her arms.

For a moment, neither of them moved. Then Emily let herself be folded into the embrace. Her breath hitched once, and she pulled back quickly, blinking hard.

"I'm all right," she said, though her voice cracked. "Just rattled."

"Come inside," Annie said. "I've got a pot of tea waiting."

She led her to the kitchen, guiding her into the cushioned chair by the stove. The tea tray was already set: two cups, honey, a wedge of lemon. Annie poured with practiced care, her hands steady now that Emily was safe.

Emily accepted the cup with a whisper of thanks, holding it between her palms like a small fire. A line of red extended from her mouth around her neck where she had been gagged.

They sat in silence a moment, the house still around them.

Annie wanted to ask what had happened—what exactly Jennison had said, whether he'd hurt her—but Emily's eyes were far away, somewhere underground, and Annie knew better than to reach for her too soon. So instead, she said, "You were brave."

Emily gave a soft laugh, shaky but real. "Felt like a sack of flour, the way he throwed me down."

"But you stayed calm. And safe."

Emily looked down into her tea. "Would've done something to help you but he said . . . if I made a sound, he'd hurt you."

Annie closed her eyes. Then reached over and touched Emily's hand.

Before either of them could speak again, soft footsteps padded on the back stair.

A wide-eyed boy peeked into the kitchen before darting across the room. "Mama?"

Emily turned, scraping her chair on the floor. "Andrew."

He hesitated in the doorway, eyes wide, face pale. "Where'd you go?"

"I'm here now, baby," she said, rising and crossing to him. She placed a steady hand on his shoulder and brushed the hair from his forehead.

"You okay?" he whispered, leaning into her for reassurance.

"Right as rain," she murmured.

Annie stood by the tea tray. "Go on, Emily. Be with him."

Emily nodded, her hand still resting on her son's shoulder. "Thank you," she said, her voice low.

"I'm the one who's grateful," Annie said.

And with that, the two servants turned and disappeared down the back stairs.

Annie went to find Daniel in the library. To her surprise, he wasn't sitting behind his desk. He was pacing.

Without a word, Annie went to his side and pressed her cheek against his chest, letting the steady rise and fall of his breathing soothe her nerves. His warmth, his strength—she let it hold her for a moment longer than usual.

Then Dan eased her away from him, examining her with a furrowed brow.

"You're sure you're not hurt? Did he touch you? Threaten you? Did Emily—?"

"Dan," she interrupted, her tone light but firm. "I'm fine. So is Emily. He tied her up, not me."

"That's not fine," he muttered.

"I know," she said. "But we're both safe now."

Still, his questions came—rapid-fire, relentless. Where had Jennison grabbed Emily? How long was she alone? What route had they taken home? Did anyone see?

Annie answered them all, each word measured and calm. When he stopped and let out a low breath, she added, "I see you're allowed to march through town with a revolver and set half the buildings on fire, but the moment I fetch a file folder, the world must stop and check me for bruises."

Dan blinked, caught off guard. "That's not what I meant."

"But it's what you *did*." She gave him a look that mixed fondness and exasperation. "I had a plan. I even had your pistol."

He frowned. "Since when do you know how to use a gun? Did you change your mind and decide they're necessary?"

"No," she said in measured tones. "But Jennison doesn't know that. In fact, you might noise it about that I held him off at gunpoint."

He let out a reluctant laugh, some of the tension in his shoulders releasing. "Fight rumors with rumors. Good idea."

She smiled then, slow and triumphant. "Glad you think so."

Before he could respond, she reached into her bag and pulled out the folders. "I brought you something."

His eyes widened. "Are those—?"

"Three policies from August nineteenth. One client from 'B', one from 'J', one from 'W.'"

He opened the top folder, scanning the date. "You must've gone through the entire cabinet."

"Every drawer."

Dan shook his head and drew her in again, voice low with wonder. "You did that. After all that happened."

She pressed her face to his cheek long enough to feel the smile tugging at the corner of his mouth.

Then she pulled back, her eyes dancing. “There’s more.”

“Oh?”

She grinned. “I found a new page in that Missouri diary. Something Iris added. And it changes everything.”

Chapter Forty-Six

Daniel

November 13, 1865

Fueled by Annie's discoveries, D.R. needed only a day to hatch a plan to restore his name. The morning it began to fall into place, he made his way from the business office of *The Times* to its pressroom.

Feeling many eyes upon him, he thought smugly, Let them all get a good look at me! Soon every single one will be answering to me instead of slandering me.

After a brief conversation with the owner, he opened the door onto the street, walked a few blocks till he got to the bank, and waited until a customer left Milton Clark's office before going in.

Milton looked up in surprise. "Is everything all right? What brings you here?" Though they had been good friends as well as business associates for years, this was the first time they had spoken since the scandal about the illegitimate child.

Milton gave D.R. a warm handshake and a concerned look. "What can I do for you?"

Shutting the door, D.R. said, "Did you know *The Times* is in trouble and can't pay their bills?"

Milton, who always made a show of keeping confidences, nodded. "We don't have their accounts like we do yours, but yes, I had heard something to that effect."

"I caught wind of it from one of its typesetters who came looking for a job. So I went over, made an offer on the paper, and it was accepted." D.R.'s satisfied nod punctuated this revelation.

Milton chuckled. "Holy Moses! Will that cut down on the mudslinging in this town?"

D.R. laughed along. "Yeah, I must admit I am sick of *The Times* attacking me. Anybody with an axe to grind can buy space with them. Jennison, for example." He dropped into a chair across the desk from the banker.

"So what can I do for you today?" repeated Milton. "I must finish something here," he explained, gesturing to a thick file on his desk.

"About the issue of the illegitimate child . . ." He summarized how Annie had unearthed decisive evidence that he, D.R., was not the father.

"Congratulations!" said Milton. "What a relief! Lydia will be so happy to hear it."

D.R. nodded, continuing, "So my purchase offer to *The Times* stipulated this: before I take ownership, they will print an article clearing my name. Tomorrow. That way no one can object that I defended myself in my own paper because I won't own it yet!"

Milton smiled at this ploy. "Strictly speaking, you're right . . ."

"But there's more. All evidence points to Jennison himself as the father."

Milton raised his eyebrows and sat back in surprise. "Well, well!" he said, nodding. "I guess that kind of fits his style, with his bordellos."

"Did you know his wife, Mary, left him, taking his daughter, too?"

"I did hear something about that," Milton said.

"Rumor has it that Mary was plenty steamed when his bars were raided for prostitution," said D.R. "But I can tell you, at one time the two of them were close. She used to roll cartridges for the Jayhawkers. He bragged about how she could beat him in a horserace. I bet he'd like to get her and his daughter back." He paused for a breath. "Those women with the child—Naughton is their name—they've lost everything because of Jennison."

D.R. outlined how, months before the sexual assault on Veronia Naughton in sixty-one, he had satisfied himself that the Naughton fellow was a true Unionist, but on a raid without Anthony, Jennison had attacked the farm anyway.

"Oddly enough, Annie found one of the women's diaries when she was shopping with Lydia." He explained about her buying the desk and his fixing the stuck drawer with the journal inside. "Those women lost everything," he repeated. "*And* they got an extra mouth to feed. A baby."

"It sounds like you're about to be done with Jennison's tricks for a while," said Milton, looking at his watch.

"Yeah. You got just a minute more? I'll be quick. It's about banking."

Milton nodded and resumed his attentive listening.

D.R. continued, "I need your cooperation on a financial transaction with Jennison. Chas and I are going to meet him tomorrow and tell him what we know. If he doesn't want to have Mary read all about his paternity in *The Times*, he's going to have to fork over a huge amount of money to support the Naughtons. As soon as I bring that money into your bank, I want the Naughton women to be able to draw it out. Can you make that happen?"

Milton steepled his fingers and leaned forward with sympathy. "I'd like to do that for you, but sometimes incoming funds have to be held for a couple days before being released. Especially large sums."

"I'll be a little short on cash for a while after buying *The Times*. But can you take my word I'll make good on the Jennison check if it bounces?"

Milton lowered his eyes and stroked his clean-shaven chin for a moment, considering. Then he smiled. "We'll make it work. I know where you keep your money."

It had been three days since Chas had tracked the Naughtons to their barn and arranged for the Sisters of Charity to shelter them for a short time. Upon learning of Annie's nighttime discoveries, he requested a meeting with the women for D.R., saying that he could provide proof of the identity of Robbie's true father. Veronia agreed to the meeting as long as one of the Sisters of Charity was present.

After leaving Milton, D.R. joined Chas as he waited at the convent in a small sitting room. Chas set a haversack on the floor while D.R. tapped his foot.

After what seemed like a long wait, the click of rosary beads signaled the arrival of the sister who ushered the Naughton family along the corridor.

"I'll amuse young Robbie for a few minutes, Veronia," the Sister of Charity said, and continued down the hall with the boy's hand in hers.

A second sister with soulful gray eyes followed the Naughtons into the room and took the fifth seat. She introduced herself as Mother Xavier.

Iris and Veronia wore skirts and blouses—simple but clean—and Iris had her hair combed to conceal part of the gash on her cheek. It was hard to tell they were related, given how Veronia stood tall and straight while Iris hunched. Both faces had sunken cheeks and circles under the eyes, but Veronia's features were fine and even, while Iris's drooped on one side.

As they took their seats, Veronia stole hateful glances at D.R. while Iris watched the door, looking ready to spring.

"How are the three of you doing, Miss Naughton?" Chas asked Veronia.

Her hands clasped tightly in her lap, Veronia replied, "How could we be anything but better off here? There are no bugs in our bedding, it's warm, and food is plentiful. Isn't that so, Iris?" She looked for confirmation from her sister, who grunted assent and began to rock in her chair.

"Safe," mumbled Iris.

"Yes," said Veronia. "It's the first time we've felt safe in many months. Years."

Mother Xavier patted her hand.

Chas leaned forward in his seat and spoke to Veronia. "After listening to your account of the day you were attacked, I had a few more questions I wanted to settle with you and Colonel Anthony both in the room. Could you please describe the man who attacked you?"

Veronia gazed off into a corner and spoke with studied reserve. "It was dark. I don't remember anything about him except that he stank of tobacco."

Iris paused her rocking to grunt but did not manage to utter a word.

"Would you mind standing up, Miss Naughton?" Chas asked Veronia. When she did, he said, "Now would it be all right if Colonel Anthony stands next to you for a moment?"

Veronia said in a tight voice, "Just for a minute."

D.R. stood beside her, careful not to touch her. Looking sideways, he could see she was tall, but still three inches shorter than he.

"What do you think, Miss Naughton?" Chas asked. "Is this the man who attacked you?"

D.R. heard her sharp intake of breath as she regarded him. Good. She was beginning to realize her mistake.

"I . . . I—" She looked to Iris for assistance, but failed to find an answer in her sister's face. Stumbling a little, she stepped back and eyed D.R. from head to toe. He hoped no one could smell the sweat soaking into his shirt.

Speaking again to Veronia, Chas reached into his haversack, "Perhaps this will help you decide." He handed her the diary with the loose page tucked inside.

Veronia's hand flew to her lips. "Where did you get this?" Her poise utterly forgotten now, she spoke in a raspy voice.

"Did you ever have a tiger maple desk, Miss Naughton?" said Chas.

"Yes. We had to sell it to buy food. I used to keep my journal in it." Understanding swept across her face.

"Mrs. Anthony bought the desk last year at a used furniture store and found the diary," said Chas. "Not knowing your sister's name, she had no idea who it belonged to."

Veronia clutched the diary to her. "Thank you."

Chas spoke. "Now, if you don't mind, would you please review the loose sheet that was placed in the diary?"

Sinking into her chair, Veronia's face paled as she read Iris's account of the cruel attack and the day after. Pausing partway through, she again took a deep breath and reached for Mother Xavier's hand.

"Did you see how you described your attacker shortly after the incident?" probed Chas.

"Yes." She closed her eyes as if pained by the memory. "He only came up to my chin. This man—" she jutted her chin at D.R. "—is much taller than that."

D.R. exhaled and sat down next to Chas.

Veronia said, "But Mr. Bauer said that Daniel Anthony was the *de facto* commander of Jennison's Jayhawkers, and they're the ones who attacked us that day."

Chas said, "What Bauer said was true. What he didn't know was that Colonel Anthony was not with the Jayhawkers that day. Jennison himself made that raid."

Iris and Veronia exchanged doubtful glances.

Chas continued, "This week I checked with some of the men who were Jayhawkers. They remember being on your farm with Jennison. And three insurance customers of Colonel Anthony's produced policies signed by him"—he gestured to D.R.—"on that day, so we know he was here in town, not in Shady Grove." As an afterthought, he added, "Jennison's quite short, by the way."

At this news, D.R. watched Veronia's face register shock and then begin to change—and not to the forgiveness he hoped to see. Instead, her eyes burned with new fury.

"So those drunk ruffians who ransacked our farm were your men?" she snapped. "Land sakes, what kind of training did you provide?"

Her voice cut through him, sharp as broken glass.

He opened his mouth, but no words came. *What kind of training did I provide?* The question echoed louder than her voice.

For a moment, the convent walls disappeared. In their place rose the flickering images of firelit barns collapsing in on themselves, of pigs squealing as they were herded off, of women screaming—not in battle, but in loss. Not enemies. Just farmers. Families. People, like in his dream.

Had he been following orders? Or had he done the work with a little too much zeal? When Jennison set the fires, D.R. hadn't always stopped him. Sometimes, he'd stoked the flames.

He remembered the smug satisfaction of claiming another "secesh" horse, the thrill of punishing anyone who dared oppose the Union cause—or who simply had more than they did.

Jennison had stirred them up, yes. But D.R. had followed. And sometimes led.

He swallowed hard. The heat in his chest wasn't anger—it was shame.

"Jennison had a way of stirring people up," he muttered, the words flat and lifeless. Even to his own ears, they sounded like cowardice. His shoulders slumped. "I'm sorry I wasn't there when you needed help. You and your family deserved better."

It wasn't enough. Nothing he said could undo what had been done. But it was the truth.

The silence that followed was heavy, but no longer hostile. More like exhaustion. A settling of the dust after a storm.

For a moment, D.R. didn't breathe.

He didn't want to be that man anymore—the one who had made war a business, who justified cruelty as necessity. Veronia's eyes wouldn't let him forget. But maybe they would make him remember something better. Something to live up to.

Someone.

Then Chas asked Veronia, "How did you end up in Leavenworth, anyway? What happened to your family and home?"

Chapter Forty-Seven

Daniel

Later that day

When Veronia explained how their menfolk had died and how Shady Grove had burned under General Order Number 11, D.R. listened in appalled silence, exchanging a grim glance with Chas. He remembered the aftermath of Quantrill's massacre in Lawrence—the charred ruins, the stunned survivors, the stench of death. Ewing's retaliation in Missouri had been brutal. What happened to Shady Grove sounded no less devastating.

"After we were driven out, we did laundry for the Fourth Regiment at the fort for a while," Veronia said, her tone clipped. "But after they moved on, things got worse. Iris got badly hurt when a horse kicked her in the head. We were homeless and hungry until we got a job at LeBonTon."

D.R. flinched at the name.

Iris paused her rocking and turned toward her sister. "Jen-n-n-nison . . . fed . . ."

Veronia's jaw tensed. "I didn't know until last week, but Jennison approached Iris more than a year ago. At first, he just gave her food in exchange for carrying messages—lies meant to damage your reputation. Iris agreed because we both believed they were true. We were convinced you"—she turned her eyes on D.R.—"were Robbie's father."

Her words struck like a slap.

"People said Jennison was your commander, but it didn't take much listening to learn he was only the commander in name. Everyone said *you* were the one giving orders. So when our farm was raided under Order Number 11, we believed you had sent the men who did it."

She gave a bitter laugh. "When Jennison offered us work and shelter, we assumed it was out of guilt for allowing you to do such things. We had no idea it was a trap—to disgrace you, to use us. But we didn't question it. Because we thought you'd already destroyed us once."

D.R. felt the heat rise in his chest and shoved down the urge to rush out and pummel Jennison. That scoundrel had not only threatened Annie and Emily and set about to systematically destroy D.R.'s reputation, he had also used a child and innocent women.

Iris rocked while Veronia continued. "But he never gave us *enough* food, so when Mrs. Anthony turned out to be so generous with provisions, we had more to eat. I think that's why Robbie's getting stronger."

Iris stopped rocking long enough to say, "Missus . . . S-s-s-sor-r . . ." She looked to Veronia for help.

Veronia said, "We are sorry to have caused Mrs. Anthony distress," she told D.R. "Your wife is a gracious person, a lady in every sense of the word."

D.R. agreed.

After Veronia sat silent for a few moments, Chas slapped his hands on his thighs and said, "Well then. We can't fix what happened to you or Shady Grove, but I think you can look forward to some better days ahead. Jennison doesn't know it yet, but when Colonel Anthony and I are done with him tomorrow, he's going to write you a check for fifteen hundred dollars."

Iris gasped and Veronia put a hand to her heart. "That's—"

"—enough to buy a house in town, and then some left over to invest. That's the intent, anyway," said Chas.

The Naughtons looked at each other, shocked. Then Iris began to speak. "N-n-n-not . . ." She struggled to voice her thoughts, but nothing intelligible resulted. "N-n-n-not . . ." she pointed her finger to the ground forcefully.

"Not here?" prompted Veronia. "Not in Leavenworth?"

Iris shook her head with energy. "See . . . Jen-n-n . . ."

Veronia nodded to her sister. "You're right. We don't want to see Jennison ever again. Especially if he takes an interest in Robbie."

"Where would you go?" asked D.R.

"Chicago." The word emerged from Iris's mouth whole and complete.

Gazing at Iris, Veronia replied, "Yes, of course. We have relatives there, but till now had no money for a fare. That would be a good place to start over."

Iris nodded.

Glad to have something to take charge of, D.R. interjected, "Then we'll cover train tickets for you, too. *Sixteen* hundred dollars total should do it, right, Marshal?" He glanced at Chas for confirmation before continuing to the women, "I suggest you leave before Jennison gets a notion to contact you. How about on the four o'clock train tomorrow out of St. Joe? I'll send a private carriage to take you to the station." The forty-mile stagecoach ride would be quite an expense, but he was beginning to feel rather magnanimous now that Jennison was in the hot seat instead of him.

Veronia and Iris consulted each other with their eyes before the younger woman nodded and rose.

Holding her head high, she said, "Yes, that would be fine. Thank you, Colonel Anthony. And please thank your wife for the food she brought us." She beckoned to Iris. "We're finished here, aren't we?"

Iris stood and shambled toward the door. As Mother Xavier inclined her head to the men, the Naughtons left without a backward glance. The Sister of Charity followed them.

After a moment of stunned silence, Chas said, "I guess that's a closed case." He sounded satisfied.

D.R., however, had plenty more to say as they wended their way through the empty corridor. "Y'know, General Sherman won the war by burning Atlanta on his March to the Sea. What the Jayhawkers did wasn't that different. It was, after all, war."

"Uh-huh," said Chas, nodding goodbye to the portress as they left the convent.

Stepping onto the sidewalk behind his friend, D.R. continued, "Don't you think they could've shown a little more gratitude for how we're going to coax *sixteen hundred dollars* out of Jennison for them?"

Chas wheeled around so suddenly that D.R. came nose-to-nose with him. "Drop it, pal. Just drop it."

Chapter Forty-Eight

Daniel

November 14, 1865

The next morning, D.R. and Chas paid a visit to Jennison at LeBonTon long before it opened. At this hour of the day, Doc looked bleary-eyed and red-nosed. The saloon also bore signs of the previous night's revelry—overflowing trash cans, bloody feathers and guts, and sticky pools of beer.

D.R. curled his lip as he righted an overturned chair in his path.

"Guess you haven't replaced the Naughton sisters yet," he observed.

Jennison shrugged and gestured for the two men to sit at the bar. "Cleaning women are easier to get than beer," he said. "Want a drink?"

The visitors declined.

"We came to talk about the women and the illegitimate child," said D.R. as Doc tossed back a shot of whiskey.

Jennison sneered. "Your whelp, you mean? From Shady Grove?"

Chas said, "I've done some investigation since you made that announcement, all according to police procedures. Both women specifically remember that a man forced himself on Veronia Naughton on August nineteenth of sixty-one. Her attacker didn't even come up to her chin, they said." He arched his brows at Jennison, who folded his arms and regarded them both warily.

"Besides that, D.R.'s insurance contracts verify that he signed three new policies on that day, and the policyholders remember doing the transactions in person. In Leavenworth." He paused to let this sink in.

Jennison cracked his knuckles.

Chas continued, "I checked with some of the Jayhawkers, who recall a raid on Shady Grove that August, the same time as the violent assault. They said you were in the thick of it." His eyes bored into Jennison's. "In short, I have every reason to believe that you are the father of the boy."

D.R. could not help clarifying the point. "That illegitimate child you mentioned . . ." Chas shot him a subduing glance.

Jennison looked stunned. "I never saw those women at Shady Grove," he said, holding up his palms. "Honest to God."

"You don't remember seeing them," D.R. corrected, "just like you probably don't remember much about getting home on the night you accused me in front of many people of fathering the Naughton boy."

As blood thundered in his forehead, D.R. jumped to his feet and thrust his face at Jennison, who stepped back. "You sorry excuse for a father," D.R. snarled. "Look at you this morning. Look at this dive. No wonder your wife left you."

Before Chas could drag D.R. away, he'd climbed halfway across the bar.

"Sit down, Dan," commanded the marshal.

Moving out of reach, Jennison said, "My saloon is none of your business. And leave Mary out of this."

D.R. stepped back but remained standing, speaking now with deadly calm. "I had a lot of respect for Mary when we were jayhawking, and I imagine she still gets news from Leavenworth, wherever she went. It'd be a shame for her, or your daughter, to learn that you fathered a child by force while you were married."

Jennison's face went ashen. "You wouldn't publish that . . . for Mary's sake, or for my daughter's . . . would you?"

Ignoring Chas's cautionary hand, D.R. leaned forward across the bar and jabbed his forefinger into Jennison's chest. "You bet I would. I have a wife too, remember? The one you escorted home. The one that you hired Iris Naughton to harass. I also have several *reputable* businesses to protect throughout this town."

In a flash of movement, Jennison produced a gun from under the bar. "Get him out of here, Goodman, before I shoot you both. Dead."

In a blink, D.R. drew and aimed his own revolver at Doc while Chas grabbed Doc's gun.

"All right, boys, calm down," cajoled Chas. "Why don't you think about this, Doc, and we'll talk again later."

"No, let's settle it now," D.R. growled. "I need to get on with my life."

"Give me your gun, D.R.," said Chas. When Dan scoffed, the officer gestured with Jennison's pistol. "C'mon. I've got you both covered now."

D.R. handed his revolver over, walked a few yards away, and sprawled on a wooden chair. "All right, I can't hurt him now," he fumed. "Satisfied?"

Chas nodded.

Jennison smirked. "Well, so maybe I am the father. What do I have to do to keep it out of *The Bulletin*?"

D.R. replied, "Well, the right thing to do would be to begin supporting your son. Financially."

"How much?" said Jennison.

The thrill of justification radiated through D.R.'s body as he answered, "Sixteen hundred dollars should do it."

"Sixteen hundred!" cried Jennison, indignant. "I haven't got that much cash."

D.R. shrugged. "Take out a loan. Or sell this dive. Or your other bar. You'll figure out something."

"All right. But it'll take me a couple weeks to come up with it."

"That won't work," said Chas. "The Naughtons need a place to live. You paid them starvation wages, and that sickly boy needs good food. They need the money now. Eleven tomorrow morning at the latest."

"Have it your way. I'll bring it to you tomorrow." Pointing to D.R., Doc said, "In the meantime, you make sure nothing of this gets in your paper, y'hear? Not a word."□

Leaving the post office and heading to *The Bulletin* the following morning, D.R. swung by the newsstand to pick up a copy of *The Times.* As a cold wind whipped at the pages, he scanned them until he found the article about his insurance contracts dated in Leavenworth the day of Veronia's attack at Shady Grove. Smiling, he continued on to his office at *The Bulletin*, noting that it was already nine-thirty.

After assuring himself business was running smoothly, he sat at his desk to begin writing an exposé of Jennison, hoping the man would fail to deliver the money on time. It would be so satisfying to nail him in print.

He was just finishing the article when Jennison followed Chas through the door. "Bet you thought I'd forget, didn't you?" gloated Doc, pointing to the clock.

D.R. gestured for both visitors to come in and sit down.

"Thought I'd bring your friend along in case you get hot under the collar and take another shot at me," said Jennison.

D.R. slid the article he was writing across the desk for Jennison to see. "Good thing you made the deadline. I was just about to hand this to the compositor for this afternoon's edition."

After a quick glance at the sheet, Jennison sighed as he removed a check from his pocket. "Had to sell my other bar, I did," he said. "But there may be a silver lining here."

"Oh, what?" said D.R.

"I always wanted a son. Mary never gave me one. But now, when I'm paying for this boy's upbringing, I can stop in from time to time and visit him. Show him a few things." He laughed and looked into D.R.'s eyes. "Like how to steer a horse with his knees so he can keep both hands free. Remember when we did that?"

D.R. tasted a bitter tang in his mouth, hating to share even one memory with this man who had brought him so much trouble.

Jennison fingered the check one last time before pushing it across the desk to D.R. Then he clasped his hands behind his head and leaned back in his chair. "Yup, a son. I never imagined it in my wildest dreams. Someone to take over my business one day. Someone to take care of me in my old age. Never in my wildest dreams." Jennison's face wore a tender expression that D.R. had never before seen.

D.R. inspected the check before placing it in his drawer, and then stood. "That concludes our transactions, then," he said. "You can have this for your records, seeing as I made a carbon copy." He handed Jennison the unpublished article he'd written and opened the door. "Thank you, Chas. Be seeing you."

Jennison crossed the threshold with his shoulders drawn back and his head high. Following him out the door, Chas nodded over his shoulder at D.R.

Chapter Forty-Nine

Annie

November 15, 1865

At dinner, Daniel was halfway through his steak, sawing at it with the same energy he brought to every problem he wanted to avoid.

Annie watched him a moment before setting down her fork. "Were you surprised when you got home and found us gone to Clarina's?"

His knife paused mid-cut. "Was I ever! I thought you'd taken Maude and left me—just like Jennison's wife."

She tilted her head. So that thought had crossed his mind. Good.

He resumed chewing, slower now. "You weren't planning to stay away, were you?"

Annie drew her shawl tighter. The fabric was soft against her arms, but it couldn't shield her from the ache inside.

"I did think about it," she said, her voice calm but firm. "This business about a mistress—it was just the final straw. A long, frightening string of things came before it."

His expression shuttered. Of course it did. He'd had enough of her "grievances" for one day.

"Yeah, but—"

She held up a finger to prevent his interruption.

"I'll always have a home on the Vineyard," she said. "If Maudie and I returned, we'd want for nothing. My father would say, 'I told you so,' and then open his wallet without hesitation. You know that's true."

He set down his fork, throat working. She guessed that her father's parting words were echoing in his mind: "If you don't treat my daughter well, I'll ruin you."

Annie picked up her napkin and dabbed at her lips. Slowly. Deliberately.

"Of course, if I ever *did* need money, I could call due the note on *The Bulletin's* startup."

His head jerked up. "You want the money back?" There was tension in his jaw now, his pulse ticking above his collar.

"I don't think that'll be necessary right now," she said, stirring lemon into her tea, letting the silence stretch between them. Then, with a slow blink, she drawled, "But I'm not sure I like the hot summers in Kansas."

His voice was too quick, too eager. "Maybe this summer you—or we—could vacation somewhere cooler."

Not on the Vineyard, though. She could see that thought pass across his face like a cloud. Her father still loomed too large in his mind.

"That would be nice," she said.

A pause. Then he asked, cautious now, "So why *did* you come back?"

She stood and walked around to his side of the table, eyes softening as she looked down at him. "Maybe Leavenworth is starting to feel like my town, too. My people." Then, with a slight smile, she said, "And maybe I love you, Daniel Anthony. Doesn't always make sense, but there it is."

He rose, swiftly moving around the table, and kissed her, ardent and full of hunger, as if that could fix everything.

She reveled in the kiss—for a moment. Then she eased back, setting her hands on his chest. "But I also came back because we have unfinished business."

He stiffened. Her shift in tone was not lost on him.

"I don't want the father of my child sullying the Anthony name with horse or cattle thieving. We need to build a family Maudie can be proud of."

She inhaled, steadying herself. "And I don't want any more livestock theft, either."

He swallowed hard. She sensed that it took effort to keep his tone even. "It wasn't stealing. We bought them from the Indians."

Annie lifted her hand in a dismissive wave. "Maybe recently. But not at first. And you know it. Those first ones most likely came from Missouri farms."

"Where'd you hear that?" His chin jutted forward, the color rising in his cheeks.

"You'd be surprised what people say about you." Her voice stayed smooth, even. "Martin Bauer. Mrs. Fisk. And men at Dexters."

He narrowed his eyes. "What were you doing at Dexters?"

She gave a slight shake of her head. That question wasn't worth answering.

"So what do you want me to do?" he said, frustration creeping in. "I can't undo it. A lot of those animals are long gone. The rest—I raised myself."

"I understand," she said, folding her hands. "But you can make amends. I was thinking a thousand-dollar donation to the Orphan Asylum."

He blinked, startled. Then gave a lopsided smile. "Happy to contribute. In installments. As *The Times* starts pulling its weight."

"That's fine," she said. But she wasn't finished. "Oh, and there's the Contraband Camp. And the Ladies' Aid. And the Colored School."

He sank into his chair as she listed them—each request delivered with the calm authority of a seasoned negotiator. She carried no weapon, but Daniel could see she was drawing lines, setting terms—and she wasn't bluffing.

The next morning, Annie rose before dawn and looked out the window with gratitude. Rain streaked the glass and blurred the outlines of the street below—an ideal morning for travelers who wanted to escape notice.

As she buttoned her bodice, she questioned her decision the night before to see them off. After all, Iris had done everything she could to cast doubt in Annie's mind about Daniel's honor.

But then she remembered the journal and the understandable mix-up about substituting Daniel for Jennison in the raids in Cass County. If she had been in the Naughtons' shoes, perhaps she would have done a similar thing.

She would go along in a gesture of forgiveness, even though there had been no apology.

After a hasty breakfast, Daniel helped her step up into the carriage where she would be dry. He wore an oil slicker to protect him from the elements when he drove. First stop: Sisters of Charity.

She nodded with approval as the Naughton sisters stepped into the carriage wearing black mourning gowns and veils that rendered them all but anonymous. But she wasn't prepared for Robbie's appearance when Mother Xavier lifted him into the carriage and settled him beside her. He was dressed head to toe in pink—bonnet, frock, and stockings. A surprised laugh rose in Annie's throat. Clever. No one would be searching for a girl.

Once they were underway, Annie placed an envelope in Veronia's hand, saying, "This is from Charles Jennison."

After Veronia nodded her thanks, Iris cleared her throat. "Misss-ter and Misss-uss . . ." she looked for Veronia for assistance.

"Mister and Mrs. Anthony . . ."

Iris clearly struggled to speak. Finally, she choked out, "Good." To assure Annie's understanding, she leaned forward and placed her now-clean hand atop Annie's, whose smile traveled all the way to her eyes.

That night, Annie could not still her thoughts enough to sleep. After a long time, she folded back the blankets, pulled on her warm robe, and padded across the hall to the tiger maple desk. There, her monogrammed stationery occupied the space where she had once kept Veronia's diary. In the soft gaslight, she allowed her hand to caress the smooth wood before beginning a letter, confident that Susan would read between the lines to infer more than Annie could commit to ink.

Dear Susan,

Remember when you admired the tiger maple desk in your room and I showed you the diary of those two Missouri women? In a strange turn of events, Dan met them in person. As I feared, they fell on even harder times later. But through an unexpected source of funds, we have been able to send them on their way to relatives in Chicago to start a new life.

I visited Clarina last week. She is well and busy. Her common-sense approach to finances continues to build on your advice about the importance of holding my own money.

We have again weathered a bad patch of pre-election mudslinging and come out stronger than ever. Maudie is sitting up on her own. Dan sends his love to you and Mary and Mother.

Yours very truly,
Annie

Annie smiled. Daniel was certainly an interesting mix. He had teased her about not giving any suffrage speeches, all the while respecting Susan and her cause. And when Annie followed Clarina's suggestion to bring him into line by leveraging her business loan to him, he had responded positively. Perhaps the women's rights campaign had merit after all.

CHAPTER FIFTY

Annie

November 16, 1865

By ten o'clock the next morning, Annie was on her way to play duets with Pia when she chanced upon her husband talking to Doc Jennison near *The Times* Building. Her heart began to pound as she recalled the day their previous argument led to a shooting. She increased her pace, hoping to forestall any violence before it developed. Reaching Daniel, she looped her arm through his in a gesture of restraint and support.

To her surprise, Dan looked relaxed and, although he did not look friendly, he didn't look hostile, either. He addressed Annie. "Doc, here, tells me that his check for the Naughtons has just cleared."

"That didn't take long," she said in a neutral voice.

"Now that I've set matters straight, I'm ready to pay a visit to my son," continued Doc, "but I don't know where he lives. None of the hotels have anybody named Naughton. Do you know where they're staying?"

"They *were* living with the Sisters of Charity," Daniel said.

"Okay, thanks. I'll call on them there." Jennison moved on. Over his shoulder, he taunted, "Too bad you don't have a son."

Annie tightened her grip on her husband's arm as she felt him start toward Jennison. "Let him go," she murmured.

Daniel placed his hand over hers. "You're right."

"What a wild goose chase you're sending him on, directing him to the Sisters of Charity," she said, turning to smile at him.

"Righting the Naughtons' wrong felt almost as good as freeing people from slavery," he said, his gaze far away.

Later, they met again at home, this time for lunch. When Daniel came in the door, Annie noticed the flush of cold on his cheeks—and the slight bulge in his coat pocket.

He didn't speak right away. Instead, he crossed the room, pressed a kiss to her forehead, and sank into the chair as though preparing to confess something important.

She waited, hands folded in her lap.

Then he reached into his pocket and withdrew a letter. "This came to the post office this morning," he said, offering it to her.

She looked at the envelope with its blocky handwriting that was, nevertheless, clear. She read it once. Then a second time as her mind absorbed the meaning.

Emily Robinson
417 North Esplanade
Leavenworth, Kansas

And the return address:

Tobey Robinson
24 Hill Creek
Natchez, Mississippi

Annie looked up, joy spreading across her face. "From Emily's husband," she marveled.

Daniel smiled. "Before I opened this, I got a separate letter this morning from a woman named Clara Barton, who said he had been found. Guess he didn't waste any time writing to Emily."

"I don't think she believed he was alive," Annie said quietly.

The floorboard creaked as Daniel shifted his weight. "Do you want to give it to her yourself?"

She nodded, watching the wind in the saplings across the street. "Yes. But I want to sit with her. Not just hand it over like a telegram."

Daniel inclined his head and, for once, said nothing.

Annie pressed the letter to her chest for a moment, as if accepting the changes it would inevitably bring. Then she crossed to the pantry where Emily was just about to descend to the kitchen.

Annie held out the letter with both hands. "Emily," she said gently, "I believe this is for you."

Want to hear how Annie discovers new courage and connection when she helps a desperate traveler on her first Christmas Eve on the frontier? Get my free short story "The Heart of Christmas" free with newsletter signup! Visit jeannegehretauthor.com/christmas to get the eBook now!

Afterword

Born of This Fire weaves the Civil War and the struggle for universal rights into the fabric of Annie and Daniel's early marriage. A wealth of nineteenth-century newspapers, letters, maps, and biographies opened the path and beckoned me forward. Where historical accounts trailed off, I used fiction to fill gaps.

Some events required interpretation—conflicting election accounts, rumors about Daniel Anthony's alleged affairs, cattle theft cases.

What's fictional: My decade of reflection on Annie's life led me to believe that only strong spiritual roots could have sustained her through this turbulent marriage—an interpretation that's purely my creation but seems entirely plausible. Emily, the Naughton sisters, and their connection to Charles Jennison are fictional elements.

What's historical: I relied heavily on David R. Phillips' research, city maps, and directories to recreate 1860s Leavenworth. Daniel Read Anthony—mayor, newspaper publisher, abolitionist—left abundant material in letters and articles. Donald L. Gilmore's *Civil War on the Missouri-Kansas Border* helped balance the pro-Union views expressed by the Anthonys and their allies.

Susan B. Anthony felt like familiar territory. As a former docent at her Rochester home, I've studied her speeches and letters extensively. Her Laing's Hall speech closely mirrors her actual remarks in the *Leavenworth*

Times. Through Ida Husted Harper's *Life and Work of Susan B. Anthony* and other sources, I came to know her public voice well enough to imagine her private one—sharp, loyal, and unshakable.

Annie Anthony proved most elusive—no diaries survive, just scattered newspaper mentions and one letter. I portrayed her as quietly resilient rather than a public crusader, shaped by her class and convictions.

This vision of Anna Osborn Anthony emerged thanks to Mary Ann Sachse Brown of the Leavenworth County Historical Society, whose research revealed Annie in charity rosters, suffrage events, and musical programs. A single note in Susan B. Anthony's biography—that Annie contributed "a very considerable sum" to her husband's publishing venture—suggested a possible source of Annie's power in her marriage.

Characters like Mother Xavier, Nettie Cochran, and Mary Gray appear fictionally but were real figures in Annie's world. Clarina Nichols also appears, though she was likely in Washington nursing soldiers during the war.

Jennison's portrayal as violent and reckless reflects historical consensus—he admitted to brutality, ran cockfights, and disobeyed orders. The accusation about Anthony's alleged mistress comes from diary entries and newspaper accounts. I did, however, take creative license in making Jennison responsible for harming Veronia Naughton and adjusted timelines for narrative flow.

Thanks to Almeta Whitis for her sensitivity read of Emily's character, and to my Word Crafters writing group for their support.

Most of all, thank you, dear reader, for joining this reimagining of how the Anthony family might have lived, loved, and endured. Visit my website (JeanneGehretAuthor.com) for more resources and articles about the Anthonys.

Interested in the sources I used to write this novel? Review them at jeannegehretauthor.com/botf-sources, or access them from the book landing page QR code below.

And please take time to review this book! Your review helps other readers like you find and enjoy it. Find direct links to major platforms, as well as the other mentioned resources, at jeannegehretauthor.com/born-of-this-fire.

Jeanne Gehret

P.S. Did you miss Dauntless Book One, *Secrets to the Wind*? Learn more about it at jeannegehretauthor.com/secrets-to-the-wind. While you're there, join my newsletter to be notified about the next book's release!

About the Author

Jeanne Gehret writes women's historical fiction that explores the emotional and spiritual journeys behind public lives, especially those of Annie and Daniel Read Anthony. Her Dauntless Series draws from years of archival research and a deep interest in how women endure—and transform—through hardship. With a background in spiritual formation and a passion for untold stories, Gehret brings the Anthony family to life through writing, blogging, and historical presentations.

Early in her career, she authored the first children's book about dyslexia, an international bestseller with over 60,000 copies sold.

Reach out to her at Jeanne@JeanneGehretAuthor.com.

www.ingramcontent.com/pod-product-compliance
Lightning Source LLC
LaVergne TN
LVHW091110080826
845145LV00008B/1865